6/23   ALL $5

Pen

CW01073101

boys of blood & bone

David Metzenthen was born in Melbourne in 1958. He began
to write fiction after abandoning a career as an advertising copy-
writer. He has lived and travelled overseas, but regards Australia and
its citizens as a major source of inspiration for his work.

David has won several awards for excellence, including the Ethel
Turner Prize in the New South Wales Literary Awards for *Johnny
Hart's Heroes* in 1996. He lives with his wife and two young chil-
dren in Melbourne.

Also by David Metzenthen

Wildlight
Stony Heart Country
Finn and the Big Guy
Johnny Hart's Heroes
Falling Forward
Gilbert's Ghost Train

For younger readers
Fort Island
The Hand-Knitted Hero
The Colour of Sunshine

boys of blood & bone

& bone

David Metzenthen

Penguin Books

Penguin Books

Published by the Penguin Group
Penguin Books Australia Ltd
250 Camberwell Road
Camberwell, Victoria 3124, Australia
Penguin Books Ltd
80 Strand, London WC2R)RL, England
Penguin Putnam Inc.
375 Hudson Street, New York, New York 10014, USA
Penguin Books, a division of Pearson Canada
10 Alcorn Avenue, Toronto, Ontario, Canada M4V 3B2
Penguin Books (N.Z.) Ltd
Cnr Rosedale and Airborne Roads, Albany, Auckland, New Zealand
Penguin Books (South Africa) (Pty) Ltd
24 Sturdee Avenue, Rosebank, Johannesburg 2196, South Africa
Penguin Books India (P) Ltd
11, Community Centre, Panchsheel Park, New Delhi, 110 017, India

First published by Penguin Books Australia, 2003

10 9 8 7 6 5 4 3 2 1

Designed by Brad Maxwell, Penguin Design Studio
Cover photography © David Metzenthen and Getty images
The sculpture, *Driver and Wipers* by C Sargeant Jagger, 1937, which appears in the photograph by David Metzenthen, is part of the City of Melbourne Art and Heritage Collection.
Typeset in 10.5 pt Bembo by Midland Typesetters, Maryborough, Victoria
Printed and bound in Australia by McPherson's Printing Group, Maryborough, Victoria

National Library of Australia
Cataloguing-in-Publication data:

Metzenthen, David.
Boys of blood and bone.

ISBN 0 14 300130 2.

1. Friendship – Fiction. 2. Reminiscing in old age – Fiction. 3. Mateship (Australia) – Fiction. I. Title.

A823.3

This project has been assisted by the Commonwealth Government through the Australia Council, its arts funding and advisory body.

The author would also like to thank the staff of the Australian War Memorial, Canberra, ACT, for their patience and most able assistance.

www.penguin.com.au

With admiration and gratitude I dedicate this book to the memory of the Australian men and women who served in the First World War, 1914-1918. In particular, I mention my grandfather, Private A J Metzenthen, Signalman and Footscray Bulldogs supporter, who fought with the Fourth Machine Gun Battalion in Belgium and France in 1916, 1917 and 1918.

The old force passed down the road into history. The dust of its march settled. The sound of its arms died. Upon a hundred battlefields the broken trees stretched their lean arms over sixty thousand of its graves.

C E W Bean, 'The Australian Imperial Force in France during the Allied Offensive, 1918', *Official History of Australia in the War of 1914–18*, Vol VI.

prologue

If Henry Lyon was able to see back down the road for, say, eighty-five years rather than just a kilometre or so, he might've seen Andrew Lansell in person, rather than just a memorial elm tree with Andy's name on it. But seen or unseen, it's possible for our paths to cross with those who have lived before – and sometimes we meet them, in a way. And the people who once lived, who were as real as we are now, have much to tell to those who listen. And Henry Lyon was always prepared to listen.

one

There was a long straight row of trees on either side of the road and there was Henry, padding along in suede sneakers and long black shorts, beside paddocks full of silence. Behind him, a fair way back, was the Volvo, blue-black in the sunshine, the nose of Henry's sailboard over-hanging the windscreen like a white spike of carefully gelled hair. The car was Henry's mother's, but it was Henry's P-plate stuck crookedly onto the glass.

Something was gut-sickeningly wrong with the station wagon, the thing running so hot that even he, Henry Lyon, who knew nothing about cars, decided he could no longer ignore the obvious and stopped amongst the sheep paddocks, no town in sight, with only the twin lines of English-looking trees leading him on to their vanishing point. So Henry was walking, sick in the stomach over the car, not mobile in any way, his phone also unwilling to provide him with a carrier.

In front of the trees were small plaques the colour of old

coins, with names and numbers clearly cast. Henry read each as he passed, guessing at the military abbreviations and numbers, assuming that these minor histories were of the men of the district who had fought in the First World War. After a few more trees and plaques Henry reckoned he had hold of the rhythm and it was steady, slow, and old-fashioned, requiring only the names and nothing else to make it work.

Lynden
Lansell
O'Bree

Davey
Bracken
Buchanan

Richards
Guilfoyle
Tregeah

And although Henry could put no faces to these names he guessed that he was walking where many, perhaps every one of them, had also passed. He looked down where the bitumen met the gravel, seeing his sneakers but imagining their boots on this track back then. The First World War. To Henry it seemed like something from the Middle Ages.

Without warning, his thoughts were swept away as a grey and blue Commodore pulled up, V-8 spitting, gold mag wheels like stars. A big guy about Henry's age, sitting in the Holden as comfortably as Buddha in his temple, checked Henry out.

'Your car back there, mate?' Buddha lifted a thumb, silver wraparound sunglasses as dark as a slit in a mailbox. 'Ya wanna lift? Getcha to the garage before it shuts.'

Henry had never hitchhiked in his life, but he didn't consider knocking back the offer.

'Yeah, that'd be great. Thanks.' He crossed the road, got in, and wondered how much he had to spill about the Volvo being his mother's car.

'Fair walk to town,' Buddha said, put his foot down, and the V-8 took off as if it had never wanted to stop in the first place.

Henry sank into the low seat, the car smelling of cigarette smoke, and some sort of floral air-freshener. .

'What's up with ya bus?' The driver asked the question as if it was unthinkable that Henry wouldn't know the answer.

'Over-heating,' Henry said. 'Just about red-lining.' Which was the extent of his mechanical diagnosis. 'I thought I'd better stop.' Elm trees flickered past, branches to the sky like arms in the air. 'I dunno though, really, what's wrong with it.'

The driver reached for smokes, juggled a lighter and lit up. He offered the pack to Henry, shoving it back on top of a P-plate when Henry declined.

'Yeah, well, it's always better to get out and walk before ya seize the bastard. Then all yer could do is nail the number plate to one a these trees and write, "here lies another dead marine. A Svedish one this time. And a bloody long way away from home, too".' Buddha grinned at the road.

Henry laughed, despite nursing a gutful of misery.

January 11 1917.

On this day, Cecelia Hainsworth, with all her love, gives this diary to Andrew Lansell. May God keep him safe and bring him home to Australia.

At dusk, night gathering in the gums, Andy Lansell led the rangy, slow-stepping horse across the dirt road and into the home paddock. He did not let the mare go straight away but stood stroking her neck, inhaling the broad, powerful, smell of her, letting her nuzzle into his shirt collar, whiskers tickling his neck. Then he slipped off the halter, stood back to coil it, and watched the grey move off toward her usual place in under the cypress trees.

'See ya in a while,' Andy murmured. 'I hope.' He lingered, hands on hips, breathing deep, watching the ambling horse. 'Hey!' he called out. 'Greta.' The mare stopped, swung her head around, perhaps expecting a wad of hay, but when she saw he held nothing she walked on.

Andy, after a while, turned for home, seeing the house sharp white against the darkening hills and blurring trees. He could smell the country; subtle, vague scents of wood smoke, grass, horses, cattle, and dirt. He listened to his boots strike, heard the muted gabble of Corellas, and the swish of his shirt. He felt the air passing over his face and hands, holding heat although the sun had set, and in his breast pocket the small notebook that Cecelia had given him bumped gently. Already she'd dated the first page and made the first entry. Already Andy knew it by heart.

He walked on, listening to the hush, memorising it, memorising everything.

two

The trees of the Avenue of Honour stopped obediently where the small town of Strattford started, which struck Henry as kind of sad, as if it had been decided long ago that the old soldiers were to be kept at a distance, that their stories were too harsh, or would take too much trouble to imagine.

'Garage's up 'ere on the left.' Buddha aimed the Commodore up the divided main street. 'You'll be right as rain with Goughie, even if he is a bit of a old stroppy bastard. And that old grey hole there is the pub.' He pointed. 'Which is where I guess you might be stayin', so I might see yer in there tonight, since I'll be comin' in with the missus. So that's Stratty, mate. Impressive, eh? Where you from?'

Henry looked across the road to the pub. *Est. 1896* was written in stone or plaster on its front.

'From Melbourne,' he said. 'Malvern.'

'Right,' said Buddha, driving into the garage to stop

between the white pumps and the office. 'Never 'eard of it.' He laughed once. 'And there's yer man and there ya go.'

A middle-aged man in blue overalls was visible through windows where fan belts hung like Christmas decorations. Buddha stuck out a hand.

'I'm Graham, but everyone calls me Trot. Buggered if I know why. Guess it could have somethin' to do with me second name being Trotter.'

Henry shook. 'I'm Henry Lyon.' He opened the car door. 'Thanks for the lift.' An idea struck him, complete and complex with implications. 'I'll buy you a beer, then. Tonight. If I stay at the pub.' Which gave him an out. He didn't have to stay at the pub.

He'd seen a Colonial Vista Motor Inn, complete with two white-painted wagon wheels stuck in a rose garden. Didn't the RACV thing his dad had taken out for him include all that kind of crap?

'No worries.' Trot pipped the accelerator. 'Catch ya then.'

Henry got out and Trot took off, peeling a short screech from the oil-stained driveway. The mechanic, with slicked-down hair and clean hands, as if he had just washed up to go home, stood in the doorway.

'Problem, mate?'

Henry was embarrassed, his mechanical ignorance again being pushed into his face.

'My car's over-heated out on the road in. But I don't really know what's wrong with it.' At least, Henry thought, he had not blown the motor up, like Trot had said. 'It was running hot, so I stopped a few k out of town.' Henry pointed approximately west. 'In the memorial trees. I'm in the RACV,' he added. 'Full cover, I think. I've got the key thing here.' He dragged out the keys with their attendant plastic tag.

The mechanic chose not to look at it.

'Long as it's paid up.'

'Yes,' said Henry, trying to please. 'It would be. I mean, it is.'

'What sorta car?' The mechanic crossed his arms as if he was bracing for more bad news.

'Volvo,' said Henry, wishing it wasn't. 'An SE 850 wagon.'

The mechanic turned away as if Henry's story was only getting worse.

'All right. Give us a minute to lock up. Then we'll go out in the truck.' He stopped in the doorway. 'You want to use the phone? Tell someone where ya are? It's in the office. I'll be back in a sec.'

Henry decided to use the pay phone; he didn't think pulling out his mobile right now would be the smartest thing he could do. He walked into the office that smelled of motors and oil, hoping his folks wouldn't be that upset about the Volvo. Walt and Marg knew he didn't mistreat cars. They'd just be relieved he hadn't crashed the thing. And later he'd ring the boys at the beach to tell them he was still on his way, or he would be by tomorrow, all going well. And then he'd ring Marcelle.

January 12 1917,
Melbourne Train.

Well, here we are, on the train heading for the big smoke. The moment has come. Had a last beer with everyone at the Strat and said our goodbyes. Boys are well. No worries so far!

Andy felt the train picking up speed over the river flats, the land swinging toward him as the carriages travelled a long bend, mauve hills creeping, solitary gums manoeuvring, the gravel bed of the McAlister River branching below like a pale old stick. He could imagine the smoke from the steam engine falling behind to fade as the sound of the train would fade, quicker and more completely than expected, and soon enough the bush would have back its quiet.

Darcy and Bob slept slumped in corners, faces on fists, legs out, boots splayed, their small bags above them in the black wire racks. They did not, any of them, look like soldiers. Andy thought of Cecelia again, home from the railway station by now, getting ready for tea, but he did not allow himself the slightest visible sign of sadness, not wanting to see it reflected back from the solemn face rocking beside him in the window.

Instead, he concentrated on the fine grain of the window's varnished frame, felt like he could see *into* it, just as he felt like he could recall *exactly* the faultless feel of Cecelia's face in his hands. Going away had swung the gate of his memory wide open. He could remember everything. He could remember each of the few fine freckles scattered across her cheeks like a loose constellation of stars. He could still feel her in the whorls of his finger tips. At least, he thought, he would get to see her again before he left for France.

The train went out onto a long trestle bridge, the road to Melbourne cutting beneath it. Andy looked down, holding a hand to the window. The road was empty, curving and luminous, looking more like a river than the river itself. Propping a boot on the armrest opposite, he grinned. The army had provided them with only one-way rail passes; evidently they thought the same way he did about the whole show — that the going away had to be dealt with before the coming back.

The motion and clatter of travel lulled him until eventually he settled back to sleep. With head propped on hand, the dusty window rattling as if it had taken over the job of diligently recording the passing of the country and the night, he and the boys slept as the train rushed on.

three

Henry could see the silver grille of the Volvo in the rear-view mirror of the tray truck. Parry Gough hadn't tried to start the wagon, but had simply attached a chain and winched it up onto his truck like a dead whale into a factory ship.

'Your car?' the mechanic asked, as they drove back toward Strattford.

'No, my mum's.' Henry watched the trees pass, the name plaques facing each other across the road in the dusk. 'Borrowed it to go up the coast.'

'Nice vehicle.' Parry Gough drove slowly into town. 'When they're goin'.'

'Yeah,' said Henry. 'I'm lucky they let me have it.' Ahead, as they rounded the roundabout, he could see the unsteady-looking front of the Strattford Hotel. 'What's the pub like to stay in?' he asked. 'Is it all right?'

The mechanic had not even hinted at a time when the Volvo might be back on the road.

'Yeah, it's good enough. Though there's the motel, if you're interested. The Rosewood. Stay at either. It's up to you. It's all covered by your membership.'

Watching the town pass like a newsreel from the 1950s, Henry considered his options. Stay at the pub . . . or the *Rosewood* Motel? Forget the Rosewood. It was bad enough to be driving Mummy's Volvo without staying at a joint called the Rosewood.

'I'll stay at the pub,' he said. 'I owe that Trot guy a beer anyway. Geez, that Commodore of his seems like it'd go.'

Parry Gough drove into the garage, the Volvo swaying.

'Yeah. About five times as fast as he needs it to.' The mechanic pulled up and hauled on the handbrake. 'Just hang on while I open up the workshop. Better keep Mum's car under cover.'

Henry looked back at the pub, seeing an old lady with white hair standing at the front door. She was badly stooped, fragile-looking in a white-flecked dress of brittle orange, but there was nothing fragile in the way she banged on the wall with a walking stick. Henry watched as the door was opened and she was let in, climbing the couple of steps whilst holding onto a handrail that looked as if it had been put there specifically for her use.

I'm in the country all right, he thought.

Henry sat in his small room, sneakers on the sill, and looked down on the main street. He held his phone, about to ring Nick, but for a minute he let himself absorb the feeling of the place. A hundred and something years old the pub was, and in the musty air, in the stillness, in the grey grain of the paint-flaked sill, he did get a sense that he was only one of the many, many people who'd looked out this window at pretty much the same things.

Actually, Henry had optimistically decided, he didn't

mind so much being stranded. Yeah, the joint was a bit rough and the plumbing groaned in a way that hinted at haunting, but he liked the caught-in-time feeling of it all. Who knew what might happen in a place like this? Well, not much probably, but still it was a kind of an adventure. He sat staring out the window until silence and stillness drifted into loneliness, then rang Nick.

'It's me,' Henry said. 'And guess what?'

Henry held off from ringing Marcelle until he'd showered in a bathroom that was like something out of a decommissioned lunatic asylum. He sat on his sagging single bed, leant against a pillow tattooed in red with the name of a laundry service, and dialled, hoping her mood might have improved since their conversation that morning.

'Hey,' he said cheerfully when she picked up, 'I hope you and Angie have a better drive up here than I did. I'm kind of like stuck. The Volvo's sick, so I'm staying in the pub till it gets fixed. I'm in a time warp. It's like a bad movie. I don't even know where I am.'

'Serves you right.' Marcelle seemed to be intent on taking up where she had left off. 'You couldn't wait three days for me. You had to go up there early. So bad luck, Henry. I hope your car costs you a million bucks.'

Henry let out a pent-up breath before cautiously going into offence, except that it felt like defence.

'Hey, *all* I wanted to do was go up for a few days with the boys because –' he sat up straighter, 'look, you guys couldn't have got your flat anyway, and your folks wouldn't have let you stay at Nick's place with us, so gimme a break. Three days. What's wrong with that? Really.' He waited hopefully.

'If you can't work it out,' Marcelle said, 'then I'm not going to tell you. See you later.' And she was gone, leaving Henry to look at his telephone as if it had let him down.

'Well, that sucks,' he said, stood up, stretched, and saw that the buildings across the road stood in golden late afternoon light. The optimistic spirit of adventure he'd felt before was fading.

Henry left the pub, bought fish and chips, and ate them on the steps of a memorial in a small, well-kept park. A swing creaked companionably and the chips were good, hot and salty, even if the fish was completely tasteless. He felt okay. He was surviving. He thought about Marcelle, felt himself to be unjustly accused, thought about ringing her, but figured she was definitely over him for the day. He'd give her another try in the morning.

On the memorial, carved into grey stone behind Henry's head, were lists of names – not that he was aware of them in the dark, although if he had turned he could've touched them, felt the remnants of gold leaf and the scabs of dried lichen. He didn't, though. He got up, binned his rubbish, and walked straight back to the pub.

January 13 1917.
Spencer Street Station, Melbourne.

One in the morning, so officially this is our second day of service. We are at Spencer Street Station. Had a cup of cold tea and a stale sandwich. Waiting for other volunteers to get in from Mildura and the Mallee. Then we march off to tents somewhere.

In ragged formation, with fifty or sixty other country volunteers, Andy Lansell, Bob Pike and Darcy Garrett headed away from Spencer Street railway station toward a temporary camp at the Lakeside football oval. The city absorbed the marchers, its locked and lifeless buildings throwing back the echoes of their boots, its bridge taking them over the river, its looming Botanic Gardens moistening and scenting the air, but to Andy it felt that the place wanted nothing to do with them.

'Where's the cheerin' crowds is what I want to know,' Darcy said. 'And why the middle-of-the-bloody-night hike? I deserve a bloody medal already. For walkin' above and beyond the call of duty.'

The city was deserted but for the marchers, the street lights casting soft, ineffectual nets. To Andy it felt like he and the other blokes were just passing through, that although they breathed the city's river-tainted air, marvelled at the width of the roads, and theorised about all the lonely, patriotic girls tucked up in bed, they were like goods destined for places and uses the city knew little of, and had no especial need to acknowledge.

'Well, *I'm* enjoyin' meself,' Bob said. 'In the company of such fine farting fellows as yourselves who volunteered 'emselves so quickly and would never complain about nothin'. Geez, here we are stridin' along, a hundred of rural Australia's finest in perfect formation. *Shit.*' He stumbled. 'I just hit a bloody pothole. I might have to go 'ome. Twisted me ankle. Gor lumme, don't tell me it's over already.'

'Come on!' a sergeant yelled. 'Yer might as well go forward as yer can't go back. Move *on*, men. And move along *smart.*'

'Jesus, who brung 'im?' Darcy gripped a one-handled bag that gaped like a mouth. 'If he really wants to be useful, he could throw himself under a bloody tram, and then we could all get on and ride. My bloody mum wouldn't like me bein' out this late at night, you could bet a bloody quid on it.'

Andy hiked along not unhappily. Things could be worse. And he was sure that in a few months they definitely would be.

four

Trot's Commodore was parked outside the pub, a red pin-point of light flashing in the dashboard. Inside the hotel, Henry could see people, mostly blokes in green or blue work shirts, ranged along the bar. He couldn't see Trot, but went inside anyway.

No one took much notice of Henry as he went to buy a drink. A pot of Vic, he would ask for. He glanced around, made sure not to stare at the few girls sitting at small round tables, and was relieved to see Trot push his way out of a door that obviously led to the toilets.

'Hey, Trot.' Henry called out, not loudly. 'Graham.'

'*Trot!*' the barman shouted, as he passed, skimming empty glasses. 'Ya wanted.'

Trot turned, big and solid in tight jeans and a white shirt, his hair combed down and damp, dull brown in the light. He extracted cigarettes from a shirt pocket as he came over.

'Mate.' He took up about twice as much space at the bar

as Henry. 'How ya goin'? How's the Volvo? Bonnet up?'

Henry had to step back to make way for Trot's elbow. 'No, I don't think so,' he said. 'Not yet. You want a beer? My shout.'

'Do I want a beer?' Trot lit a cigarette and managed to scratch his nose without burning his eye. 'I do, but I'm bloody drivin'. You know the story. P-plate bullshit.' He looked across the bar. 'But if Janine could be *persuaded* . . . yeah, get me one. A VB. She'll be right. Thanks. '

Henry could see a girl with long straight brown hair and olive skin sitting alone at a table. At the table next to her, in a far more comfortable-looking chair, was the old lady Henry had seen going into the hotel earlier. Trot dragged his wallet out of his jeans.

'I'll get Janine a Scotch and Coke. Since that was what I come over here for in the first place.'

'I'll get it,' Henry said promptly. 'You helped me out today. Thanks. Otherwise I'd probably still be walking.'

Trot put away his wallet. 'Yeah, all right. Ta. Then come'n meet the girl. What's ya name again?' Trot's big freckles joined up around a grin. 'I'm good on cars, mate, but that's about it.'

'Henry.' Henry fished around with two fingers in his pocket for another note to add to his five. 'Henry Lyon. Or Hank. Whatever. Henry, mostly.'

'Henry'll do,' Trot said. 'That I can remember. Thanks, mate. And I am *lookin'* forward to this nice cold pot.'

'What'd ya have to sit here for?' Trot hissed at his girlfriend, tilting his head at the old lady who sat behind him with a tiny beer glass in front of her and, Henry saw, a vase of fresh white carnations. 'Anyway, Janine this is Henry. Henry – Janine.'

'Hi, Henry.' Janine took an empty glass off the coaster in front of her, replacing it with the full one. 'Beer, Trot? So I'm drivin' now, am I?'

Trot sat next to Janine, Henry opposite, close to the old lady, in what smelled like a cloud of aged perfume, flowers, and powder.

'Henry bought 'em,' Trot said, 'so what could I say?' Trot folded up his sleeves. 'His car's in Goughie's garage. Overheated out in the Avenue. So is that a surfboard you've got on top of the Volvo, Henry? Or somethin' else?'

Janine thanked Henry for the drink, Henry noticing how brown her skin was and in contrast, how icy-blue her eyes. In a vague way she reminded him of Marcelle, although Marcelle's hair wasn't as straight or as long and her eyes were green. Greenish.

'No, it's a sailboard.' Henry guessed he sounded like a bit of a wanker. A sailboard *and* a Volvo. Still, he went on. He was proud of the board. 'It's a wave jumper. I'm going up to Saint Helena. A few of my mates are up there.'

'Any girls?' Janine sipped her drink, a gold charm bracelet catching the light. 'Or is it just the boys?'

'Just the boys, so far.' Henry folded up the edges of the cardboard coaster. 'My girlfriend's coming up in a few days with one of her friends.' *All going well*, he was tempted to add.

'I love that place.' Janine pushed hair away from her face. 'It's beautiful. You should have a nice time.'

'Yeah, well, hopefully,' he said, and added a smile. 'But my girlfriend isn't exactly all that happy with me at the moment. So I'll have to see how things turn out.'

Trot sculled his pot. 'Yeah, there's always some problem. Another, Henry? Since we aren't drivin'. Who's hungry? Chips? Packet or plate?'

'Plate,' Janine said. 'Get two. And vinegar.'

Trot returned to the bar and Henry took a decent mouthful of beer. It was good, golden and cold, with a creamy head.

'It's a nice pub.' Henry nodded his approval.

'Lucky,' Janine said. 'It's the only one in town.' She smiled and rattled ice-cubes with her straw. 'No, it's okay, I guess. What's your girlfriend's name?'

'Marcelle.' Henry felt something adjust inside. He wished that she was here, or at least, not angry with him. 'She thinks I should've waited to drive up with her.'

Janine gave Henry a short steady look.

'Not surprised. You guys and your mates.' She moved her chair in closer to the table and looked past Henry's shoulder. 'Hello, Miss Hainsworth,' she said loudly. 'How are you this evening?'

The old lady turned carefully but decisively, as if she had been waiting for this enquiry. Henry received a glance that held the weight of a stare.

'I am well enough, Janine.' The elderly lady wore a gold watch so old, Henry saw, that it seemed to have lost its colour. 'How are you? What do you do now? Do you have a job yet?'

'I do reception work at the Rosewood Motel,' Janine said. 'It's not full-time, though. I help Grace Carter three days a week. It's good. It's fine.'

'And what about him?' She turned a finger toward the bar. 'Mr Trotter. The one getting the beer.'

Henry reckoned the old lady was perhaps the oldest-looking person he'd ever seen. Her face was small and pale, and not so much wrinkled but folded in places, as if her skin had never been exposed to the sun.

Janine sipped Scotch and Coke, Henry seeing, as she tipped her head forward to drink, that her hair was parted dead-straight. She put her glass down.

'He's going to start a course at Blaggalong TAFE this year. Forestry. Plantation management. So it should be good.'

Henry liked the way Janine talked. It was clear and direct;

she looked straight at whomever she talked to, and gave short, sharp answers. He could not imagine her ever telling a lie.

'And who are you?' Miss Hainsworth turned in her chair, to better make Henry the focus of her attention. 'What do you do? Where do you come from?'

Henry smiled involuntarily.

'I'm Henry Lyon.' He fiddled with the buttons of his shirt. 'I'm, ah, from Melbourne. I'm going to go to university this year to do Arts and Law. My car's broken down here. I'm just staying until it's fixed.'

'Did you say Lansell?' There was nothing shaky about the old lady's voice. She did not speak softly. 'Lansell is a very well-known name around here.'

'No, my name's Lyon,' Henry said. 'My dad's a Canadian,' he added, which was certainly true, although he had no idea why he had said it.

The old lady seemed to pay no attention to what Henry had just told her.

'The Lansell's were property owners,' she continued. 'Horse and cattle people. Very well known. How old do you think I am?'

Henry hid behind another polite smile. He would've liked not to have to answer the question. He had no real idea how old she was. Old. Her hair was wispy and white and her eyes were colourless, the pupil and iris seeming to have merged, and her wrists were so knobbly they looked deformed.

'Eighty-two,' he said recklessly and shrugged, wondering if she hoped he would over or under-estimate.

'I'm one hundred and one,' she said curtly. 'One hundred and one. You think about that. I was born in this town in 1899.'

'Really?' said Henry, impressed. 'God. One hundred and one. Wow. Before cars. Gee, things would've been different then.'

Janine continued to rotate ice-cubes with her straw, traces of sympathetic amusement flickering on her face.

'Miss Hainsworth,' Janine said to Henry, 'knows more about this town than anyone else *ever* has. She's our very own living, local, legend. She ran a drapery store in the main street for fifty years. You're a legend, aren't you, Miss H? Do you want another shandy? I'll get you one. Or do you want a cup of tea?'

Miss Hainsworth shook her head. 'No. No, thank you, I don't want either.' Again she focused on Henry. 'You look a bit like a Lansell anyway. He does not.' She wagged a finger at Trot who was returning from the bar. 'I was to marry Andrew Lansell. A long time ago. Sixty years before you were born, I would have no doubt. His family bred horses and cattle out on the road there. He was a great rider, Andy. He took after his mother, Annaliese.'

'Andrew Lansell was killed in the First World War,' said Janine, in a way that seemed to Henry to be designed to placate the old lady. 'He was barely twenty. He fought in France. His name's on the memorial over there in the park. And he has a tree out in the Avenue of Honour. Where your car broke down.'

'Are you staying in the hotel?' Miss Hainsworth asked Henry. 'I live here, you know. My family owns the premises. Of course I get special treatment.'

Henry wanted to laugh, but didn't.

'Yes, I am.' He spoke loudly and clearly, as Janine did. 'Until my car gets fixed.'

Trot put a beer down in front of Henry.

'And that could take a while. Knowin' Parry. Back in a sec, folks.' He went back for the plates of chips, but stopped to talk at the bar, appearing to be in no great hurry to return.

'I saw the little plaques,' Henry said to Miss Hainsworth. 'My dad's grandfather was in the First World War.' He spoke both to Janine and Miss Hainsworth. 'In the Canadian army. We've got some photos and my old man's got his medals somewhere. He didn't get killed. He got gassed or something, and they sent him home.'

Janine set her drink and the salt and pepper shakers aside in preparation for the arrival of the chips. 'Miss Hainsworth lent me Andy's diary,' she said. 'It's really interesting. You know, in France, and before they got over there. It's quite an amazing story.'

There was a note in Janine's voice that struck Henry. In fact, there were a couple; one that he felt was of her genuine interest in the diary and another of – well, he couldn't help thinking it was a subtle warning, or a perhaps it might have been a subtle invitation.

'Sometimes I look *at* the words more than I read the writing,' she added. 'It's all in pencil and he filled it out nearly every single day except – well, you know, almost every day. On some pages you can see his fingerprints when his hands must've been muddy.' Janine looked at Miss Hainsworth, who appeared to be waiting for Janine to go on. 'It's a beautiful thing, isn't it, Miss H? You can tell a lot about Andy from it, can't you? Him and Bob and Darcy.'

The old lady stood shakily. Henry shifted a chair out of her way. He felt like he should jump up and shift *twenty* chairs out of the way for her. It was obvious she meant to leave.

'Janine might show you the diary,' she said to Henry. 'I would allow it. If your great-grandfather was there you might be interested. The Canadians were well thought of by the Australians. They were very good fighters.'

Henry nodded, pleased. 'I might go out and look at the trees again tomorrow,' he said, as a way of accepting the compliment and to show he did also respect the boys from Strattford. 'Since I'll be in town for the day. At least.'

Miss Hainsworth seemed not to have heard. 'Well, good night. It's late. I shall go.' She turned to Janine. 'You can tell Graham it's safe to come back now.'

Janine laughed and put a hand on Miss Hainsworth's arm. 'It's nice to see you, Miss Hainsworth. I'm glad you're well.'

'I'm alive, anyway.' Miss Hainsworth set off toward the glass doors, the burly drinkers parting before her.

Janine let out a breath and visibly relaxed. Trot returned with the chips.

'The good news,' he said, 'is that the coast is clear, but the bad news is the chips are cold. Ah, well.' He sat. 'So how did that go, Henry?'

'He was very polite.' Janine nibbled a chip. 'Did you mean what you said about going out to the Avenue tomorrow, Henry? Andy's tree is only about a k out. On the left hand side. It'd only take you twenty minutes.'

'Yeah, I might.' Henry shyly took a chip. 'It's not like I've got that much else to do. And I guess I said I would.'

Trot moved the plate closer to Henry. 'She'll know if you don't. She's like an eagle, mate. Once she dobbed me into the coppers because I had a bloody brake light out. I mean fair suck of the old sauce bottle.' Trot took a handful of chips. 'Nothin' much goes on here that *doesn't* get noticed, one way or the bloody other.'

January 14 1917,
South Melbourne Camp.

Third night in tents. Got a fair mix of city and country fellows in. Plenty of jokers. Darcy's making mates everywhere. Hard to believe we're going to travel ten thousand bloody miles for this. Shown where France and Germany are today! Some blokes didn't know. I had a rough idea.

Andy and Darcy stood outside their tent, the night starred and cool, and made strange by the honking of a swan.

'He's up late.' Darcy sucked on a cigarette. 'So here we are then. In the middle of a bloody footy oval. Well, centre half-forward, anyway. Nice grass.' He scuffed at it with a boot. 'Be a good ground this, with a bit more water on it.'

Andy nodded. He'd been lost for words, in a way, since they had left Strattford. Always used to being under a large sky, he had expected Melbourne to enclose him, but it felt limitless and unknown. The honking of the swan drew loneliness from him, made him think of marshes, of the land at night that radiated out from where he and Darce stood, past the lines of white tents, beyond the city, through the bush, to Strattford, where in the blackness on the road there was the hanging wooden sign at the property's front gate, the sign that he'd recently painted, black on white, saying *Kooyong*.

'Well, we're into it,' he said, which was all he could think of to say. 'It's all ahead of us now, I guess.'

Darcy flicked his cigarette. 'Yeah. So when d'you reckon we get our hands on their bloody rifles? Bein' in the army, as we are.'

Andy stretched, felt a release of energy, and was suddenly pleased at the prospect of doing something fair dinkum. Yeah, it would be good to nestle into the stock of a decent rifle and shoot. He'd always liked guns, their dangerous precision, the seriousness of them, and the satisfaction of using one small, well-aimed piece of lead to bring what was far away within reach.

'Soon, I would say.' Andy could see the heavy, jagged top of a type of palm tree etched against the darkness. Funny plant, he reckoned. Strange city. 'It'd be a priority, I believe.'

'Think you could shoot someone?' Darcy's coat rustled as he crossed his arms and scratched his ribs. 'Whadda ya reckon? I can't see it as bein' all that hard. I reckon I could do it now.' He lifted his arms, sighting down them. '*Bang*. Bye-bye, Fritz.'

Andy did not have to think. 'I just hope we get the chance. Be a joke to have gone through all this business and miss the boat. Like, if it ends.' But once he'd spoken he began to think. Firstly, it wasn't going to end. The battles over there just seemed to be getting bigger — but if it somehow did end, missing out on killing someone was probably not the worst thing a bloke might have to live with. So they'd joined up and never fired a shot? So what? But shoot someone? Sight on a bloke and fire the type of bullet you'd use to put down a horse. Could he do that? Yeah, he could. After all, it wasn't as if anybody on the other side would hold back on him.

'Yeah, I could, too.' He tried to find words. 'Like, I mean, it's legal. Like bloody duck season.' He laughed, felt a spike of guilt, and wanted to re-set the balance. He knew he had never thought of what they might end up doing as being anything other than serious. 'That's the job, eh? Killin' Germans.'

Darcy dug into the turf with his boot heel.

'Yeah, it is that. And maybe pretty bloody soon.'

'True.' Andy turned, the rows of tents cloud-white in the darkness. 'Go back for a cuppa tea, will we?'

'Yeah,' said Darce. 'Why not? Since there's no beer.'

They walked to the mess area, Andy not unaware that in the utter peace of the night there was the subtle sensation of being on borrowed time. All of them were; the boys wandering around the oval, the boys sitting and smoking, the boys coming down to Melbourne on the trains, the boys heading out to Port Melbourne to the ships, the boys out at Broadmeadows getting stuck into their training. The war would be waiting for them all.

Andy wondered, as they stood in line in the mess tent, what Cecelia might make of him and Darce coming to the conclusion, barely two days away from home, that they felt they were quite capable of killing blokes. Even if all they'd seen of the enemy so far was nothing more than a few square inches of German homeland on a map. But that, he thought, was what Cecelia and just about everybody else, wanted them to do. Kill Germans. That was why you joined up. It was no secret what the job was. You were given a rifle. It was up to you to use it.

five

After a milk bar breakfast of a toasted cheese sandwich and an orange juice, Henry walked back up the main street. He went past the Rosewood Motel, where Janine worked, and headed out of town. Beyond a couple of shops that looked barely open for business and eight or nine plain-looking houses, every one with its own barking dog, Henry was in the country. A herd of black and white cows gazed at him from behind a slack barbed-wire fence. Fifty metres further on, the Avenue of Honour began.

Henry walked, looking for Andy Lansell's plaque, feeling self-conscious. It seemed an odd thing to do; his car in Strattford garage, bonnet up, Parry Gough into its guts like a surgeon, whilst he was out here immersed in the past, steered into it by an old lady of a hundred and one. Still. He liked this place. He liked the twin lines of anonymous old gnarled trees that were both memorable and forgettable at the same time. Everything, the elms, the paddocks, the wispy grass brushing the bent plaques, the quiet, the shadows, all conspired to only whisper the names of the old guys. Not too many people in the passing cars, Henry thought, would be paying much attention to the place at all.

Walking, he thought about Marcelle, and felt a spark of resentment. It was a bit over the top that she had wanted him to wait in Melbourne just so they could drive up together. Somehow it seemed too serious and couple-like, as if she was purposely setting out to wreck his freedom. With the sides of his sneakers he scuffed sharp lines in the gravel, triggered by guilt rather than anger, as he realised he didn't know if he really wanted her to come up to Saint Helena at all.

The trees continued on in their sometimes-faltering march into the near distance. Henry felt as if he was in an airy tunnel. Summer-dry leaves crackled, the names of the men and the numbers of their battalions passed, until Henry eventually found a plaque for one Pte A R Lansell, complete with battalion number, soldier's number, and a small raised cross.

So what did happen to you, Andy Lansell? Henry thought. All those years ago. But A R Lansell's plaque, the tree, and the Avenue were not about to give up answers to someone like Henry. It was like looking at the rusted cogs of machinery long-abandoned; any explanation of history was too long seized in time. Henry gazed around, the wind hot on his face.

He could imagine a paddock – no, a field – like the paddocks around here, but more churned-up, and the grey images of soldiers moving, picking their way forward through a grey landscape. He could not imagine it being sunny, but he could imagine gunfire and men going down as the others moved on into whatever it was the old war footage never showed. He had to try harder to picture the wounded as they lay, feeling the coldness of the ground, their equipment digging into them as they waited for help, but the camera seemed always aimed into the impenetrable grey mist where the men went forward.

Henry looked back toward town and saw, across the road, a stand of cypress trees in the corner of a paddock. The trees were big and old, with massive trunks that bore long silver scars where branches had either fallen or been stripped away by storms. The shadows of the trees lay deep and dark, at odds with the sunny openness of the paddocks. Henry was drawn to the place. It seemed the cypresses, foreign and ancient, standing apart, old and damaged, held more of a sense of rememberance than the trees in the Avenue. They seemed more of the time of the war, their darkness hinting at death, secrets, and the unspoken.

Henry crossed the road, heading for the old windbreak. He looked for farmhouses, but saw only a few twisted fruit trees and a collapsed tank stand where a dwelling had once stood. Carefully, he climbed through the fence and walked into the darkened place, aware of an aura of abandonment and age. It was a wild corner where it seemed neither people nor stock had been for a long time. In the shadows, Henry kicked around in the powdery dirt, having no idea what he was hoping to feel or find, but when he unearthed the rusted crescent of a horseshoe, he picked it up and rubbed its pitted curve.

Andy Lansell had horses, Henry remembered. Miss Hainsworth had mentioned that in the pub. So, who knew? Maybe it was one of Andy's horses that had dropped the thing. Maybe it was Andy who'd hammered it on the horse in the first place? After a minute more in the shadows, Henry tossed the shoe in under the trees, and went back out onto the road.

The mood of the place stayed with him. Out here, the past did not seem so far away. And Henry guessed if he'd been around when Andy was, there was a fair chance he would have gone off to France as well – and seen first-hand what the darkness of the trees could only suggest.

Henry set off back to Strattford, a sinking feeling slowing him up when he thought about the Volvo. Whatever Parry Gough was doing had looked major, and major meant expensive. Henry pulled out his phone, figuring it was best to get this call to his dad over and done with as quickly as possible. Walt answered and Henry explained the current situation.

'All right, Henry,' his dad said, 'you're doin' fine. Now if you could give me this guy's number I want to speak to him.'

'I haven't got it on me.' Henry talked as he walked. 'But I'm heading up there now so I'll get back to you in a few minutes.'

'Okay,' Walt said, 'I'll be here.'

Henry then rang Marcelle, to be told by her mother, in no uncertain terms, that she was out and wasn't expected back all day.

'Strike two,' Henry muttered, and wished he'd brought some water.

January 24 1917,
Broadmeadows Camp.

At the firing range today. All is hot work and the place is as dry as a chip. Doing much drilling, marching, bayoneting, physical exercises and so forth. The boys all in high spirits and holding steady for the job that lies ahead. Dragged Darcy from a blue with a not very good but very big cook. Darce says he would have prevailed eventually. Doubtful.

Andy, lying down, settled the weight of the rifle evenly into his hands and screwed his elbows down into the canvas groundsheet.

Calming his breathing, he aligned fore and backsights and brought the bead to bear on the distant black and white target. Gently he took up pressure on the trigger, aware of the steely smell of gun oil, the cool wooden stock against his cheek, and the point of the picket foresight like a steadily-held pin about to puncture the black inner ring of the target.

He fired, the rifle kicking, and although at three hundred yards he could not see where the bullet had hit, there was a small tear in the target on the left of the inner ring.

Without haste, he drew the rifle bolt back to eject the spent cartridge, pushed the bolt forward to seat a fresh round, and thought of nothing other than what he was doing. Up and down the range, rifles fired, an endless loud smattering that sent smoke rising toward the sky that arced over the Broadmeadows camp like a roof; a sky so clear and so blue that once, when Andy did look up, the impression he got was that the day might be endless, that it would be fine to stay here forever, methodically loading and firing at a target he had no way of knowing if he'd hit or not.

He fired his last shot and for a moment looked past the targets to the paddocks that lay beyond. The country was dry, hazed with heat, and silent. He could not, he simply could not, imagine England or France or Germany or Flanders. There was only this country and these paddocks, holding him not by force but by spell. So, if he was to fight, already he knew that it would not be for England or for France. The reasons he would fight were far closer to home than that.

He stepped back from the firing line, his twenty rounds spent, and let the next man take his place.

'Ta, mate.' The lanky private eased himself down. 'I'll see what damage I can do, if any.'

Andy walked back to where others sat cradling their rifles and talking. He raised a hand to catch Bob's attention, Bob coming over slowly to sit down.

'Hot, eh?' Bob looked down the line of prone men, the soles of their boots dusty in the sun. 'I'll tell yer, I just saw one feller put one through the brim of his bloody hat.'

Andy fished his diary out, but the heat had taken away any idea of what he might write. He sat with the pencil poised like a blunt dart. Bob tossed a twig at him.

'Write about all them dunny holes we dug today, if you're stuck for an idea. That'll make interestin' readin' if yer ever get captured.'

Andy grinned and leant more comfortably on his hip. The firing from the line was sporadic.

'D'you ever think,' Bob said, watching the long line of soldiers, 'that there's probably some German blokes over there doin' exactly what were doin' right now? I just hope we're the better shots.'

six

Henry walked away from Parry Gough Motors with an instant headache. The work being done looked serious, time-consuming and expensive. Even his sailboard had been taken off the roof rack. Probably to get the bonnet right up, he decided. Parry Gough had told him to come back in the afternoon for a further progress report. Henry, crossing the road, was looking forward to that about as much as a trip to the dentist.

He bought a chocolate milk, drank it whilst checking out a shop full of all-terrain farm bikes, then went back into the pub, almost knocking Miss Hainsworth over in the entrance.

'Steady on, Mr Lyon,' she said, gripping the banister for support. 'More speed and less haste. Or is there a fire?'

Henry stopped in his tracks. 'No, there's no fire, Miss Hainsworth. I was just, I don't know, you know, just going up to my room.'

Miss Hainsworth appeared to think about this. Henry stayed where he was, aware that he was expected to do so.

'How is your motor car?' the old lady asked finally.

'Um, not too good.' Henry could say that with certainty. 'But Mr Gough thinks he'll probably get it done pretty soon. I, um, went out to the Avenue of Honour today,' he added. 'I saw Andy Lansell's marker. It's nice out there. The trees and stuff. The paddocks.'

If Henry had expected a great reaction to his statement he did not get it. Miss Hainsworth only nodded.

'If you will wait here,' she said, 'I will return to my room and bring you something to look at. A photograph.'

'Yeah, sure,' said Henry. 'I'll wait.' Talking to the old lady was like talking to the School Principal. You did what you were told without question.

'You can sit on the stairs,' Miss Hainsworth said. 'I am neither quick nor hasty nor formal. I shall be at least a minute or two.'

Henry sat down to wait, sunlight coming in through a few high windows, dust particles glinting, the sounds of traffic distant. He guessed Nick and Marcus would be sailing today, or if they weren't, they'd be swimming. The beach was like a jewel up there. He wished he were with them. Miss Hainsworth reappeared clutching a framed photograph that was about the size of a large book. Henry stood.

'Sit.' The old lady handed him the picture. 'That is Andrew Lansell and some of the other boys from Strattford.' Miss Hainsworth stood holding onto the curled end of the bannister. 'The photo was taken in France, near Corbie, in July, 1918. A short while before the big Allied offensive.'

Henry nodded, although he had no real knowledge of what she was talking about. He stared at the picture.

Andy Lansell was sitting on the railing of a small bridge with six other diggers, the photo so clear that Henry could see the reflection of grass overhanging the water. Henry could see a gap where one of the men had lost a tooth, he could see the outline of pocket books or cigarettes in the soldiers' tunic pockets.

Henry could also see Andy wasn't as big as some of the others, but he looked fit and capable, and although all the others were grinning, he wasn't; he seemed to be looking at something distant, or as if he was watching something the others did not see. It was a look too powerful, too piercing, for the photograph. Andy Lansell didn't appear, Henry thought, all that friendly. His eyes were as steady as a cat's, his face was even and strong, he sat with his hands loose, but Henry could imagine them clenched.

Henry saw that the trees behind the men had leaves like stars, the branches rough-barked, thin, and whippy. The soldiers, apart from Andy, looked right at the camera, grinning affably as if anyone was welcome to join them, that this war business was nothing more than a walk in the park. Just believe in us, cobber, they seemed to be saying, and eighty-five years'll go up in smoke because it's only a bit of bloody time standing between you and us, and time's nothin' if you truly believe, if you truly want to be one of us. And for a moment, Henry did.

Henry studied them as they looked out, caught in time, cigarettes in angular hands, young – not all as young as Henry, but they were not old, and they smiled as if they knew things that Henry could know, too – but he was looking at them through the years, them in their lives, him in his, and that was that. He wondered what they did after this moment on the bridge. What happened when the photographer said, 'done,' and they all stood, dusted off their pants, and moved off, flicking butts into the stream and laughing. What lay in store for them beyond the picture? What happened in the next hour, or week, or month? All hell broke loose, probably.

That was the thing, Henry realised. To be on the bridge, to be able to smile that smile and wear your hat like that, you had to put yourself in the way of something so huge and relentless that you might simply be obliterated. But to be on the bridge, a grinning gambler with those other grinning gamblers; well, it might have been worth it. Although Henry guessed the whole thing was not so simple as the men were doing their best to make it look – something lurked in the darkness of the trees, within the reflections in the water, in the smiles and open faces.

'It's a great picture, Miss Hainsworth,' he said, and handed it back. 'They look like good guys.'

Miss Hainsworth accepted the photograph, clutching it in a blotchy hand. To hold it seemed to cause her pain. Henry offered to carry it for her, but she declined.

'It is light,' she said. 'It is memories that weigh you down. Perhaps I shall see you again, Henry. Janine Walker might show you Andrew's diary if you are interested. She has it, for one reason or another. Goodbye, Mr Lyon.'

'Goodbye, Miss Hainsworth.' Henry nodded, feeling like an actor in a Channel Two drama his mum might watch. 'It's been nice to meet you. I guess I might see you around. Depending on my car and stuff.'

Miss Hainsworth appeared not to have heard.

'I don't think people really have any idea what that war was like,' she said. 'They didn't see it, so they don't believe it. I have the feeling it was like nothing on earth.'

Henry nodded. 'Yeah, it sounds like it was. That's for sure.'

Henry stared uneasily into the exposed silver cylinder pots that shone under the harsh fluorescent light. Parry Gough didn't speak, as if he wanted Henry to take in the full implication of what was being undertaken.

'Not as bad as it looks,' he said eventually. 'Believe it or not. I spoke to your old man an hour ago. Again. He wanted to know how things were goin'.'

Henry accepted this information. 'How are they going?' he asked bravely. 'It looks serious.'

'It's just a motor.' Parry Gough wiped his hands on a towel draped over the exposed blue duco. 'Better than some, worse than others. I'll start puttin' it back together shortly. Might be a bit late when she's done. I dunno how ya feel about drivin' at night. How far ya goin'?'

'Saint Helena Bay,' Henry said.

Parry Gough re-laid the towel. 'Four hours. I'll be finished here about dinner time. Have a think and come back then.'

'Okay. I will.' Henry looked at his sailboard lying in a corner on a couple of flattened cardboard boxes, and received a small charge of pleasure. It was a good board. He couldn't wait to be sailing, hammering out to sea, settled in his harness, aiming for a wave. He might try and get up to the beach tonight. See the boys. Kick back in comfort and forget all this. 'I'll come back, then,' he added. 'Thanks.'

The mechanic nodded, as if the word 'thanks' had been the most important part of the conversation.

Waiting to cross the road, Henry heard a car horn blast and turned to see Trot's Commodore completing a U-turn. Henry waited. Trot drew up.

'Still in town, mate?' Trot's car burbled, a vibration in the vehicle like the life in a flighty horse. 'Parry got the head off it, yeah?'

Henry guessed that was what Parry Gough had certainly done; the head being the motor head, he presumed.

'Yeah.' Henry glanced at the garage. 'But he reckons he'll have it all back on tonight. I might drive up the coast after I pick it up. Be about four hours from here, wouldn't it?' Which was a long drive in the dark. Henry knew his folks would be dead-set against it. To him it sounded like an adventure.

'Fair hike,' Trot said evenly. 'Not all that straight, either. Ah, why don't ya go tomorra?' He flicked up a hand. 'Come down the pub again. We'll go for a drive. Me and Janine'll take ya somewhere. Come on. Shit, mate, live dangerously.'

Henry wasn't used to such direct, friendly invitations. In Melbourne the people he knew tended to be a bit more evasive. They wanted to get a good idea of someone's true colours before they'd offer anything as much as a light for a cigarette. But Henry didn't mind Trot's lack of cool. It was kind of good to feel like they were partly mates already – even if Trot didn't appear to be one of the smoothest dudes in the state.

'Yeah, well, I might.' Henry guessed he would. Breaking down again or getting lost would be bad enough, but driving off the road would be a hell of a lot worse. 'I'll see. What time'll you get there?'

'Oh, after tea.' Trot shifted back behind the sports steering wheel. 'Anyway, see how ya go. Hey, I forgot to give ya this.' He picked up something from the passenger-side seat and held it out. 'Janine sent it. It's Andy-boy's diary. She said she saw you headin' out to the Avenue this mornin' and thought ya might want to take a look at it. Just leave it with Miss H. if you decide to head off.' Trot smiled, showing not the whitest or straightest teeth Henry had ever seen. 'Just leave me out of it. Catch ya.' And he drove away, the noise of the Commodore washing up against the shop windows in waves.

Sitting on the floor in his room, Henry decided that he would stay another night. It just seemed easier to go with the flow and the idea of the night drive had become more ominous than adventurous as the day wound down. Besides, he'd never spent time any time at all in a country town, and things were happening. That he held this diary proved it. Plus there was also something good about not doing what Nick and Marcus expected he should do, which was just get in the car, and drive.

Henry opened the diary at the very first page, the type dark and small. An odour of age, mushroomy and cool, rose.

Bound and printed by Gathercole Bros Spencer Street, Melbourne, Victoria. Henry read. He turned the page. *A R Lansell* was written compactly in grey lead pencil. *77th Inf. Batt. AIF c/o Kooyong, Cordner's Lane via Strattford, Victoria, Australia.*

Cordner's Lane. Henry had seen that. He'd seen it this morning, a narrow road that speared off into farmland, quite close to the windbreak of trees where he'd poked around. Not that that meant much, he decided, but in the space of twenty-four hours he'd seen this guy Andy's picture, his memorial, met the person he was going to have married, probably seen where he had lived, and now he had his bloody diary to read.

Henry looked at Andrew Lansell's name written neatly on the inside cover of the diary. There was nothing flash or fancy about the writing, except that each capital letter was slightly elongated, and all letters leant to the right. It was efficient-looking writing, the writing of someone capable and determined. For some reason, Henry decided it didn't look like the writing of a born soldier.

'Well, I'll read your book, Andy,' Henry murmured, then felt an instinctive, almost superstitious urge to change his tone. If you don't mind, he thought.

Henry turned a page and ran his eye over the first half-dozen entries that were separated from each other by hand-drawn lines. The very first entry was written by Cecelia Hainsworth herself. Henry could hardly believe it – but there it was, dated January 11 in 1917.

On this day, Cecelia Hainsworth, with all her love, gives this diary to Andrew Lansell. May God keep him safe and bring him home to Australia.

It sounded a bit like something out of a marriage ceremony, Henry thought. He read on, feeling as if he was tracking Andy and his two mates as they went to Melbourne for training at a camp in Broadmeadows – which would all be houses now, Henry thought – before they were seen off at Port Melbourne, taking a ship called the *Arapiles* to England.

Henry carefully turned the pages, then skipped quickly through diary entries, passing over days, weeks and months where nothing much seemed to be happening. He was keen to find reference to the fighting – but when he did, the entries were simply and disappointingly written, without detail. Henry was hoping for action and stories of people killed, but Andy's recording of his frontline experience seemed to be an exercise in self-control and understatement.

September 23 1917, Henry read. *We're in this up to our necks. One hell of a stunt. Mud. It's shocking. Be lucky to see this one through, I reckon.*

And that was it, at least for that battle. Henry put the diary down and went to the window. Looking across the roofs of Strattford he could see the distant trees in the Avenue of Honour, but it wasn't the trees he was looking for. Henry was looking for open land around Cordner's Lane where Andy had ridden his horses and lived and worked, and whilst he looked, Henry was thinking about where and how Andy had died, because that had also happened.

Henry wondered how the diary had been brought back from the war. Did someone take it out of Andy Lansell's pocket after a battle? Or in a hospital? Or was it found later amongst his stuff? Well, it had come back, all right, but how it came back was one part of the story that Henry guessed he'd never know.

Henry tried to imagine what it would be like to pick up someone who was dead; maybe take an arm, a still-warm wrist, and help carry the person to a rough hole and lower them in. They'd be heavy. There would be blood and wounds. You'd shovel the dirt in carefully. At the start. He could imagine. And then they'd be gone.

_____

March 10 1917.
Broadmeadows Camp.

Two days until embarkation for England. Boys in fine fettle. Hope ship is same. Weather warm. Northerly blowing. Dusty.

Andy sat with his sleeves rolled up, a late afternoon breeze riffling over his forearms. Around the camp, men strolled, stood, and sat, the white bell tents tethered in lines, the smell of smoke and cooking floating off into the pine trees.

'Well, *tomorra*,' said Darcy, sitting on a fruit box, letting the word hang.

'Yeah, tomorra.' Bob looked off into the middle distance, the sun faintly tingeing the tents, trees, fences and paddocks with gold. 'To-bloody-morrow. I hope it's a nice day. I hope it's a nice ship. I hope I don't spew me guts out halfway up bloody Port Phillip Bay.'

Andy was calm, his breathing slow, his nose clear. Tomorrow they would sail away, away from Australia, for England. It was as if the world was tilting them toward something that was going on a long way away. But it was going on as he sat here, and even though it was vague and unimaginable, it was real and he could feel it was real, as real as the bayonets and the faultlessly milled blue-grey barrels of their rifles.

Andy pictured Cecelia at home, sitting on the veranda of her parents' new house at number 4 Clovelly Street, feeling the same golden afternoon sun he was feeling, one hand up to shade her face as she waited to be taken to the station. Andy could almost conjure up her scent, like a mix of flowers and peaches and something else that was so essentially female it could not be described. And she would be impatient, her voice cutting back through the taut flywire into the cool interior of the house. Andy could almost hear her.

'Come *on*, mother! Let's go.'

Then Evangeline Hainsworth, as overdone as a Christmas tree, would appear and Cecelia's old man, Vance, in his usual dark blue suit, would carry the bags to the station. Andy could picture the train rolling in, breathing smoke, round-bellied and snorting like a big black pig. And then Cecelia would be on her way to see him for the last time for a . . . fair while. And that was being optimistic.

It felt like he was losing her, that's what it felt like. He could imagine her so clearly; all five foot three of her, her tiny waist, her face so clear-skinned and delicate, and those grey-blue eyes and the way she looked at him, coolly, but pleased to see him or pleased *with* him or some-such-bloody-thing. And now — *Jesus* — after taking so long to find her, he was losing her. Yes, he'd seen her a week ago here, he'd see her again tomorrow, and at the wharf the day after that, then he wouldn't see her again for a bloody long time.

He looked across the camp, men moving, men sitting, the pointy, tooth-shaped tents incised against the sky like fifty miniature circuses. Yes, he could cope with not seeing her for a while — years maybe — but he did not want to even think about not seeing her ever again.

He thought of her hair; ash-blonde, long and curling, hair really too beautiful for anyone grown-up, but there you go, she had it, and the curves of her face, like — like he didn't know what. But beautiful. To him.

'Well,' said Darce, pushing out a shiny boot that was lightly coated with fine grey Broadmeadows dust. 'It was our choice, boys. Silly bastards that we are. Now, who's got a smoke for a poor old digger down on his luck?' He looked at Bob. 'Bobby-boy? There's no point in bein' tight now. We got a long way to go together, cobber. Share and share alike. Mate.'

Bob tossed a cigarette into Darce's lap.

'Don't leave the country.'

Andy laughed quietly. The camp, the afternoon, the smell of Darcy's cigarette, the lines of tents, the sound of wind in the pine trees, the sight of a magpie gliding — all things, *everything*, seemed to Andy to be of significance. He felt a sense of recognition and identification with what was around him, although he knew it was not that all these things were so special in themselves, but that being alive and being in Australia was.

He felt that the journey had begun, that life was leading him somewhere, that everything, even as he sat here, was changing. He took out his diary, but it was not possible, as usual, to write what he was thinking, so instead he'd write what was happening. And so he wrote something that was true, but it was only a small part of the truth.

seven

The Volvo was parked outside Parry Gough's workshop, again looking like something out of a brochure for the perfect family car. Henry walked past it into the office, where Parry formally presented him with the bill, all two pages of it, pinned to a clipboard.

'It's a bit of an *essay*,' he said.

Henry skimmed the first three items, skipped the rest, turned to page two, and went straight down to the bottom line. Eight hundred and sixty bucks, underlined twice. And seventy-five cents. Like a kid, Henry had walked into the place with his wallet in his hand, so, there being no point in pretending he hadn't, he plucked out his Visa card. Parry took it with pinched fingers.

'Credit check okay, Henry? Just a phone call. Hang on if you would.'

Henry would hang. He looked around. Fan belts looped, the Michelin man was as fat as ever, there were no calendars of nude girls. The card'd be fine, although Henry was not about to tell anyone that his dad kept it well topped-up for emergency use just like this. Parry Gough put down the phone.

'You're fine, Henry. There are adequate funds.'

Not quite as adequate as they were, Henry thought.

'Good,' he said. 'Thanks for the work.'

Henry followed Janine and Trot out of the Stratty pub. The night was cool, a half moon navigated a sea of stars, the Commodore sat poised.

'I'm not saying the Stratty's *not* a good pub,' Trot said, 'but darts *and* the dogs *live* from Sandown? I don't think so. Suggestions anyone?'

Henry certainly had none. He had to think twice to remember what state he was in. He looked at Janine, who was pretty dressed-up, he thought, for a night at the pub. She wore black pants, a kind of a deep crimson cardigan thing over a white T-shirt, and her hair, cut dead-straight just below her shoulder blades, shone, even under the streetlights.

'We should've gone to the Valley,' she said. 'But it's too late now. Too far. We could've all gone to Hazey's.'

Trot unlocked the passenger-side door for Janine.

'Still can. Get in. Let's go.'

Janine got in, but didn't shut the door. 'No, takes too long. How about we take Henry out to McQuarry's? We haven't been there for months.' Janine smiled at Henry. 'It's a tiny little pub. It's ancient. Not much goes on there, but it's nice.'

'Sounds good,' said Henry. 'Sure. No worries.' He remembered he hadn't rung Marcelle. That was something he figured he'd better put right.

'And it's a nice drive,' Trot added and sucked in a big breath. 'The *open* road.'

'Trot, could you hang on for a sec?' Henry took out his

phone. 'I just have to ring my girlfriend. It'll only take a minute.'

Trot glanced back. 'Only a minute? Geez, you're sorted.'

Henry got out of the car, dialled, and after a few rings Marcelle answered.

'So where are you now?' she asked. 'Or is that a secret?'

'Strattford.' Henry was annoyed. 'And if you'd driven up with me you'd be stuck here, too. So what's happening down there?'

'Angie's dad doesn't want her to drive up.' Henry heard a chair move. 'Her car's not very good. So we're going to fly. He got us these special tickets. Only one-way, though.' Marcelle laughed, which made Henry grin. 'You'll have to pick us up at the airport the day after tomorrow. Think you can handle *that*?'

Henry, for the first time in days, felt something like happiness coming back into their conversation.

'I *might* be able to. I will just have to check my *sched-ule*.'

'Yeah, you'd better.' Marcelle's voice had lightened. 'I'll ring you tomorrow. Bye, Henry. Don't talk to any girls, okay?'

'Promise.' He hung up and got back into the car.

Janine turned in her seat. 'So, Henry. Everything under control?'

Henry, Janine, and Trot sat in the small country pub that Henry thought might once have been a farmhouse. There were bars in various rooms, the place had a large front veranda, and the walls were hung with old photographs of huge logs on bullock drays, river boats that used to supply the small inland towns, and football teams that had won grand finals played decades ago. A lone guitarist was setting up an amplifier in front of the biggest fireplace Henry had ever seen.

'So did you read much of the diary?' Janine asked him across a table newly made from old timber. A fingertip would fit in some of the nail holes. 'I just thought you might like to see it.'

Henry had given the diary back earlier in the evening.

'Yeah, I did,' he said. 'A bit less than half, maybe. It's really interesting even if it is just kind of notes.'

Janine pushed aside a menu that seemed to consist mostly of varieties of pies.

'You get the feeling that old Andy wasn't into giving the full story, don't you?' She hesitated, her hand hovering. 'It isn't *quite* what I expected, I guess, but it makes sense when you think about it.'

Henry did agree. Most guys, him included, didn't trust diaries – for one reason or another.

'Yeah, it was probably bad enough to *see* what happened,' he said. 'Let alone write it all down.'

'Absolutely.' Trot flexed his arms over his head then put one big elbow down on the table. 'So you're off up the coast tomorrow, Henry? Should be nice. The weather's stayin' warm, it seems.'

Henry nodded. 'Yep. All goin' well with the car. Why don't you guys come up? If there's a spare room, Nick won't mind.' It was an impulsive invitation and, he realised, perhaps unworkable, but he kept on going. 'I'll ask him when I get there. It's a big house and look, even if it doesn't work out, maybe you guys could stay at a motel or something?' He knew suddenly the offer wasn't sounding so wonderful. 'If you can give me a number I'll check it out and ring you back.'

'Well, yeah, maybe,' Trot said doubtfully. 'What d'you reckon, Janine?'

Janine hesitated. 'Only if you're sure it would be okay, Henry. You check with your friend and give us a ring.' She took a card from her purse and handed it across. 'Call me at work. I'm there Monday, Tuesday, and Wednesday, eight tilll five.' She sat back. 'Yeah, call us, Henry. We might be able to come up. But only if it's definitely okay with your mate.'

Henry put Janine's card into his shirt pocket. Perhaps he'd spoken too soon, but it was done now. All he could do was ask Nick.

'See what happens, then.' Trot held the menu up as if he was showing Henry a scorecard. 'Now let's order some food before they run out of wood for the stove.'

Henry watched Trot take off up Strattford's main street, the Commodore's lights flashing in shop windows like so many speed cameras. For a moment he stood watching the car go, letting the atmosphere of the town settle around him. It was a strange feeling to know that Andy Lansell had walked right over the spot where he, Henry, was now standing. But Andy was certainly gone from here now, and had been gone for a long time. Henry wondered where his grave might be and what it might look like – and if anyone had ever visited it.

March 12 1917,
Broadmeadows Camp.

Ship sails tomorrow. The Arapiles. *Rumour is roast beef for tea tonight. Families at camp today. Nice to see a bit of skirt around the place!*

Andy walked arm-in-arm with Cecelia around the perimeter path of Broadmeadows camp, his face sometimes touching her hair. He was finding it hard to think of things to say; whatever he came up with seemed as insubstantial as the dandelion seeds that floated away as his boots brushed them — but he felt that in a way there was no need for words, that their *real* selves walked on ahead or behind them in silence, understanding how his going away might affect them in the future.

'I know you have to go.' Cecelia measured her words, her face tinged with pink in the afternoon heat. 'And I knew you would.' She flashed one of her rare smiles. 'Although I wish you — *none* of you — *had* to. But there's no way out, is there? For you boys.' She glanced across the open grassland to where the sprawl of tents and huts stood, a line of horses, and carts and some motor cars along one side of the road. 'And all the others.'

'No, there isn't.' Andy looked up the track where other couples walked. He could smell cigarette smoke. Most of the boys smoked. 'Unfortunately.' He grinned, trying to knock the seriousness out of the word, and got hold of her hands. 'Because *you* mean more to me than all of this.' He tipped his head toward the camp, not prepared to release her hand for the sake of the army. 'And the bloody rest of it. But the war's makin' all the rules at the moment and so that's bloody that.'

Cecelia reclaimed her hands, holding them in front of her as if she was cold.

'We just have to get it out of the way and then everything will be fine.' Her eyes held the brightness of the day. 'I think it will work out, Andy, I think it will. In the end.'

Andy had to steady himself. 'You're right.' He looked away, blinking, to take in the sweep of the camp, the colours of the visitors as bright as flowers, bringing a festive air to the place that was otherwise dressed in tones of the earth. 'And if I do get through, then on we go, full-steam ahead, eh?' He felt emotions sweep upward, a surge of hope alongside a sense of desolation. 'Together.'

'We're together now.' She took hold of his tunic and drew him forward.

They kissed, Andy with his hat held in one hand against her

back, the summer-dry landscape stretching away from them as far as the eye could see. Already he was locking this moment into his memory to be taken away and kept for as long as he lived.

eight

The morning was bright, Henry driving happily, shades on against sun glare that seemed atomic. He was thinking about the days ahead: the sailing, the waves, the beach, hanging out at Nick's place on the hill – all of it was going to be good. He thought about Marcelle and felt a surge of anticipation that was tempered by worry.

He'd never been away with her before, and even though they weren't going to be actually staying together in the same house, this holiday seemed to be a big step forward. Yes, he liked her a lot and yes, when he saw her he wondered how he'd got so lucky, but just how serious did he want things to get?

No one else had a boyfriend or girlfriend coming up. Everybody else was free to kind of just hang loose, have fun, and maybe that's what he really wanted to do, too. It was kind of easier, that was for sure. And a lot less serious. Henry chewed at the side of his thumb and spat out a fragment of skin.

'Ar, come on,' he muttered, brought his right hand back down onto the wheel, sat up straighter, took a deep breath, and felt better, at least, for not chewing his thumb. As soon as he saw Marcelle things would be fine. He imagined her smiling and smiled himself.

March 13 1917,
Troop ship Arapiles, Port Phillip Bay.

All our goodbyes said. We are now on board and on our way. It is funny to watch the land go by so steadily. We are on a decent deck with portholes. Could track the ship to England by lolly papers and fag ends going over the side. Very rousing to hear national anthem sung at dock. Cool night. Boys excited.

Andy, marching down the dock, caught sight of Cecelia madly waving a flag in the ship's giant shadow, but he was trapped in the ranks of moving men, and although there were only a few yards between them, he could not get to her. Already he was passing, looking back but staying in time, distance and discipline forcing him to turn to the front and march on.

He was in two worlds; this one of wharves, ships, soldiers, officers, and orders that pressed home its claim on him as the other world behind him that promised life, love, and secrets faded like mist, relinquishing its hold to the higher power. It seemed wrong.

There was Cecelia, *his*, found at *last*, and so completely offering to him what he was offering to her, which was everything — but here was the ship, rising over him, stoked and waiting, with only the hawsers holding her back whilst the things spoken and unspoken between those staying and those going were now as irrelevant as regret, and as fragile as promises. And then he was on the ship.

'I would remind you at this point,' said Bob, hands out as they clumped up the bellying gangplank, 'that it was us goats that actually did volunteer for this, you know.'

Darcy spat. 'Yeah, well, there's two sides to that argument.' The boys came to a halt, the line of embarking troops zigzagging up and along the ship's decks, the line behind snaking back down the gangplank and wharf. 'I guess anything's possible when you're pissed. But I didn't think it'd lead to this.'

Andy grinned, high up on the gangplank, waiting for his turn to go on into the ship. He swung around like everybody else to look, knowing that somewhere down there were his parents, Cecelia, and her parents. He stared until he found them and he waved hard, as everybody else waved hard, seeking their people, everyone in the grip of a kind of universal fever created by the desire to go, the desire to stay, and the power and pull of every-thing that their lives had been so far and might be in the future.

'Bloody hell.' Darcy squinted hard. 'This is bloody crazy. One minute yer can't wait to get away from the bastards, and now none of us can bear to bloody go.'

The crowd seemed to be part of the wharf, the wharf part of the city, and the city, starkly exposed by the merciless sun, seemed to be generating the power that was commanding the boys to leave. It felt to Andy like he was above what his life had been up to this point. And he realised, with what felt like fear or panic, that per-haps he had stood on Australian ground for the last time ever. He had been cut loose from his country by his country, and was at the whim of the wider world.

'Well, no one can say we didn't do the right thing.' Darcy's flat-mouthed look was one of resignation and obstinacy. 'Not now they can't. Here we are, everybody. Up here.' He waved. 'We're goin'. We're off. Good bye-ee. Get fucked.'

Below, Andy could still see, he was sure, Cecelia's dark blue hat and her upturned face. And it struck him that although he had kissed her at the camp, and had held her hands, and they had talked for a long time, it was only with this unassailable distance between them did he know he had been right about her and she about him. It was the distance that did it, the impossibility of overcoming it. He loved her, all right. He did, despite what had happened with Frances-Jane. That incident he would blame on patriotic fever and forget. With a last wave he moved into the ship, feeling the diary in his tunic pocket, full of blank pages waiting for his future to be written.

nine

Henry imagined as he drove what it would be like to leave Australia for the war. Maybe leave it for the last time ever. How would that feel? Like you were being cut in two, he reckoned; part of you would want to be going on the adventure, even if it was an adventure you might not come back from, but the other part of you would be looking at the people, at the sky, at the land, at the place, and feeling as if you'd die without it. Imagine never feeling summer heat again. Never seeing your house, or your parents, or all the girls you knew, or your girlfriend. How would that feel?

Too bloody complicated to think about at this time of morning, he decided.

Instead, he thought of Andy Lansell and his mates taking their last look at land from their ship. They'd be at the rail, eyes trying to tell them that they could still see it until everybody knew for sure that they couldn't, and then they'd turn away not knowing what to say, and that'd be that – but today

Henry wasn't looking for the last sight of land, he was looking for the first sight of water. And coming around a corner, balanced on the tops of ten thousand ironbark trees of the Arkine National Park, there it was, that deep, heart-felt blue of the ocean.

Henry turned onto the paved driveway of Nick's house and saw the two boys unloading sailboards from the back of Marcus's utility. He honked. Marcus, big and bare-chested, waved and Nick, in an Hawaiian shirt and sandals, gave Henry the finger.

''Bout time, ya dud.' Nick tossed a wetsuit on top of a sailboard. 'It's almost bloody winter.'

Henry grinned and parked off to one side, easing the car up to the retaining wall and carefully putting on the handbrake. The water was too good to believe. He sat back, relieved to have made it.

March 18 1917,
Arapiles, Indian Ocean!

Last sight of land today. Reckon we can still smell it. Not so rough away from Great Aust. Bight. Well and truly on our way. Boys out looking for Southern Cross. Plenty of games, drills, and lectures to keep us busy.

Andy looked out over the smooth surface of a canvas-covered lifeboat toward the coastline, a remote pastel line of scrubby sand hills abruptly fronting the sea. The air was startlingly clear, cleansed by the salt, the wind, or the ocean, he reckoned. Up and down the ship men loitered, smoking and talking, spitting over the rail, looking every few seconds in toward the shore. Some, arms folded, just stared.

'Hope she just doesn't tip over,' Darcy said. 'What with every simple-minded bastard over this side. God strike me.' He blinked as if he had dust in his eyes. 'Funny how me last sight of Aussie is gunna be somethin' I don't even recognise. I've never been to the bloody beach in me life. Not a friggin' gumtree in sight.'

'It's the thought that counts,' Bob said. 'Like, imagine bein' off in the dunny, Darce, and then you come up on deck, mate, and she's gone. Missed out on your last look at the mother country because you'd been too busy wipin' your dirty little botty.'

Andy leant on the rail. Below, the sea surged in swathes and solidly heaved, yet it raced down the side of the ship like blue-green mercury, sending up a dull hissing roar that constantly changed but hardly lessened. He looked to the land, distance and dusk dissolving shape and colour, until the difference between coast and sky was hardly recognisable. Watching this, the boys spoke less, Andy straining to see until he had to admit the land was gone, might've gone right underwater for all he could tell.

'And then the fat lady flatulated.' Bob lifted his hands as if he had just stopped playing the piano. 'And said, "Boys, I will see you all again shortly." Or at least, I hope that's what she bloody said.'

ten

The boys rigged their boards on the beach, bent over their work like tribal craftsmen as they tightened sails, knotted away loose ends, and slid sail battens into sleeves. Four or five riders were already out, Henry listening to the sizzle of boards and the slap of sails as they turned close to shore. Sand, lifted by the wind, bounced over his own sail like popcorn in a pan, and in his stomach he felt anticipation rise.

For a moment he looked out to sea, the water grey-blue under a cloudy sky. A few surfers waited in the line-up on the bar break, a couple of boogie boarders mucked around close to shore, but no one swam. The wind had blown most people off the beach, except those who were walking, and those who didn't need the sun for what they liked to do. Which, in Henry's case, was to sail fast and get air.

'Come on.' Marcus was ready to go. He picked up his board, see-through sail looking like a large triangular magnifying glass. 'Well, I'll see you guys out there. I can't wait here all day. I'm gettin' old.' He walked to the water and waded out, pushing his board until spent waves washed above his knees, and then sailed away.

Henry thought about Trot and Janine back in Strattford. What day was it? Monday. He didn't know what Trot would be doing, although he guessed it would have something to do with his car, but Janine would be at the Rosewood Motel in a little office somewhere behind the two white wagon wheels, being helpful. He almost laughed. It didn't seem quite the right job for her. Yeah, she was friendly, although she didn't seem naturally *helpful* – but in a town like Stratty though, he figured, you probably took whatever halfway reasonable job came along.

'Hey, Nick.' Henry was never sure how Nick would react to requests. 'Look, these people I met in Strattford on the way up. Janine and Trot –'

'Y-e-sss?' Nick stood his sail in the sand, frowning up at a few wrinkles that crossed the fabric. 'What about 'em? Your new best friends.'

'Yeah, them.' Henry pulled down an ankle zip. 'Would it be okay if they came up to stay for a couple of days? With us. In that spare room. Not your folks' room. You know, they were pretty good to me down there. I mean, they *don't* have to stay at your place. Although it'd be good if they could. They're pretty cool.' Henry didn't think cool was quite the right word.

Nick knelt over his board, his straight streaky hair wriggling as he set his mast into place.

'They wouldn't bring anyone else, would they?' He sat back on his haunches. 'I mean, like half a bloody footy team. You know my folks – I'd get killed. Then sued. '

'No, they wouldn't.' Henry could not imagine Trot and Janine rolling up with uninvited mates. 'No way. They're, you know, good. Besides, there's no one else down there. It's a ghost town.'

Nick got up, wearing a new sleeveless orange and black wetsuit that made him look, Henry thought, like some sort of pseudo-superhero. Carrot Man.

'Yeah, well, all right.' Nick rolled his arms around, his underarms pale compared to his shoulders. 'But if they're not cool they'll have to go. You know the old man.' He lifted his board by a foot strap, preparing to drag it to the water. 'So what's the girl like?'

'Oh, you know, pretty nice.' Henry didn't have to think. 'Yeah, she's good. She's funny.' Was Janine funny? He couldn't remember, rightly. 'And Trot's a good guy. Which is good, because he's a big mother.'

Nick shrugged. 'All right. Why not? So when are Marcelle and what's-her-face getting here? Or should I say, *flying* in?'

Henry had to laugh. It was a joke, the girls catching the plane.

'Tomorrow. One o'clock, I think.' Henry picked up his board. 'Hopefully she still won't have the shits with me.'

Nick picked up his board. 'Yeah, hopefully she won't. Still. Whatever. It'll be good to have her here. She's a good unit.' Nick raised dark eyebrows that nearly joined in the middle. 'You're lucky. Come on, let's go.'

Henry felt a tic of nervousness as they carried their boards into the shallows. Marcelle's arrival would complicate things, but, on the other hand, to have a girlfriend at the beach would be pretty special. Yes, it would work out. Nick was right. Henry steadied his board, the wind at his back, stepped on, sailed out, set himself for a small wave and took off, knowing that this moment wouldn't last, which made it even more beautiful.

March 24 1917,
Arapiles, Indian Ocean.

*Engine trouble today. Bobbed around like a cork for two hours. Made
many of the boys sick — me included. We are once again underway. Saw
a whale. Said good morning to ship's captain. Saluted, of course!*

Andy stood at the ship's rail next to Bob, feeling far healthier after
vomiting. The slow rolling motion of the *Arapiles* was unlike anything he'd experienced, except perhaps when he'd climbed high
into a tree that heeled with the wind, the sky close and clear like
it seemed now. He spat, watched the waves march on by, each
armoured with a steely sheen and possessing strength he couldn't
even guess at. Cigarette smoke and ash streamed on the wind,
soldiers on the decks everywhere.

'Hey, Andy.' Bob leant on the rail, his long back lowered so that
he looked like a horse pausing at a trough. 'You remember that
Fund Raiser we went out to at Springthorpe? D'you ever see that
girl again? She was a cracker. And her friend. That was a good
night, as I recall.'

Andy remembered the dance and he remembered Frances-Jane
Kelly. Clearly.

'Yeah, it was a good night.' Something lodged in his chest.
Guilt was part of it. 'But no, I never saw her again.' From where he
stood the ship's bow could be seen plunging in slow-motion, as if
the *Arapiles* was about go into a death dive, but she always rose on
the next wave to imprint herself on the horizon. 'Yeah, she was
nice, Frances-Jane Kelly. Too nice, in a way.' He didn't explain.

'Yeah,' said Darcy, a boot up on the rails, 'yer don't want 'em
too nice. I mean, apart from Cecelia, that is. You know.' Darcy
glanced up at the ship's bridge. 'Yer reckon this bloke knows where
he's goin'? There's not a fuckin' lot out there to steer by. We could

be goin' around in bloody circles. Be funny to end up back where we started from.' He watched he sea. 'Although I guess that'd be the general idea, in the long run.'

Bob granted Darcy a complimentary jab in the ribs before returning to picking grey paint off the ship's rail.

'So you went all right with this Frances-Jane Kelly then, Andy?'

'Yeah. I did.' Andy felt the heat in his cheeks meet the cool ocean breeze. 'Like a bloody idiot. I bought the bloody engagement ring for Cecelia the Monday after, if yer really wanna know.'

A seabird, as large as an eagle, skimmed the waves, its wings like scimitars.

'A guilty conscience –' Darcy pretended to shoot the bird, 'often brings out the best in a bloke. Bang bang. If you get my drift.' He flicked the tip of his nose. 'Well, it was a Patriotic Fund Raiser. She was just doin' her bit the best way she knew how.'

Andy watched the waves, but did not see them.

'Well, I won't be goin' back to Springthorpe again,' he said. 'I don't think.'

eleven

'I knew we should've driven up to the Tathra pub.' Marcus surveyed the band assembling on stage, picking up shiny guitars, the drummer seating himself behind a small drum kit. 'My dad could've got a gig with these guys.'

'Can he play?' Nick set his beer back on the table.

'No.' Marcus took his drink from the tray. 'But he's got a better haircut.'

The band twanged into action, the boys looked at each other, but it was live music of a sort, the bowls of chips were hot from the kitchen and the drinks in the Pacific Hotel were fairly priced. Nick, always the most critical, seemed to be enjoying the band the most.

'They're like something out of *Pulp Fiction*,' he said. 'This could be a parallel universe.'

Marcus hunched forward. 'I don't think your medication's kicked in Nicky-boy, you're way out there.' He watched a girl walk past until she disappeared behind a salad bar. 'Hey, any you guys see the weather tonight? A big low's coming. Nine eighty-five. That's low. That's very, *very* low.'

'When?' Henry hoped the system wouldn't only bring rain. Wind was what they wanted, although he knew it wouldn't please Marcelle and Angie too much.

'A couple of days, I guess.' Marcus scooped his change off the table and poured it back into his pocket. 'By the time it gets up the coast.'

The band stopped, the applause, slow to start, was quick to die down. The singer announced a break and walked off, dragging a comb out of a back pocket. A good percentage of the crowd began to drift toward the poker machines.

'Just as long as it doesn't blow the babes off the beach.' Nick stuffed his wallet back into his pocket. 'It'll be oh-kay.'

April 11 1917,
Arapiles, Colombo, Ceylon.

First sight of a foreign country today. Colombo, in Ceylon, it is called. Boys very excited. Colombo is a large town and very green with trees. Those at home will have trouble picturing us here! Fresh fruit and vegetables coming onboard. Little black fellows dive for coins. They can swim like fish. It is warm.

The ship, blacked out, darker than the darkness, ran like something spectral until gradually she slowed and eased into the port of Colombo, her smoke falling on her decks, the sun rising over the low-lying city.

'I don't bloody believe it,' Andy said, eyes narrowed. 'Another bloody country.'

'Yeah.' Darcy turned his head, cocked a hand around his ear. 'Listen. I can hear an elephant.'

Bob Pike stood with arms folded and looked at the land, his tongue pushed into his cheek. He shook his head in wonder.

'Well, that is bloody staggerin', I must say. I mean that is just bloody *staggerin'*.' He glanced at Andy. 'So this has been here *all* the time, then? Ooga Booga Land? Mate, that bush looks *thick*.'

An army captain, immaculately uniformed, complete with hat, came along the deck. In a badly scarred hand he held a tin of cigarettes.

'If you find *that* staggering just wait a bit.' He flicked open the tin, offered it around, then snapped it shut. 'Because pretty soon you'll see places where you won't have to imagine anything at all.' The captain lit Darcy's cigarette and then his own. He blew out smoke. 'Because the unimaginable will happen right in front of your very eyes. Not that I want to put you off or anything. Enjoy the morning, men.'

With beetling brows Darcy watched him swing away.

'Anyway,' he said, 'as I was saying before we was *rudely* interrupted, we would'a never have got 'ere if we didn't join up, eh?' He breathed in deeply, savouring the moist woody smell of earth and vegetation that unfurled over them. 'See? We've all broadened our bloody minds. And maybe later, with a little bit of luck, we might even get to see some nice black girls with big bare bums.'

Andy looked down into the water, its emerald green depths impenetrable, and then he looked at the land that was a deeper, darker green. The place, he thought, was amazing. He didn't understand the sea, but he could feel the pull of the land, even if the force of this place was entirely different from the land and bush he had grown up with at Strattford.

'You're right, Darce.' He tried to take it in. 'We got here, anyway. It's amazing.' The sight of this, another country, real and rock solid, was as mysterious as it was striking. 'And it is right bloody *there*.' He had never felt such curiosity. The humid tropical air, laden with salt, affected him like a drug.

'And we're *right* bloody 'ere.' Darcy tapped ash. 'Pity they couldn't drop us off and pick us up on the way back. But then we'd have to miss out on the war and that probably wouldn't exactly suit their plans.'

'No, the bloody pikers.' Andy laughed at his own bitterness, but still he wondered how they'd managed to lose control of their lives so easily and so comprehensively. 'Hey, I'd even give 'em back the price of me ticket.'

It was all pretty much inevitable though, he figured. From that first morning the boys went ashore against the Turks, the pressure to join up was like a steady wind that swept across the paddocks, across the school yards, up every street in every town, and in through the front door of every pub. You boys have gotta go, you boys have gotta go. And under their breath they had murmured, 'Yeah, yeah, we bloody know.'

'We might get through this, you know,' Andy said, almost experimentally, the thought a surprising source of pleasure. 'We might just walk through it and go home.' He thought of the farm, the horses, his life, Cecelia, their future. 'Then get on with the rest of it. In peace.'

'In *one* piece,' Bob said. 'Preferably.'

'And talk about it in front of the fire at the fuckin' pub.' Darcy flicked his cigarette, watching as the wind held it up before sweeping it down into the sea. 'It could 'appen, you know. God works in funny ways. He let stinkin' Carlton win the bloody flag three times in a row, didn't he?'

twelve

After breakfast, Henry went outside to ring Janine. The sky was a cool, austere blue, the only clouds small and unmoving, ragged and separate, like puffy white kites. No sign of a storm. Henry stopped on the road when Janine answered, then began to explain himself.

'You know, my car was –'

'Yeah, I know who you are, Henry.' Janine laughed, her voice slightly harsher on the phone. 'I mean, I know everyone's as thick as two short planks in the country, but – what'd you say your name was again?'

Henry bypassed the joke. 'Nick says it would be fine if you guys came up for a few days. He checked it out with his folks. There's a room here. It's even got a shower. It's pretty nice.' He could feel himself about to blush. 'You know, we're pretty casual. We don't do much. Just hang out really. Why don't you talk to Trot and give me a ring back later? I'll be here for a week, at least. Come up. It's nice. Got a pen?'

'I'm a receptionist, Henry,' Janine said. 'You know what I'm saying?'

Henry gave her his mobile number. 'It'll be good. Trot'll like it. I mean, so will you. Call me later, if you can.'

'It sounds lovely. So is Marcelle there yet, Henry?'

Henry felt his stomach give a by-now familiar little dip.

'This afternoon. On the plane.'

'Well, that's good,' Janine said. 'And thanks, Henry. Hey, if we come I'll bring the diary up so you can finish it. Anyway, I'll ring you back as soon as I can. Talk to you soon, bye.'

Henry said goodbye, decided to keep walking, and headed down and around the inlet, buying a take-away coffee on the way. Finding a picnic table to sit on, he watched the boats and the water, a guy in yellow waders tending an oyster lease. He hoped Janine would bring the diary. He did want to finish it. He wanted to know the steps and places and things that took Andy to his end, and even though the notes in the little book were simple, and there wasn't the battle stuff and gory details he'd hoped for, he wanted to see how the guy's life unfolded.

Henry finished his coffee and started back around the inlet, thinking that Andy's story was a strange one, because although he, Henry, was reading toward an end he already knew, it was pretty obvious that the end wasn't quite the end at all. Otherwise Janine, Miss Hainsworth, and he, and Trot even, would not still be talking about it eighty-five years later.

Henry's phone rang as he crossed the bridge. It was Janine. He stopped, looking down into green water where seaweed streamed in the current like black flames.

'We'll drive up on Friday, Henry,' she said. 'If that's all right with you guys.'

'No problem.' Henry looked down the inlet, sparks of light on the water, the boats, the roofs of the houses. 'All systems are go.'

★ ★ ★

In the afternoon, Henry, Marcus and Nick drove out to the airport by the inlet to pick up the girls.

'Nervous, mate?' Marcus asked as they sat outside drinking Coke.

'You ought'a be,' Nick threw in, a comment that Henry ignored, knowing that it was said in Nick-speak, with no intention or meaning.

Henry *was* nervous, though. As soon as the skinny white plane flew into sight, he stood up, then sat down to watch it land and slowly taxi to the terminal.

'There they are!' Marcus squeaked, his hands to his chest, as the passengers made their way down the few steps. 'It's Kylie *and* Britney!'

Nick stood. 'Get your autograph books out everybody. They're in disguise, but it's really them.'

People in the small crowd smiled. Henry watched Marcelle coming across the tarmac, black bag over her shoulder, sunglasses on. She held her hair back against the breeze, slight-looking in a plain mauve cotton shirt that pressed against her. Henry smiled, at her and at himself, it felt like. He could see she was smiling, too, and so was copper-haired ironic Angie, who obviously thought this was a something of a stunt.

'Well go and *kiss* her, Hen-rair.' Nick pushed him forward. 'She's *your* rock star.'

Henry figured he'd better not walk out onto the tarmac, but when Marcelle was ten metres away, shyly he went.

'That's the way!' Marcus's voice boomed from behind.

'Hey,' Henry said, nodding. 'How are you going? It's good to see ya.' He leant forward and kissed her to applause from the boys.

'So what about me?' Angie offered her face, Henry obliged. 'Right,' Angie added, facing determinedly ahead. 'That's that done. It's now *holiday* time.'

Weather wet, cold, windy. England! Letters from home. Some news. Have begun trench warfare training, bombing, etc. Food lousy. We are very busy mostly.

Through a quarter-paned window, Andy and Bob watched the rain coming down as if the clouds were collapsing. Stuffed sacks for bayonet drill hung from a wooden beam, like dead men on a gibbet, and beyond, like a hastily-filled mass grave, the mounds of the rifle range disappeared into sodden green fields and drizzly grey distance.

'Lovely, little England *is*,' Bob said, rubbing the mist off the glass, 'the colour of an old bloody tin tank. Exactly. This is just *lovely* weather.'

Andy folded his letters. The weather and the day, he thought, didn't look all that much different to Stratty when a mid-winter southerly was blowing up out of the Strait. And the news he'd just got from home, he thought, wasn't about to brighten it up – at all.

'At least we're not out in it,' he said, gloomily. 'I'm surprised they haven't sent us out to dig a fuckin' trench.'

Bob studied the landscape, but what he looked for appeared to escape him.

'Maybe France'll be better.' He cleared his throat like an actor preparing. 'You know. Brighter. *Cheerier*. In the trenches. All the boys singin' a few songs around the billy, then every now and again, hopping up to pop off a few caps at Fritzy. We could keep a scoreboard on the wall. Like billiards.'

Andy held his letters up. 'Well here's another bit of news to brighten up ya day, mate. I just got a letter from Miss Frances-Jane Kelly of Springthorpe, and guess what? I'm gunna be a father.'

Andy pushed the letters down into his tunic pocket and crossed his arms. 'Jesus Christ. I might as well go and shoot myself right now and save the bloody Huns the trouble. A bloody baby, mate. That's bloody torn it.' Andy felt something beyond despair, grief almost, for what he'd done. 'My bloody card's marked now.' He felt as if his life was slipping away and he was powerless to stop it.

Various parts of Bob's long face moved in various directions. He moistened his lips, put his tongue away, moistened his lips again, then moved around as if he didn't know where he should be standing or how.

'Bloody hell, Andy,' he said eventually. 'I dunno what to say.' Suddenly he stuck his hand out. 'Congratulations!'

Andy, eyes slit, accepted the offered hand.

'Yeah, thanks, mate, but I don't know if congratulations was exactly what I had in mind. I just hope Cecelia's as happy when she finds out.' He swore, spitting out the word as if it was a broken tooth. 'And her bloody parents. And mine. *Fuck* it, I'm an *idiot*. Perhaps they could all have a party over at the bloody Hainsworth's to celebrate? That'd be a riot.'

Bob hesitated, as if he was considering whether or not he should offer a suggestion.

'Yeah, but does she *have* to find out?' Bob moved a step closer. 'Couldn't you just send Frances a few quid and tell her to keep quiet, and that you'll keep on sendin' it as long as she shuts up? Jesus. How would Cecelia ever know? It's been done before, mate. You're not the first to 'ave jumped the fence. She doesn't ever need to find out. A bit of smoke and mirror work, mate. Sleeping dogs.'

Andy gestured to Darcy, who was standing around a wood stove with other soldiers drinking tea, and looking at postcards.

'No, she'll find out,' Andy said. 'Because I'll have to bloody tell her. Because I don't want to make it any worse than it already bloody is.'

Bob shuffled around, his boots grinding, not convinced.

'Ask Darce before ya do anythin' too heroic. No point fallin' on ya sword just for the sake of it. We're in enough danger of that happenin' as it is.' Bob motioned across to Darcy. 'Eh, Darcy. Get over here. Andy's got some news from home.'

Darcy wandered over, holding a white tin mug, a cigarette stored behind each ear.

'What?' He shivered, glanced outside, looked disgusted and then ignored the view. 'Lor lumme, boys. It's bloody freezin' over this side. Whyn't ya come over to the fire? Cropper's got some lovely postcards. Not quite the type yer'd send home, but very nice all the same. Some of those French girls are marvellously put together. And it's not too hard to see where all the hinges are.'

'Andy's got some news.' Bob had managed to clamp down on any sign of humour. 'And it's not particularly good. At all. Really.'

Darcy slid a cigarette out from behind an ear, stuck it in his mouth and searched his pockets for a match.

'What? Bloody Cecelia hasn't pulled the pin on ya has she, mate?' He lit up. 'Shit. Don't tell me the fuckin' pub's burned down?'

Andy dragged his letters out, flicked through one of them, handed Darcy a page.

'No. Worse. Read that.'

thirteen

In front of Henry and Marcelle, the sand, quartz-coloured and smooth, sloped to the water, and the sky at the horizon was a serene pearl-grey. Waves, low and non-descript, battered at the shore and seagulls stood looking steadily out to sea. Marcelle pulled a white windcheater over her knees as a buffer against the breeze.

'Oh, I love this,' she said. 'What a beach.'

'Yeah, it's nice, all right.' Henry watched the waves like a skier would look at snow, with estimation and appreciation in equal parts. All the same, the expanse of the ocean and the crescent of coastline, added depth to his mood.

'It's funny when we haven't seen each other for a while,' Marcelle said. 'Isn't it? It takes us a while to get back to where we were.'

Henry nodded and plucked at a stubborn stalk of dune grass. He hoped they could. Abandoning the grass, he took hold of Marcelle's hand, but the angle was wrong or something was, and he let it go. She withdrew it without comment.

'I'll have to practise that,' Henry said. 'We'll – ' He couldn't think of anything to add, and the gap in conversation that followed had an awkward edge.

They watched the water, its endless movement, Henry knowing the waves hid rips and sandbars and holes and gutters. It was still beautiful, though, he could see that.

'Not long until you start uni,' Marcelle said. 'Henry Lyon . . . the *lawyer*.'

Henry tipped his head to the side, as if he could better imagine himself from a slightly skewed angle. A first year *law student*. Yep, that'd be him. It sounded all a bit too serious, too straight, and too *smartly*-dressed, but it was locked in now. And there was no point bitching, because he was the one who'd picked the course, and had worked bloody hard for a couple of years to get into it.

'Yeah, well, who knows what that'll be like.' He felt a spark of conversation. 'Any news from that office you wrote to?'

Marcelle nodded. 'They'll give me an interview when I get back from here.'

'You'll kick arse.' Henry guessed she would, although he wasn't exactly sure what she might do in a sharebroking office, but anyone could see how smart she was. 'You'll be a share market superstar in a couple of months flat.'

'I'll be lucky if they let me do the photocopying.' Marcelle pushed her hands into the sand to make prints. 'I mean, it's only a twelve month thing, Henry. But maybe it'll work out.'

'It will. You're the goods.' Henry could feel that between them something was, well, not wrong, but kind of flat.

He also knew that if they tried to talk about it they would only succeed in making things worse. Maybe tomorrow, when she'd settled in, things would get better. When she'd had a day at the beach. He watched her watching the sea, her chin on her knuckles, her eyes green and clear like a reflection of the water.

'You're wat-*ching* me,' she said.

'I wouldn't want you to try to run away.' This he meant as a joke, but guessed it didn't come out as intended.

Marcelle lifted her chin off her hands and picked up her sandals from where they lay beside her. Henry could see that she had collected a few more freckles over the course of summer. They dotted her cheekbones in two fine converging flocks and made her eyes look even greener. She stood and gently slapped at her skirt, knocking loose the clinging grains.

'I think it's you who's the one doing the running away.' She turned toward the wooden walkway that wound its way back through the dunes. 'Come on, let's go back to the flat, and see what the others are up to. We'll only end up arguing if we stay here for much longer.'

May 19 1917,
Salisbury Plain, England.

Sunny day today. Went into local village for afternoon tea. Heard good rains at home. Met Otto Padgett from old Stratty state school days. He is doing Signals Training, semaphore, etc. Nice fellow.

Andy had the English darkness to himself. In misty stillness, he stood on sentry duty outside the armoury, his boots scraping on concrete, the camp in front of him enveloped in blackness but for the glow of a few electric lights and behind him, adding their own particular quality to the night, hundreds of weapons racked in readiness for whatever killing drills were planned for the troops in training.

If he turned he could see, through barred windows, rows of Lewis light machine guns, the sinister black bulk of Vickers heavy machine guns, and rack after rack of Lee Enfield rifles, the wooden stocks ranging in colour from honey-yellow through to dark brown, all set off by grim gun metal and the inhuman slivers of fixed bayonets. The tools of the trade, he thought. His new trade.

The Great War, the English papers were calling it; and the idea that Andy was forming of it was something huge and black, something endlessly and massively churning like monster threshing machines dragging back and forth over destroyed ground, throwing up smoke, fire, bodies, and earth — because the war *had* to be like that, he reasoned; it had to be bigger and more violent than anything that had taken place before, because every day *everything* that the Allies had in the way of man-power and armaments were being sent up to the front, and everything in the way of man-power and armaments that the Germans had were being sent up to their front, there to meet head-on.

At Southampton dock, Andy had seen thousands of troops disembarking from lines of ships to rapidly form up and march away, holding a rifle, each with the sole purpose of getting to France, getting to the front, crossing no-man's-land and coming to grips with other men whose sole purpose was to — Andy took a step to the left, turned away from the armoury and instead made himself think of Frances-Jane. He thought of her perhaps sitting on her bed or walking down a shady track, with his baby inside her, maybe a son, maybe a daughter, and for a moment was struck by the simplicity and the goodness of it, then all the other implications came charging back.

He was in strife. And so was she. That much he knew, but he couldn't do much about it from over here, and there was no way to get back. Well, there was. There were a number of ways, but none of them worth considering. He reckoned he'd brought enough dishonour on himself and his family as it was. All he could do was take the blame, wear the consequences, and send money. And let the pieces fall where they would.

It was strange; he had been brought over here to kill people. In fact, they were going to pay him six bob a day to do it – and that was all quite fine and dandy, and he'd do the work if the other bastards didn't get him first – but to father a baby at home to a girl he wasn't married to, was a foul and despicable crime. He spat into the English darkness. Then he spat *at* the English darkness, and made up his mind that if he ever got home, for as long as he lived, he would walk down the main street of Strattford with his chest out and his chin up, and any bastard who felt they might want to try to score a point would go down for the count. Fuck 'em. Everything was so cut and dried for those that weren't coming over here to put their head on the block.

He would not disown the kid – he would bloody own *up* to it. And he'd look after it in whatever ways he possibly could. In one way he knew he already was. He spat again, with pride and anger.

fourteen

The day was still and hot, the sky a brooding grey. The boys, after swimming across the mouth of the inlet, holding their stuff high, headed up the beach to meet Angie and Marcelle. Marcus walked beside Henry.

'Good to see the girls, eh?' He bounced a tennis ball. 'How's it all goin'?'

Henry had to laugh. 'Oh, a bit on the quiet side. You know. We're working a few things out.' He watched kids in the surf, boogie boards flying. 'Maybe just she and I'll go out to tea tonight. Or I'll go 'round to their flat or something. She's – I –' Henry grinned, as there was nothing else for it. 'I dunno. There's a few things we need to work out.'

Marcus bounced the ball as they walked, catching it one-handed.

'Suggestion.' He held up the ball. 'Beach cricket. Nick's got the bat.'

Henry looked at him. 'Geez, why didn't I think of that?

Beach cricket. You're a genius.'

Marcus accepted the compliment. 'I thought you'd be impressed. There they are. I can see 'em just up there.'

Henry could see Marcelle lying on her front on her towel. He took a deep breath. Don't throw it away, he thought. You'll regret it.

They played beach cricket, Marcelle finishing the game by catching Henry out.

'Well, it's swim time.' She tossed the ball toward the towels. 'Who's coming in?'

Henry began to unbutton his shirt, looking up at the road that ran behind Marcus's house. Through a gap in the ti-tree he saw a blue and grey Commodore that he figured had to be Trot's.

'I think that's Trot's car going up to your place, Nick,' he said. 'Maybe after I've had a quick swim I might get goin' back. I said we'd be there about four, four-thirty.'

'Henry the *social* director.' Marcelle dropped her hat onto her towel. 'Anyway, I'm going in. You guys do what you like.' She set off toward the water.

'Hey, *I'm* swimmin'.' Marcus, poised to head down to the water, stopped. 'But I'm thinkin' we'd better do it quick because that down there looks like a storm, I would say.'

To the south, a castle of black cloud stood over the hills, its edges trailing away, too moisture-laden to keep up. Lightning, blue-white, spiked earth-ward and thunder responded, grumbling. A few people had already begun to move off the beach.

'You guys go and meet your new friends or whatever,' Angie said. 'I'm going in with Marcelle.' She jogged off down the slope. 'Hang on, Marce. I'm coming!'

Henry watched the girls cautiously make their way out

into the surf, screeching in the waves. He looked back up the hill but couldn't see Trot's car. He would have a swim, he decided. Then go back.

Walking in to the surf, he hoped he hadn't made a mistake by inviting Trot and Janine. No, it'd be fine. It'd be good to have them here. The more the merrier. Henry ran, ploughing his way out until he caught up with the others, dived under a wave, and came up laughing. The surf had built over the last hour and was now regular and strong.

'It does *not* get much better than this,' he said, waiting for the next wave.

'Nope. No way.' Marcus let the wave smash him, disappearing in the tumbling white water.

Marcelle ducked neatly and came up, skin glistening.

'You boys are so simple,' she said. 'Truly.'

Henry surprised Trot and Janine by coming up from the beach via the garden and out onto the paved driveway. Nick and Marcus followed on behind.

'Henry Lyon, the camp leader,' Nick said, using the bright green cricket bat like a walking stick as he climbed the steps. 'Goes where none have gone before.'

'Henry Lyon, the camp ranger,' Marcus added. 'A true leader of men.'

Henry ignored them. 'Hey, guys. You got here, then.' He shook hands with Trot and kissed Janine quickly on the cheek. 'Good drive up? Car go all right?' The Commodore sat by Henry's Volvo, wearing a coat of rust-coloured road dust.

'Beautiful.' Trot tossed his keys. 'Less than a tank, door to door.'

Henry introduced Nick and Marcus as thunder rumbled and a few big spots of rain slapped onto the pavers.

'Time for a beer then.' Marcus kicked off his thongs.

'We'll give you guys a hand with your stuff before the rain really starts.'

'Thanks.' Trot inserted a key into the boot lock. 'Haven't got that much myself. But Janine's got a couple of tonnes.'

The storm moved in, the beach and hills blurring to grey and black, the trees around the inlet ducking and diving like boxers brawling.

'Do you sail or surf at all, Graham?' Nick handed Trot a beer then sat on an armchair of imitation suede.

Trot carefully opened the beer. 'Nah, a bit of fishin' is about it. I brought a rod up, actually. I'd break a surfboard. Into about fifty pieces.' He sipped. 'Janine likes the beach, don't ya, mate?'

Janine sat demurely in the other chair, knees and feet together.

'Yeah. To lie on. I don't do anything sporty. Reading a trashy book is about as far as I go. We're from the bush, remember.'

'You're pretty brown, though.' Nick folded the cuffs of his jeans, the storm had dropped the temperature by fifteen degrees. Henry wore a windcheater. Only Marcus refused to acknowledge that it was no longer hot and wore a white singlet. 'You look like you *live* on the beach.'

Janine struck a pose, her face on the back of her hand.

'I'm just *naturally* olive-skinned, I guess.' She looked past Nick to Henry. 'Did your girlfriend come, Henry? Marcelle?'

'Yeah, she's here.' Henry pushed up his sleeves. 'She and her friend, Angie. They've gone back to their flat. Maybe we'll all go out for tea tonight?'

'I'm keen.' Trot nodded. 'Meet the woman.'

'I bet she's nice-looking,' Janine said. 'And smart.'

Henry acknowledged that that might be the case, but was keen to change the subject.

'Did you bring the diary?' He hoped this was a reasonable thing to ask. 'I wouldn't mind having another look at it.'

Janine passed some biscuits that she and Trot had brought.

'Yeah, I did. I'll get it for you later. It's in my bag.'

'Diary?' said Nick, coming in from the kitchen to neatly hop over the arm of a chair. He put his bare feet up on the table. 'What diary? Or should I say, *whose* diary?' He raised his eyebrows. 'It's not your sister's, is it, Janine?'

Trot loosed off a laugh and hoisted his can in readiness for immediate drinking.

'No, mate,' he said, 'but it is one hell of a *long* story.'

'Henry'll fill you in –' Janine put her can down on the table. 'But right now I think we should get off our bums, and go for a walk up the road to that wharf, because the rain's stopping and we should be outside.'

Henry looked out of the window. He thought the rain might be easing off, but he didn't know whether it was exactly stopping. Janine hitched at her skirt.

'You guys can't sit here all day drinking.' She waggled a finger at the lot of them. 'As much as you think it might be a great idea.'

Henry saw quite clearly that Marcus and Nick liked Janine already. They'd go along with what she said. They were glad she was here. Nick jumped up, performing, as usual.

'Yes, *enough* drinking.' He clapped twice, standing to attention like a ringmaster. 'Chop chop! Let's go for a *walk*!' He patted Janine on the shoulder. 'This is *good*, Janine. You're saving us from ourselves and we need that. Especially that *lazy* bastard, Henry.'

June 8 1917.
Le Havre, France.

It is hard to believe that we have landed in France. The people are very dark-haired and dark-eyed. We have some marching in front of us and more training here. It is interesting to hear a foreign language. The French language is easy on the ear. Boys in good spirits. Bloody hungry! Darce wants frogs legs.

With the collars of their greatcoats turned up, the boys looked out over the English channel as the troop ship wallowed on toward France.

'They reckon you can hear the guns as soon as you land,' Darcy said, 'if it's still. Ya can hear 'em if they're layin' down a barrage. Boom boom boom.'

Andy felt a ripple of excitement. It was the same feeling as he had when he was breaking a horse and was about to get on it for the first time. Anything could happen: it mightn't, but it could. But he'd always got on. He looked at his hands, which were not big by farming standards, but they'd been shaped and strengthened by work. He was pretty good with his hands, really. He could build yards, fences, sheds, a bloody house if he put his mind to it, but it was the work with the horses he liked best. The horses brought out the best in him.

As he leant on the ship's rail, he thought about leaning on a wooden rail at home, watching some yearling running around, trying to judge if it would be any good. That was where he should be; home with the horses, on the farm, and he hoped, as long as he didn't lose a couple of legs or something, that was what he'd go back to when all this was finished.

He looked out over sea that was a sullen, bitter green. If he could get back to the horses in close enough to one piece, the rest of it, somehow, would work itself out. It might not be perfect, it might not be what it would've been, but he knew he could live with it. A couple of medals wouldn't make it any harder, either, in keeping a few gobs shut around town.

He thought about Cecelia, and how she had cried every time he saw her over the last couple of weeks before he went — crying because he was going, and crying because she believed things about him which he knew were no longer all true.

Yes, he had made a big mistake with Frances-Jane — a mistake too big to ever be forgotten or forgiven, yet even though the trouble he'd caused was huge, he could not help but remember what it had been like with her after the dance. She had been like heaven on earth. He remembered every pale angel's curve of her. Her skin, her body, her way of moving was like something from another world. Beautiful then, and probably just as bloody beautiful now.

He could see quite clearly how he had made a liar and a bastard of himself over her. And he'd done it for something less than love — but he reckoned, here and now as he looked over the bitter sea, that he did love her in a way, maybe just for allowing him to make love to her, maybe just for giving him a glimpse of something he actually hadn't quite believed existed.

You could, Andy reckoned, love people for different reasons and in different ways. And at different times. You'd be an idiot to think anything different, but you'd be more of an idiot to think you'd ever be allowed to get away with it. So, people would have to be told, and soon, because later might be too late, over here. He would tell the truth. Let everyone at home gather it up and do with it what they would.

Andy caught sight of one of the battalion sergeants approaching.

'Boys.' Sergeant Ripper stopped and prized loose a cigarette from a mouth like crevice. His face, courtesy of a former career as a welterweight boxer, was as flat as a plate. He stood as if he was commanding the centre of a ring. 'How are we all?'

'We're well, Sergeant,' Andy replied.

'Yeah, we're bloody well, Sergeant,' added Darcy.

'Top form, sir.' Bob rolled a shoulder. 'If perhaps not a little bit on the cool side. And I must say I do have a bit of a cough, thank you for enquiring.' Bob coughed politely into his fist. 'But nothing to trouble yourself with, Mr Ripper, I don't think. Just a passing thing.'

Ripper ignored Bob and pointed toward the low-lying coast, his cigarette pinched like a drawing pin he was about to push into a wall.

'If yers'll all take a look to the front you'll see for yerselves la belly France, where, you'd better start believin', there is a whole bloody war waitin' for yers to win. Not that I want to scare the pants off yers or anythin'.'

'Bloody hell,' said Darcy. 'Just us, Sergeant?'

Ripper spat, tucked his chin in, and looked at the boys from under a well-hammered brow. He was a small man who had long ago worked out that size did not define men.

'No, Private Garrett. I'll be there as well.'

'That's a relief.' Bob Pike delicately squeezed the bridge of his nose. 'You know, because as I said, I haven't been feelin' too well lately, Sergeant, what with the cough and so forth.' Bob tapped his chest. 'Continental weather and my chest. Very bad.'

Ripper grinned, as if his missing front teeth were part of a display of what a real soldier should look like.

'Ah, don't worry, Private Pike. A good prod in the arse with a bayonet'll soon have ya up and at 'em.'

Bob nodded agreeably. 'Thank you, Sergeant. At the thought of that I'm feelin' a lot better already.'

Andy laughed and got a mouthful of cold air for his trouble. Sandwiched between his two mates, with France just a few miles in front, and with blokes like Ripper around, the decision to be made between Frances-Jane and Cecelia seemed to be something that could be put off for a short while. Suddenly reality was separating itself from imagination, and what was happening at home was becoming less significant as the mutterings of the guns grew clearer.

'Ya hear that?' Ripper stared at the low dark line that was France. 'That's the bloody starter's guns, that is. We'll be off and runnin' sooner than youse can shake a bloody stick at it. All right, boys. Look after yerselves.' Ripper moved off, heading for the next group at the rail.

Andy watched the shore as the troop ship closed in, remembering years and years ago, when he, his sister and his parents had caught a steamer to Saint Helena Bay from Lakes Entrance. He could still remember the Saint Helena wharf, jutting from a steep scrubby hill out over water that was blue-black and his mother laughing, holding her hat. He wouldn't mind going back there again, he thought, with Cecelia, if he ever got the chance. Or with Frances-Jane, if she accepted the proposal he knew he was honour-bound to make.

fifteen

Henry could hear the waves thundering but he couldn't see them, the surf beach hidden below houses and stands of ti-tree. The rain had eased as if the clouds had just about been shaken dry, but the wind continued to blow hard from the south-west, the hills shouldering clouds of battleship grey.

'That's some swell by the sounds of it,' Nick said, as they walked in a loose group along the road. 'Hear it, Marcus? A comment?'

'Yeah.' Marcus walked on, hands in jacket pockets. 'Get stuffed.'

The wharf stood at the end of the road, timbers blackened by the rain, a few cars in the car park and a couple of bikes leaning against the rails. Seven or eight people stood out on it, wearing rain slickers. The sea, black, rolled by in swells, graceful and smooth, each appearing to be about the size and length of a freight train.

'Holy *shit*.' Marcus stopped in the middle of the road. '*Look* at the waves.'

Henry stopped to watch a swell rise and break in a booming, bursting, avalanche of white. Slowly, he started to walk again, the five of them making their way out onto the wharf, the hissing, sloshing sounds of the backwash a sinister whisper.

'Bloody *hell*.' Nick coughed out a kind of a strangled laugh. 'They're almost runnin' up into the dunes. What d'you reckon? Two metres. Three? *Four*?'

Trot released Janine's hand and held his own as high as he could above his head.

'Well, I go about six foot somethin', and those things have to be *way* over my head. I'm callin' 'em haystacks, mate. They're huge. You wouldn't go out sailin' in 'em, would ya? You'd have to be mad.'

Henry looked at Nick and Marcus. He had not even thought about sailing. The waves were massive and the wind that was blasting moisture from his eyes moaned.

'It is *extreme*,' Henry said. 'And that's an understatement. To say the least.'

'The least.' Marcus shrugged.

Nick stood facing directly into the wind, the tail of his shirt flicking, spots of rain dotting his face.

'Yeah, it *is*,' he said, 'but it's also perfect. The wind's blowing straight up the beach and the sets are as clean-as. We *might* be able to handle it. There's no chop. Don't pull the pin yet. God. Take a look at it.'

'But the waves are very *big*, Nicholas.' Marcus spoke like someone from Playschool. 'And the water is *very* dangerous, Nicholas. And besides, d'you see any *locals* out?'

'No.' Nick stared at the distant beach, the narrow line of sand, and the empty car park beyond it. 'So we'll be the first. So what? Look, it's rolling. It's as regular as clockwork.

They're good waves. You guys can sail. Shit. You're both better than me and I reckon *I'd* give it a shot.'

'You wouldn't, would you, Henry?' Janine stood next to him, Trot on her other side. 'And I don't even know how good a sailor, or surfer, or whatever, you are.'

Henry managed to keep a grin together for a couple of seconds. Just the suggestion that they might go out in it had lifted his pulse rate. The waves were clean, as Nick said. But they were also very big, as Marcus had pointed out.

'I don't know.' Henry felt that he couldn't totally scrub the idea. He was supposedly the best sailor of them all, so he guessed he was the one who should be considering sailing the most. 'They're good waves. But they're bloody big.'

The waves *were* spectacular. Sculpted by wind, tide, and storm, they were surf magazine centre-spread material. The wind was side-on, twenty-five knots plus, and dead-steady. You couldn't get better than that. Yes, you might get more wind and bigger waves, but you'd be hard pushed to find conditions like this anywhere else in the country.

They watched from the wharf, no one saying much, Trot letting out a breath every now and again as a wave turned over, curling immense green shoulders.

'I think we could,' Nick said. 'It's big, but it's perfect. It's not exactly monstrous.'

Henry put a sneaker up on the timber and pushed his hands into his jacket pockets. He did have to concede that there were long gaps of clear water between swells. There would be no problem sailing out and back.

'Yeah, it's good, all right. Yeah, it is.'

Nick flicked Henry's jacket. 'Yeah, we all agree that it's good. So what are we here for. That? Or a bloody ham sand-which? C'mon.' He turned as if the decision had been made. 'And we'll pick Marcelle and Angie up on the way, Hankster, so you can show 'em what you're made of.'

Henry figured, after that little speech, that really he had no choice. All right. They would sail. Well. Bring it on. He almost laughed at that.

Sailing out was never going to be the hard part. All Henry had to do was lift his mast, let the wind get in under it, and he would shoot away across the sudsy water like an arrow from a bow – but it was the timing that was critical, the idea being not to slam straight into a wave that was coming down like a crashing B-52 bomber.

The plan he had was to hit the first wave well after it had broken, smash through the fading white water, then get to the next swell before it was a vertical wall. That was the plan. Behind him, he could hear Marcus splashing out and swearing as the wind got hold of his sail, ripped it from his grip, and smacked it down. Henry glanced back.

'You right?' He had to talk loudly to be heard over the wind and crashing of the waves. It was like thunder, all encompassing.

'Ah, no.' Marcus retrieved his rig and stopped a few metres behind. 'But I'm here. Off ya go, Hank. I'll be right behind ya.'

Henry could hear the rasp of fear in Marcus's voice. He could feel it in his own throat, the sound of the waves reinforcing the danger.

'No, stick here for a minute.' Henry knew that he was the best sailor of the three, and that Marcus was probably the worst, despite what Nick claimed. 'You watch how I go. And if it works then give it a fly.' Henry had to raise his voice. 'Look, it's bloody big. I mean, are you up for it?'

Marcus checked his harness, checked his sail, then crossed his eyes.

'Shit, yeah, Henry. I'm *havin'* a ball.'

Henry shoved a foot under a foot strap. Marcus had a point. This was about ignoring fear.

'All right. See how I go.' Henry stepped up and leant back, the board accelerating as he hooked into his harness, his sail set like a wing.

He felt strong and in control, confident almost. They're only waves, he kept thinking. Only waves. Just stay bloody upright. Deliberately, he leant back, spilled some air, dropped speed, and bent his knees to absorb the shock of a metre of oncoming white water.

It hit him hard, burying him, but he made it through and sailed clear, immediately setting himself for the next wave that had already risen to chest height, not hollowed-out, just massive, like the roller of an over-sized road-maker rolling faster than any road-maker ever should.

'Deal with it,' he muttered, unhooking his harness.

Henry was sailing fast, hanging well out over the water, in good shape, in flat water that now was rising into the long shadow-dark face of a wave that had lifted frighteningly – and then he was on it, airborne, knowing instantly that he had flung himself far too high, was in trouble – and was proved right, smacking down in a catastrophic mess of booms, sail, board, arms, legs, one foot loose, one trapped – yet it was okay.

Nothing knocked him out, smacked into his face, broke his arms or legs, or held him under. Floating free, he looked out to sea, instantly judging that he was clear of the strike zone. The next wave would lift him, but it would not break on his head. Which was a great relief. The one after that, if it was bigger, might, but this next one wouldn't. If he nailed his water-start in the next twenty seconds.

Henry pushed his mast tip into the wind, grabbed the booms to trap a cushion of air, then suddenly saw that he had seriously miscalculated the physics of the oncoming wave. It was rising higher and faster than he expected, and that he was going to get smashed was obvious. Fear arrived, dense and heavy, Henry acknowledging it without guilt or panic. With a roar the wave came down.

The impact had a universality about it, as if the force of it had registered on an international scale for serious power, a marine scientist somewhere raising an eyebrow and taking note. Henry had never been smashed by anything like it, the wave absorbing him and his board, sending them over the falls before grudgingly releasing him into churning white wash. His board it took with it like a hostage.

Henry surfaced, looked behind, and saw another wall of water on its way. Be cool, he told himself. Just dive, which he did, the force of the wave less than the last as he was now twenty metres closer to the beach.

Slowly, he began to swim, in foam that simmered and fizzed – then as it began to drag out, he forced himself to relax, ploughing on for the beach only when another incoming wave neutralised the current. Fifty metres away in the shallows he could see his board, its mast, sail, and booms sticking up like bits of a collapsed clothesline.

In a way, he hoped it was damaged so that he could withdraw with honour. Again the inexorable drag of out-going water accelerated, but Henry remained outwardly calm, and waited for the next wave. It came, and he swam with it, knowing that to those on the beach he was nothing but a bobbing head in a vast foamy plain, but he was okay. He had his flotation vest on, he knew the beach, he was not in a rip, and in another ten metres or so he reckoned he'd be able to stand and that would be one beautiful Robinson Crusoe moment.

Unexpectedly, his feet touched bottom, the sea seeming to have granted him a favour. With relief, he began to porpoise-dive in, seeing that Marcus and Nick were rescuing his board and beyond, Trot, Janine, Angie, and Marcelle stood like the wind-whipped survivors of a wreck.

At least he had set an example – of what not to do. But

he knew that some part of him was not going to let him pick up his board and drag it up onto the sand. He'd have another go at it, however unwise that seemed to his more rational self. Aware of Marcelle, he stopped, dipped his head under, and swept his hair back.

'How's the board look, boys?' He felt strangely weightless as he splashed through the shallows. 'Trashed?'

Marcus checked it over. 'Nah, it looks okay. Surprisingly. But what about you? Shit, you got hit by bloody Africa.' He let Henry take possession of his sailboard. 'I couldn't even get out. I got smashed by the shore break.'

Henry felt better now. His strength was returning. He had his board back and in one piece.

'I might have another go at it.' The last thing he wanted to do was sound like a hero. 'I reckon I can judge it a bit better than I did last time.'

'You're off your rocker,' Nick said, with no trace of irony. 'Marcus and I are up for a cold beer and nice lie down. My hands are still shaking.' He held them up and Henry could see quite clearly that they were. 'Hey, it was a dumb idea. Come on. Get out.'

Henry almost complied.

'No, I'll have another go.' He cleared his nose into the water. 'Don't worry. I feel all right.' He grinned at their wet-dog faces and he even managed to raise a laugh. 'No, I do. I bloody do.'

Henry made it out through the shore-break, reassured by a couple of other crash-helmeted riders cutting past, sails curved. Fifty metres beyond the breaking waves, he felt completely safe, the swells lifting him like broad black road humps, the wind patterning them with delicate chop. But the idea wasn't, he knew, to avoid the waves but to embrace them, to sail with them, on them, in them.

'Come on, pal,' he muttered, then turned in a sure-handed jibe, coming out slowly, needing time to make a hundred judgements that finally would have to be sifted down to a couple of crucial decisions: which wave to take and when to go for it.

Henry let his board bog down, allowing a couple of swells to roll on underneath, before selecting what he hoped was the least formidable of the set. Leaning back, he matched it for pace, aware of its gathering momentum, then suddenly he found that he'd made the smoothest of transitions from fear to joy and was sailing effortlessly.

He cut down the wave's face, and along its constantly curving bottom before shooting back up to hang, in its sound it seemed, then dove down to power away from the pounding white water. The way ahead was all-clear if he wanted to bail out, but he stayed on as simultaneously the wave evolved in front and died behind, until eventually its force was gone, and he cut straight back out to sea, ready to tangle with another.

'Oh, *yeah!*' He leant back in his harness. 'All *right.*'

In front of him, the sea was threateningly dark and dirty, but the waves beyond were amazing, and that they were big and dangerous and fantastic was a good thing. He settled back, confident. This was a great day. This was one of his best.

June 9 1917,
France.

Well here we are. Boys have gone mad with French Fever. All girls seen get decent or indecent proposal. Train slow as an old wet week. Better get us off before someone starts shooting.

Troops thronged the railway platform, the dull gleam of rifles everywhere like pickets of a moving fence, haversacks hefted as the train crawled into the station on clouds of steam, its whistle met by cheers of sarcasm.

'The only time you'd ever want one to be late,' Darcy said, his kit spread on the ground as he finished his cigarette, 'or not turn up. And she's right on time. Wouldn't happen if I was in charge, no sir-ee. You boys ever notice how the trains run out of Stratty when I was at the station?'

'Yeah, Darce.' Andy was loaded-up, ready to go. 'Late. Very late. And don't even bother comin'.'

'That's right.' With disdain Darcy watched the train move by, clanking and screeching. 'You can't say I didn't do me level best to slow down the pace of modern life. Hey, at least this thing's not pullin' cattle cars.'

'Not bloody far from it.' Bob stood, shoulders hunched against his load, his rifle held two-handedly, butt-to-the ground as if it was a staff. 'I would be tippin' she won't have a bar.'

The train stopped, creaking as if it was loose at every joint, the wet coal-flavoured air cut with a hundred shouts as corporals and sergeants strode like dogs chivvying sheep, ordering the men to stand back and wait.

'And watch those bloody rifles. You might have to use them one day.'

'Good point, Mickey.' Darcy granted a passing corporal a nod. 'Pardon the pun. And just where is bloody Flanders by the way?' He bent at the knees to pick up his kit. 'And what the hell've they got planned for us when we get there? Bloody lunch, I hope. That breakfast was shit.'

Like a Jack-in-the-box, Ripper turned up, a smile spreading like rings across a snaggy pool.

'Planned for yers, Private Garrett? Why, they've got a party planned. A fuckin' big party, pardon the French. So don't forget your dancing shoes and pointy hat. And save me some bloody cake.' And with that, Ripper was gone, leaving the boys to shuffle toward the carriages.

'Streuth, Ruth,' Bob said, his long face creasing up like a concertina as he came within six feet of the door, 'that *stinks*.'

Andy sniffed, the broad smell of antiseptic layered with other more sickening undertones seemed to fill his head. A soldier with a face like a pirate turned, rifle held in a hand tattooed with a swallow.

'Used as a hospital train, mate.' He was hook-nosed and dark-skinned, and smiled to show jagged teeth. 'But don't worry, fellers. Ya can't catch death. Come on, in yers get, and we'll all get used to it togevver.'

The soldiers boarded, the boys cramming into a compartment, a rifle butt smashing a window as someone tried to turn around.

'Whoops,' the infantryman said, surveying the damage. 'Now I'm in trouble. D'you think they'll still let me go to the war?'

Andy piled rifles into an overhead rack, squeezed into a seat, and listened to the yelling and laughing that reminded him of lunchtimes at school. Already the air was rough with smoke, swearing and spitting, but he couldn't have cared less.

Being used to spending his days working out in the paddocks alone, or with the old man, he found he had soon settled into his place as a part of the battalion, where there were a thousand blokes who'd back him up, just as he would back any of them. It felt like he was part of the biggest football team in the world. Ripper poked his head in, slouch hat pushed back, and grinned his usual satanic grin.

'All comfy are we? Good.' He squeezed into the compartment. 'Now –' he held up a finger, 'I don't want any of you boy scouts carvin' your names in the windows, orright? Because bayonets and knives is for the sole purposes of killin' the enemy, not for fuckin' up the lovely old French woodwork, orright?'

The train gave a throaty, determined whistle, wrenched itself forward, the boys cheered, and Sergeant Ripper, as soon as he had got a light from Darcy, withdrew.

Andy looked out at the passing town, saw washing, a dog in a yard, grimy lace curtains trailing out of an upstairs window, brick walls and slate roofs, and wondered how a war could be going on sixty miles away while nothing out of the ordinary, it seemed, was going on here. He thought about Strattford.

At home he guessed his old man would be out in the paddocks or around the sheds, his mum might be walking down to the Fiveways Store or cooking, and the horses and cattle would be paying no attention to anything but grass and water and the prevailing wind. Whenever he thought of home now, it was without subtlety. The greater the distance and the longer the time he was gone, the more his mind presented him with broad images, like photographs or paintings.

He had to make himself think of the lesser things; the wrenching sound of the gate into Eaglehawk paddock, the smell of fresh-cut hay, the feel of the front bar at the Stratty pub, the warmth of the kitchen after a morning in the paddocks, the sound of the chains of the dogs dragging over the ground. It was harder and harder to focus on the small things. The war was taking the farm away from him and there was nothing he could do about it.

Watching the brick houses give way to flat fields, he thought about Cecelia and Frances-Jane, never able to think of one without the other, and instead of the indescribably buoyant feelings Cecelia used to arouse in him, and the intense pleasure of remembering Frances-Jane, he felt himself close to despair. The unrelenting grip of regret seemed only to be tightening. And he had yet to write the letters.

sixteen

In the morning, Henry went in search of orange juice and Panadol and found Trot in the kitchen, a tea towel slung over his shoulder as he wiped down the bench. The sight of the orderly kitchen brought Henry an instant measure of relief from his headache.

'You're a legend, Trot.' He rubbed his temples, squinting in the sunshine that found its way between curtains. 'That's worth a million bucks. You had anything to eat yet? The fridge's full of whatever.'

'Nah.' Trot dropped the tea towel on the bench. 'Thought I might go fishin' since the day looks all right, and get a bite to eat at the coffee shop at the wharf. Janine's gunna get some groceries later. She's still sleepin'. I guess we had a few last night.'

'I guess we did.' Henry went into the pantry, grabbed a loaf of plastic-bagged bread as if by the ear, found the Vegemite, reappeared, and dumped them on the bench.

'Toast first. For cleaning up, Trot, whatever we got is yours. The coffee shop isn't always open, anyway. Want some orange juice?' Henry swung around, feeling unsteady on his feet. 'Weeties? Panadol? Eggs? Help yourself. Bowls are down there. Cereal's here.'

Trot hesitated, took out a couple of blue and yellow cereal bowls, and handed one to Henry.

'Ta. Geez, you killed that wind surfin' yesterday. How'd ya learn to do that?'

Henry took the milk and margarine out of the fridge. Yesterday, he reckoned, was probably the best day out on the water he'd ever had.

'I've been at it for a while.' He measured out cereal. 'The old man used to have a yacht down at a yacht club, so I got a sailboard instead.' He did not want Trot to get the wrong idea. 'Like, it wasn't a big yacht. Just a sixteen-footer he used to sail with another guy.' Henry looked around for the sugar bowl – or had it been broken? No, that was something else.

'Takes guts though,' Trot said. 'Those waves were bloody huge.'

Henry guessed it did at some level, but it wasn't as if he hadn't been sailing for years.

'You've just gotta tell yourself not to freak out.' Which was true. He poured milk. 'And like I said, I've been at it for a while.' Henry was keen to divert attention from himself. 'I mean, d'you play footy?'

Trot nodded, spreading a solid layer of sugar on his Weeties.

'Yeah, Seniors. Spoons? Ya got any?'

Henry found two.

'Ta.' Trot sat on one of the kitchen stools. 'Yeah, but in Stratty, mate, if ya can do up your laces they put ya in the firsts. And ya can't get drowned playin' footy. Although the grounds can be bloody wet.'

'Still,' Henry said, 'it's kind of the same thing. Just the hits come from different directions. Like, you can get smashed playin' footy, eh?'

'True. And I have been.' Trot gave his cereal a bit of a stir. 'Hey. Here she comes. Sleepin' beauty.'

Janine, in a blue kimono, came up from the lounge and into the kitchen, her hair wet and combed straight. She looked a lot younger, Henry thought, without make-up.

'Hi, Henry.' She dabbed at her nose with a bunched-up tissue. 'How are you this morning? You were very funny last night.' She crossed her arms, pushing open a fold in the front of dressing gown, Henry seeing the rounded side of her breast before the fold was removed. He ignored it in his best Henry Lyon fashion.

'Was I?' He couldn't really remember and so pulled what he hoped was an appropriately neutral face. Outside, he saw the rain seemed to have washed the whole world clean. 'I'm not usually.' He could remember Marcelle saying something about him showing off just before she and Angie left. 'Trot's going fishing,' he added. 'He's already cleaned the kitchen. It's unbelievable.'

'Yeah, he's not too bad.' Janine cast a critical eye over him, bulky in a red flannel shirt and green tracksuit pants. 'Underneath his fantastic wardrobe.'

'Yeah, absolute superstar.' Trot rinsed his bowl and rested it to drain. 'Hey, kid,' he said, 'go get us some groceries this mornin', will ya? Take the car. I'm goin' fishin'. Me wallet's by the bed. Some things for dinner or lunch or somethin'. Do we use the dishwasher here, Henry, or what?'

'Shit, yeah.' Henry slotted bread into the toaster. 'Nick's old man owns a bulk store. Appliances we do. But you take your car.' Henry pushed the toast down. 'I can drive Janine into town or we can walk. If you've got rods and stuff to carry, the wharf's a bit of a hike.'

'Yeah? Sure?' Trot stretched. 'Okay. Just don't let her buy a hundred buck's worth of chocolate.'

The day, Henry felt, had an edge of brilliance to it, the sun varnishing one side of every tree, house, and boatshed with light whilst simultaneously drawing sharp black shadows from the other. He walked with Janine who wandered along the road, hands up under the front of her windcheater, dawdling like a school kid.

'Your friend, Marcelle, Henry,' Janine said. 'She seems nice.'

Henry faltered. He'd been thinking about Marcelle, but not for the last ten minutes.

'Yeah, she is.' He smiled, pleased, and thought of Marcelle with affection. 'She gets kind of moody,' he added, in a way to balance things up. 'She reads stuff into things that isn't always there. I'd better go up there this morning and see her. She kind of likes me to be around a bit more than I am I think.'

In front of them the water was green, glass-bright, and the narrow strip of sand across the inlet looked as white as salt. Janine took her hands out from under her windcheater.

'Ya wanna hear a secret, Henry?' She lifted her sunglasses and winked. 'You'll know what I'm talking about, kind of.'

'Will I?' Henry smiled, although he felt as if the conversation had lurched into risky territory. 'Well, you know, if you think you should tell me.'

Janine pointed to a park, its swings and slide dull with dew.

'Let's go in there. Off the road for a minute.'

Henry let her lead the way, the inlet sparkling in front of them like some sort of heavenly road. Tide's coming in, he thought absently. Surf would be building.

'This secret,' Janine said, walking on breezily in front, 'is a fair-sized one. Or at least *I* think it is.'

Henry was not about to argue. He had the feeling Janine was a very much sharper person than he had originally thought. They arrived at the flat-topped sea wall, damp sand below, the salty smell of exposed seaweed rising. A family of purple crabs clattered away. Janine grinned as she dumped her bag on top of the wall.

'Don't look so worried, Henry. It's not a *huge* scandal.'

'Okay.' Henry felt entirely in her command. He looked back up the hill toward Nick's house and was somewhat relieved to see he and Janine were out of sight. 'Well, if you think you should tell me, you know, well, I'd like to hear it. Sure.' He crossed his arms, prepared to listen.

Janine slapped his elbow. 'Oh, Henry, you're *too* bloody nice. You're like Trot.' She returned her hands to their place back up under her windcheater. 'Anyway. *Stop* frowning. You look like a beetle.'

'Right.' Henry's poked his fingers into his forehead. 'I won't. That's what my mum says. That I look like a beetle.'

Janine leant back against the wall and let the sun fall full on her face, as if she had to draw the required amount of energy from it before she could start.

'Well, you know Andy Lansell in the diary?' She did not give Henry time to answer. 'And the Miss Hainsworth engagement thing and all that? You know the basic story anyway, right?'

Henry nodded. 'Yeah, *basically* I do.' He wondered where this could be going exactly.

'Relax, Henry.' Janine tapped him again with her knuckles. 'This isn't "Sale Of The Century". Well, *anyway*, you know Andy never married Miss H because he never came back . . . but guess what?' Janine's voice held an emotion Henry couldn't identify. 'He's actually my great-grandfather. So there you are.' She folded her arms. 'There's a little bit of history for you. He's not s'posed to be, but he is, if you get my drift. So there's your secret for the day.'

Henry had the sensation of three or four streams of thought spinning in his head like the reels of a poker machine.

'Andrew Lansell is . . . your grandfather?' Even that statement he realised he'd got wrong.

'Great-grandfather,' Janine said promptly. 'Yes, he is.'

'But –' Henry blinked widely. 'So how's that work? I mean, he never came back. He got killed. So . . .?'

'Before he left.' Janine shrugged. 'He got a girl called Frances-Jane Kelly pregnant. He met her just before he left for the war. His family looked after her – well, they gave her money and things until she married someone else. Andy's war mates helped her as well, apparently.' Janine looked up the hill where gum trees stood tall amongst the houses. 'And then later *her* daughter went back to Strattford because she'd been left a house in a will and – you don't need to know all that stuff, but that's the story.'

'So –' Henry was still stuck between at least a couple reels of thought. 'But what about Miss Hainsworth? What did she do when all this was going on?' The story seemed riddled with unknowns. 'I mean – how did you find out?' Henry wondered if this was a reasonable thing to ask.

'My mum told me last year.' Janine shrugged. 'When I turned eighteen. Andy didn't write it in his diary, obviously. He didn't mention it because I guess he knew that diaries get read by other people.' Janine turned to Henry, the reflection of the sun in her dark glasses. 'I wish he *had* written about it. It would've been nice to know what he really thought – well, I *guess* it would.'

Henry nodded slowly. Not many guys would ever write that sort of stuff in a diary, he thought. They might talk about it to their mates, but they'd never write it down.

'So does Miss Hainsworth,' he said carefully, 'know about,

ah, you? Um, this?' Henry felt the story to be elusively hovering, a ghost of itself in time. 'Do you think?'

Janine shrugged, her hair shiny and dark under a sky that was holiday-brochure blue.

'I dunno, Henry. Sometimes she tells me things as if I'm kind of special to her. Other times she's been pretty hard on me. Which would make sense, you know, if she knew.' Janine put her hands on the wall behind and lifted herself onto it. Henry decided to do the same. 'A couple of times she's tried to get me to leave Strattford to do something else, you know, for my future, but she's *never* not been nice, really.' Janine brushed sand off the wall with a flat hand. 'I reckon she probably knows Andy got someone pregnant, but I doubt she'd know I am *who* I am.' Janine picked up a tiny spiral shell someone had left on the wall. 'Otherwise I don't think she'd talk to me. She's got a long memory, Cecelia. Maybe she just thinks Frances-Jane went off and had the baby and that was the end of it. But it wasn't. It isn't.'

'So, you wouldn't tell her then?' Henry hoped this was a fair enough question.

Janine paused, Henry waited.

'Ah – I don't know.' Janine carefully placed the shell back down as if it was an ornament. 'But probably not. I mean, she's so old a lady and it all happened such a long time ago, I don't think that there'd be any point *in* telling her. I mean, it *was* a scandal back then. She would've suffered over it. Let sleeping dogs lie. That might be smartest.'

Henry couldn't formalise what he was thinking. Images of the Avenue of Honour and the cypress trees and Andy's plaque merged. The blurry weight of eighty-five years pressed down.

'But in a way she might want – you're – does Trot know?'

Janine flicked her hair back and laughed. 'Oh shit, *no*. My God, I don't know what he'd think and I'm not about to find out. That's one of the reasons why I'm calling it a secret. I mean, he's had Andy Lansell pushed at him for the last ten years by Cecelia. So maybe he might not want to live with Andy Lansell's great-granddaughter for the rest of his life.' Janine's eyebrows arched. 'If Trot and I go on like we are, you know what I'm saying. But I don't think there's much to be gained by telling him or Cecelia, do you?'

'Well, no,' Henry said. 'No. Well, I don't know. I mean, maybe Cecelia would like to know – about you? Like, it did happen eighty –' Henry wondered if he'd gone too far. 'It's tricky.'

'It is.' Janine slid off the wall. 'My problem, anyway. Come on, we'd better get going. Enough scandal for one day, hey?' She looked at the boats in the inlet as if she was checking they were all still there. 'God, this is a nice place. I'm glad we came. Thanks for asking Nick for us, Henry. It was good of him to let us come.'

'Yeah, he's a good guy.' Henry saw a beer bottle on the ground, picked it up, and lobbed it into a bin. 'So are you, you know, happy that Andy Lansell *is* your great-grandfather?'

Janine's smile was instantaneous. 'Yeah, I am. I mean, the very first time I saw his photo – *before* I knew all this stuff – I thought he looked so *Australian*. With those clear eyes that could look forever.' Janine's eyes were lit with what Henry thought was a kind of serious good humour. 'And if it wasn't for him, I wouldn't be here, would I? So, yes, I love him.' She spoke with certainty. 'And I could not bring myself to hate him for making love to someone just before he went off to fight. Not that I approve of that kind of carry-on generally, though.' She grinned. 'You're the first person I've ever told this to. Sorry. I guess I shouldn't have really laid it on you like this.'

'No.' Henry spoke quickly. 'It's fine. It's amazing.' He didn't think he could really blame Andy, either, for making love to a girl before heading off to the war – because that seemed like about the best thing as compared to about the worst. 'I'll read the rest of the diary,' he added. 'You know, while you're here.'

'Sure,' Janine turned out onto footpath. 'I hoped you'd say that.'

June 23 1917,
Etaples Training Camp.

Hard yakka here for the boys. They call it the bullring. Training hand-to-hand fighting, marches with full-kit, square-bashing, obstacle runs, the bloody lot. Fit, though. Ready to go. Can hear the guns on the wind.

Andy could feel a hint of moist warmth radiating from the earth wall. He stood looking at the neatly dug trench that was strengthened with timber and sandbags and did not feel as if he was in a completely strange place. He was from the bush; he was used to dirt, he'd dug ditches and post holes, put in crops, helped make dams, he loved the bloody stuff, but he made damn sure to keep his rifle clear, the tiniest clod capable of jamming the weapon.

He stood listening to the muted sounds of equipment rubbing and clinking as the men in the line waited, and above them all the continuous song of a hovering lark seemed to suggest that it was not too late to turn back from what was proposed, that there were other more benign things that they could be doing. His new tin helmet was heavy and exerted pressure on his neck.

'I feel like bloody Brer rabbit,' Darcy muttered. 'Give the old fox a fright, but.' He twisted his rifle. 'Ten inches of bayonet up the bum and a couple of slugs for good measure.'

Bob and Andy exchanged looks, shook their heads in amazement, which Darcy took as an appropriate response.

'Just keepin' the troops amused,' he said. 'In our last moments before we confront the menace of the dirty Hun.'

Along the trench Andy could see an uneven line of helmets, tensed arms, and the backs of bare necks as the men faced the front, looking down at the fire step they would climb up onto before going right over the top for the mock attack.

'Ten seconds, boys.' Ripper's eyes never left his watch. 'Get ready, men. No muckin' around. Right. *Seven*. Six. Five. Four. Three. Two. *Go!*'

Andy climbed upwards through the sound of cheering and shouting, one knee on the solid hump of sandbags, then he was over the top and out in the open in a broad field, cool air in his eyes as he went forward with hundreds of infantrymen in a long mostly straight line. The air shivered and cracked with the rattle of machine guns, the enemy trench partially hidden by mounds of dirt, rusty belts of barbed wire, and a few concrete block houses complete with active gun ports.

Smoke drifted, yellow and grey, Andy running through skeins of it, feeling it in his throat as he stopped, dropped, and fired a blank at a soldier who disappeared. He ejected the spent cartridge, pushed home another, closed the bolt, stood, and ran on.

Around him soldiers leapt up from holes like dead men come to life, khaki-green figures in smoke, a light machine gun chattering to Andy's left, blue smoke rolling as the gunner swept the ground.

'Into the trench, boys!' Ripper yelled. 'Go!' He gestured with a bent arm. 'Come *on!* Remember that these bastards are bloody *Germans!* Then take those bloody pillboxes. Go!'

Andy and Darcy skirted the hand-dug shell holes, running hard, heaving for breath, seventy pounds of equipment jogging up and down on their backs like bags of cement, shovel handles up like insect antennae. Ripper seemed to be everywhere and nowhere, a disembodied voice like some avenging demon coaching his crew.

'Jump in boys! Bomb those strong points! Bayonets up! Don't

stop! Run and fire! Move and fire! Block with those bags! Work together!'

Andy stopped at the trench, fired, jumped in, almost fell, staggered upright, then moved along between its planked walls, working his rifle bolt as he looked for dugouts. Small groups of soldiers crouched at corners where the trench zigzagged, hurling fake grenades, then charged forward into smoke and noise, only to come to a shambling halt as a whistle was blown three times. Andy leant against a section of trench strengthened with woven branches, struggling for breath, feeling as if he might vomit. Spark-coloured stars floated in front of his eyes, blood pounded in his hands and head, he wore a layer of heat and sweat like a second tunic. Above him, Ripper appeared, strangely colourless against the skyline, and calmly statuesque.

'Very good, boys.' The sergeant lit a cigarette, disposed of the match, and looked comfortably down on the men in the supposedly captured trench. 'And if yers can all do that sort of work a bit further on up the road, we might actually manage to kill a few of the bastards. And that, of course, is what this six bob-a-job caper is all about.'

Bob caught Andy's eye as they rested against the wall, tin hats crooked, sweat running. He cleared his throat and spat.

'I can see a few problems with this actual jumping *into* an enemy trench,' he said quietly. 'One being that the other bastards'll probably be in it. Another being they probably won't like it.'

Andy nodded. His hands seemed to swell with each beat of his heart. He felt a kind of a mad elation, as if the road they'd embarked upon had suddenly dipped down so steeply that there was no question of ever turning back or aside.

'Yeah, not bright,' he said. 'There seems to be somethin' kind'a lacking in the planning.'

'Yeah, it's called imagination.' Darcy dumped his pack. 'And the element of surprise.'

seventeen

Henry spent the afternoon with Marcelle at the pool at her apartment. Mostly they talked and swam and when Marcelle read, Henry was content to gaze off into the middle distance and think of nothing too much at all, although he was well aware of her beside him, the musky smell of warm skin and sunscreen drifting. There were only three other people at the pool and they were across the other side, staying out of the sun.

'Go upstairs?' Henry suggested at one point, his hand on Marcelle's wrist, his heart beating hard, as the sun edged across the sky toward the rim of the hill. 'Angie's at the beach.'

Marcelle didn't reply or shift her arm, but Henry felt, or thought he felt, a tension move through it.

'Why not?' he asked bravely. 'I mean, come on, it's a beautiful day.' Henry wasn't sure what he meant by that. 'Come on. Please.' He let fly with a grin.

Marcelle shifted her legs, raising her knees, bringing them together. She let her book fall face-down on her stomach.

'I don't know, Henry,' she said, and scratched the top of one foot with the toes of the other.

'You don't know what?' He didn't like the sound of this, as if they were moving reluctantly, but moving all the same, toward some problem between them that Marcelle could see, but he couldn't.

'I just don't know.' She lifted her hand, then put it back down on the white plastic armrest. 'It's just that something's not working out all that well between us, Henry. I mean, I thought you'd want to spend, like, all your time with me up here, and there are other things. I just don't think you're kind of one hundred per cent into this, are you?' She looked at him, with her sunglasses on, and picked up her book as if she might go back to reading.

Henry scratched his shoulder. He didn't know how to answer. He didn't think he'd done anything particularly wrong. Well, he couldn't see that he had. Yes, he could feel that maybe he wasn't the most adoring boyfriend, but he didn't think he *had* to be – like, not all the time. Like, were they about to get married?

'Hey, I'm allowed to spend a *bit* of time with my friends, aren't I?' he said, purposefully avoiding the word 'mates'. 'I don't try and stop you seeing Angie, do I?'

'It's not really that.' Marcelle ran her fingernails along the armrest, her face shaded by the wide brim of her hat. 'It's like you're kind of caught up in too many other things to fit me in.' She looked him full in the face. 'You *like* me and all that, but I'm just *one* thing in your life, and that's not quite how I think it should be. There's your mates and sailboarding and there was school and basketball, and now there'll be uni, and where will I be in all that exactly? In your schedule?'

Henry could sense the accuracy of what she was saying,

but felt that he had to deny it anyway. It wasn't *totally* accurate, but he could tell by the way he was feeling – which was dismal – that there was certainly some truth to it.

'But –' What could he say now? That he would spend all his time with her and that they should take things *really* seriously? He couldn't say that.

'I'm not a hobby, Henry.' Marcelle draped her sarong over her legs. 'But that's how you treat me and I won't let you. We're supposed to be together, not meeting whenever it suits you.' She looked at the glittering pool and did not take her eyes from it. 'I think I might go home. I think I might catch the bus. I don't feel really very happy up here.'

'Go *home*?' Henry was struck by a real and sudden sadness. He knew that it was possible that he had let Marcelle down in a big way.

He watched her take her sunglasses off, wipe her eyes, and he swore to himself and at himself. He got hold of her hand.

'Look, don't go home,' he said. 'Please. I mean, I'm sorry. This is your holiday as well, okay? Marcelle, I'm really sorry. I am. If – don't go. I don't want you to. I'm a prick, but please, don't go.'

Marcelle wiped her eyes with a fingertip and started to gather her things.

'I'm going up to the flat.'

Henry stood up. 'I'll come with you.'

'No you won't.' She would not look at him. 'You go home to your place and I'll talk to you later.'

Henry didn't want to leave. He felt responsible – no, not responsible for wrecking her holiday – that was soft. He felt *guilty* about wrecking it, because he'd seen the writing on the wall, and he'd ignored it. It was his fault.

'All right,' he said, feeling right now as if he might never see her again. 'I'll go.' Everything, it felt like, had changed. The day felt different, the whole town felt different, *he* felt different – as if he'd discovered himself to be someone not very pleasant.

'I'll call you later,' he said. 'On your mobile. I'm sorry, Marcelle.'

She pushed her feet into a pair of white leather thongs that Henry had not seen before.

'Yes, all right.' She walked to the gate and he followed, the two of them standing together as she pulled up the latch. 'I'll see you later.' She took the path that led to the units, leaving Henry to take the path that led to the road.

'Okay,' he said. 'I'll ring.'

He left the apartments and began to walk down the hill. The view of the town seemed to have a bright coldness about it, as if he had been excluded.

Trot drove the Commodore with Janine in the front and the boys in the back. The road, running beside the local airport, widened into three lanes and Trot indicated, pulling out to pass a slower Falcon.

'Go for it, Trot,' Marcus said. 'Turbo, baby.'

Janine turned to speak around the headrest. 'It has no turbo,' she said patiently, as if she was discussing the sharing of colouring books between the children in the back. 'It has everything else, but no turbo.'

Henry saw that the Falcon had also sped up, the middle-aged driver staring dead-ahead, both hands on the wheel, the blonde woman beside him looking annoyed.

'He no want to be passed,' said Marcus, looking out his window. 'He put foot down.'

Trot's big knees pumped as he changed gears, the Commodore hesitating for a split second before leaping like a greyhound from a box, V-8 blasting, Henry enjoying the primitive thrill of speed and unleashed power. For a moment he stopped thinking about Marcelle.

'See ya later, *sucker!*' Nick waved out through the back window. 'You have just been embarrassed by the Trot Holden Commodore V-8 Racing Team.'

Henry felt the Commodore not so much slow but cease to accelerate, the speedo needle dropping back quickly from one hundred and forty kilometres an hour to just over one hundred. The Falcon passed as if making a last charge for the chequered flag.

'Ohh, *Trot.*' Marcus sadly watched it go. 'Geez, *that* was a bit disappointing. I mean, that thing was actually a *company* car.'

Trot laughed, checked his mirrors, and moved over to the left.

'Yeah, but I only ever really push it when I'm by meself. Besides, with you three over-sized rich bastards, this thing was going' like a pig. Is this the pub? Golf club, whatever.'

A large building, white-roofed, stood on the highest point of a golf course that was so green the grass fairways looked like a linked series of lagoons.

'Yeah, Trot.' Henry leant forward. 'Go right, then down there, and park next to the fence.'

'Too easy.' Trot swung into the carpark, drove down the road, and turned into the first available space.

With a banging of doors, everyone got out, Henry straightening his shirt, seeing that beyond the golf course was a lake and in the lessening light the water was a beautiful solemn grey, the black grids of oyster farms exposed in the shallows, graveyard straight. There was something about knowing Janine's secret and looking at this view, with hardly a house to be seen and the trees unmoving in the dusk, that made Henry think of Andy Lansell.

Andy might've been gone a long time, Henry thought, but the story was still real, and continued on, in a way. He thought about the place Andy was buried and imagined it to be cold, bleak, and windswept.

'Come on, Henry.' Janine waited, anchoring Trot to the spot, their arms linked. 'Give yourself a break. You can go round and see her tomorrow. I'm sure things will've worked themselves out a bit by then. It'll be all right. I guarantee it.' Henry caught up. He hadn't been thinking about Marcelle, but he began to now.

'This motel you work at, Janine,' Marcus said, sitting down after returning from the bar with drinks, 'is that a long term thing or are you gunna do something else?'

Henry had wanted to ask the same question, but, weighing it up, he'd decided it was a bit iffy. Maybe she liked working at the exclusive Rosewood Motel? Maybe that was *exactly* what she wanted to do for the next ten years. Not everybody, he knew, had their sights set on living the big life like Marcus, like Nick, and like Henry himself did. A career, whatever *that* was, was not something all people wanted. Jesus. Nick's older brother was a dope-smoking surfer living in Bali who called himself a photographer. Not that there was anything wrong with that.

Janine lit a cigarette and tossed the matchbook back onto the table.

'I would like to travel,' she said, 'which is just *so* original, I know. Not that I've got any money.' She looked at a line of attention-seeking poker machines, then focused on the edge of the table where her matches sat like a tiny fallen bird. 'Yeah, I guess I am in a bit of a rut, but that's all right.' She smiled upwards as she drew the ashtray toward her. 'I mean, I'll probably wait a couple of years for Trot to finish his course, then maybe we'll go somewhere.'

'Might have to swim.' Trot opened a bag of chips and poured them into a wooden bowl. 'Because I won't have a lot – *correction* – I won't have *any* money after I've finished me course, either.'

'Win it on a poker machine.' Marcus pulled out notes and coins from a pocket. 'Like I am. Watch me. Anyone comin'?'

'Oh, you loser.' Nick stuffed chips into his mouth. 'Of course I am. Come on, chappies.' He took more chips as if they were rations for the journey. 'Lucky day.'

Trot stood. 'You up for it, Henry? Janine? C'mon. Invest a couple of bucks, make a mill.'

Janine held up her cigarette. 'I'll finish this. Henry, you keep me company. I want to talk to you about Marcelle for a minute.'

'Uh-oh,' said Trot, backing away from the table. 'I'm out of here.'

Henry pretended as if he was going to get up too, but generally when girls asked him to do something, he did it. He stayed where he was. Marcus sat down, put his chin on his hand, and leant forward attentively. 'No, I find this sort of shit really interesting. Go on, Janine. Fire away.'

'Get lost.' She waved her cigarette. 'Look. Nick needs a hand to lose his money.'

Marcus did as he was told.

'So, Henry – ' Janine ground out her cigarette, 'what's the problem with Marcelle? If you don't mind me asking.'

Henry didn't mind. He was glad to be given the chance to talk.

'Basically,' he said, 'she thinks that I'm not into it, properly.'

Janine bit her lip. 'Are you?'

'I'm not sure.' Henry looked up at the ceiling. It had millions of tiny holes in it. For ventilation, he guessed. Or maybe sound-dampening. 'I guess that sometimes I'm not. Well, I mean, I like her. A lot.' He wanted to explain. 'But you know, for God's sake, how serious do you have to be? I like to do other things as well.'

Janine took a single potato chip from the bowl.

'So would you mind if she went off and did a lot of other

stuff? I mean, it's when someone feels second best, you know, that problems kick in.'

Henry acknowledged there might be truth in that.

'She says she might go home on the bus. Early.' He felt shame, or something close to it. 'I mean, I've told her not to. I'm going to go down and talk to her again.' Henry put his elbows on the table. 'I talked to her on the phone today. She hasn't made up her mind. Yeah, no, I think I've stuffed up.'

Janine settled further into her chair. 'It's not easy, is it?' She smiled, then instantly dismantled the shape she'd made with her hands. '*Unless* it's going *really* well, then it's a cruise. But try not to let her go home on the bus. That would be my advice.'

'Yeah.' Henry agreed with that totally. 'That'd be bad. And my fault. Maybe I can get Angie to say something?'

Janine shifted her hair away from her face. Henry could imagine how thick it would feel if he held it. And cool.

'Change of subject,' she said. 'So what d'you think *you'll* be doing in five year's time?'

Henry was surprised by the question, but he knew, because he'd thought it over many times before, that in five year's time he'd be finished his course, all going well, and hopefully he'd have a job in a law office.

'I guess I'll be a lawyer,' he said. 'If I go okay.'

Janine glanced over to where Trot, Marcus and Nick crowded around a poker machine, having pooled their funds, it seemed. Trot was thumbing the coins in, Marcus was pushing the buttons, and Nick was attempting to persuade the machine with a subtle smack or two.

'That sounds good.' She raised her eyebrows. 'I'm sure you will be. You're a person who does what they say they will. And Marcelle? What are her plans?'

Henry folded a circular beer coaster in four then flattened it out again. Did he always do what he'd said he would? Maybe. Probably. But not with Marcelle. He might not have promised her anything, but he'd let her down all the same.

'She wants to be a share broker, like her old man,' he said. 'And he drives a big black BM so I guess he knows what he's doing. She's going to work in a share broking office this year then do an economics degree. She's pretty sharp.'

'She makes me feel like a loser,' Janine said. 'God. Lawyers, guns, and money. Geez, you guys. What about Marcus and Nick?'

'Marcus is doing a building course.' Henry scraped together what chips were left in the bowl. He'd buy some more in a minute. 'And Nick's doing a science degree. He wants to make a billion in bio-technology.' Henry laughed and spilled chips. 'But he'll blow up the lab first. Or get busted making drugs.'

'You boys –' Janine moved a shoulder, 'you're all so – I dunno. Like you've all got it sussed.' She tapped the table. 'Come on, let's go see the losers.'

July 6 1917,
Northern France.

Heading to the front. Not directly. We stop here, we stop there. Can hear the guns all the time now. Australia seems very distant. Strattford is like a dream. Seeing some great horses. Big matched teams. France feels different, but hard to describe.

The boys marched under a wispy blue sky from one small village, red-bricked and slate-roofed, to the next, past workers bent double in the flat fields, large woven baskets like full stops at the end of every row. The sound of artillery was a distant, eerie rumble, as if there were giants at work somewhere over the horizon and that if the boys stayed where they were, the war might remain unseen forever.

'Where we're goin's a pretty quiet sector,' Ripper said, cradling his rifle, muzzle sheathed, as he tramped in rough time. 'But dependin' on what might be planned, or what might *happen*, eventually we'll move up from behind the lines into supply trenches, the reserves, and then on into the front line. So the idea from here on *in*, fellers, is to get as many of them in as many, in *any*, way possible.' The Sergeant bestowed a smile on those close by as if he was presenting five pound notes. 'Then there's less of them to get us. Ya see the logic in that, doncha? Anyway –' he looked away toward the low grey line of the horizon, 'you'll earn ya pay, one way or the other.'

Andy's head was hot and itchy. Under his haversack he could feel sweat. His rifle had rubbed a tender spot on his collarbone and its stock clicked like an unreliable clock against his collar badge, but all the discomfort, including the knowledge he had letters to send Cecelia and Frances, were not enough to over-ride the sense of excitement that hovered like static electricity.

'I'd like to stop now.' Darcy extracted a thumb from under a strap. 'And wait for the pie cart to catch up. This hikin's gone past a joke. I could be quite happy snoozin' in that paddock right there. In that grassy corner.'

'Well, just ask,' said Bob. 'I'm sure Ripper'll be right.' He nodded, slouch hat worn low. 'Looks like a nice little town comin' anyway, so I guess we'll all be into the pub for lunch, a few pots, and a game of darts.'

'Yeah, Bob,' Andy said. 'You'd be on the money there, mate.'

The village ahead seemed to have imploded into low red heaps of rubble, although the road, arrow-straight and cobbled, lanced through it like a backbone that would never buckle. The colours of destruction, bright split bricks and dusty splintered timber, made Andy think of the intestines and bones of a butchered animal.

'Rooted,' said Darcy, surveying the couple of acres of shattered buildings. 'Like me. Absolutely.'

The troops moved through the ruins on the relentlessly straight road, brick walls blasted apart on either side, rafters supporting nothing but air and a few scabs of slates, the place smelling not of death or decay but of pulverised stone. It was a bit like, Andy felt, walking through a play on a stage, the walls of a few houses and shops rising and real-enough, but flat like the scenery painted on canvas that it had been his job to move between acts for the annual Strattford high school show.

'Nothin' a few barrers of mortar and a few dozen bricks wouldn't fix,' a brawny-necked soldier said. 'These Frenchies are just plain bone-bloody lazy. I could have this joint cleaned up in an afternoon.'

The rubble, piled hip-high beside the road, served to direct the movement and sight of the troops forward. In front, Andy could see long lines of waiting transport teams, the horses standing out to him like nothing else, the deep colours of their hides pulling at his vision whilst thoughts of home, of his horses grazing in pale grass at Kooyong, led him on to think about Cecelia coolly regarding him from under her wide-brimmed Melbourne-bought hat as she sat in the shade of her veranda, and then he thought of Frances who had glowed like moonlight in the darkness, irresistible and available, desire an overwhelming force between them.

Andy marched on, head down, listening to hundreds of pairs of boots crunching, the land opening out again into fields empty and sick-looking, scarred with old shell holes, turned over or abandoned to the armies, it seemed, to do with what they liked.

'She's warm.' Bob looked for the sun, which shone through torn clouds. 'Funny. I didn't expect it to be. I thought it'd be – I dunno. Cold. Freezin'.' He shrugged the shoulder that his rifle wasn't on. 'Not like this. I didn't expect trees. I didn't expect nothin'. But there you go.' He pointed. Poplar trees stood like fine colourless feathers in short, formal, lines. 'This is like bloody Thorpedale or something. Without the cows.'

'Bloody *smells* different.' Darcy sniffed hard, nostrils closing, his nose sharpening. 'Smells like bloody mud. And *look* at it.' He tilted his head toward the roadside. 'It's just some hopeless, useless, fuckin' flat shit that someone's said'll be good enough for a battle. I mean, *look* at it. Worth fighting over? That? Strike me. These Fritzies must be more dense than I thought. Not to mention us, for comin' all this way to the bloody party.'

Andy looked, not at the land but at the boys' heads, their hair below their hats all the mixed colours of a herd of horses, men in a line going up to the line, whatever exactly the 'line' was. It was something though, Andy knew; the line was definitely something – the line was something that he could not truly imagine, but it was certainly real, and he and the boys would go there, and then they would go beyond it, through whatever was there and arrive, perhaps, somewhere on the other side.

Suddenly, it felt like all his life he had been marching to the line, that there really had never been anything more important and bigger than the line, that the line had always been waiting for him, had always been there, the horizon of the new world, the final place of all places he would go – and then, hopefully, go back from, to places known, old, and understood.

The company halted, having come up behind waiting horse and mule teams. The order was given to fall out, the boys walking off the road to rest, unslinging packs, leaning rifles, cigarette smoke colouring the air that smelled of animals, stores, and equipment. Andy sat, arms draped around his knees, and looked. For as far as he could see the road was busy.

'Dunno what the hold-up is.' Darcy leant against his pack, boots splayed, hands behind his head, a cigarette dangling. 'But I'm bloody grateful.'

Bob lowered himself onto the ground that was covered with weeds and rank grass.

'Word is,' he said, 'we're waitin' for fourteen ambulances of wounded to get past. So how do you feel now, ya lazy hard-hearted bastard?'

''Bout the same.' Darcy blew a stream of smoke onto the face of his watch. 'For I cannot change what happens more'n a donkey ride away from my front door. Jesus. Look at that. Half past one.' He showed his watch. 'It's way past my bloody lunchtime. I'd be asleep back home, if I was at work.'

Andy savoured the rest. For a moment he felt like he was completely still while all around him everything was on the move to the north. He felt calm and quite happy. Time seemed to be passing slowly. He knew they'd been lucky already; the winter gone had been the coldest for a hundred years and they'd missed most of it. He'd heard stories of fields full of frozen men, British, German, Australian, and French all together; of troops dying of exhaustion, in muddy greatcoats weighing seventy pounds, of trench feet and frostbite, and huge battles fought over ground as hard as steel, the shells exploding onto it, thousands of iron fragments flinging out for hundreds of yards – and then the tellers of the stories would stop and shrug. You imagine the rest, mate. I can't tell you. So Andy, in a way, was pleased to be where he was, warm, safe, and quietly hopeful.

He looked up into sky grey-dappled with cloud. There was no explaining this, or anything, really, he thought. There was no sense in it. You were just here doing what you were doing, for one reason or another – and some places were good, and others were a hell of a lot worse. What you had to do, he figured, was take what was happening to you and deal with it according to your own rules. Put your stamp on it. Make it yours. And then you might see some sense in it, or get some sense from it. Or you might not.

eighteen

Henry, in bare feet, stood at the open window of Trot's Commodore. Trot, holding an unlit cigarette, squinted up into the sun that was high over Henry's shoulder.

'Come with us.' Trot went to turn the car off. 'It's just a few ks up the road. We'll wait. Have a fish off the wharf, a drink at the pub. They catch sharks up there and everythin'. I've got a spare rod ya can use.'

Henry scratched the top of one bare foot with the other. The slashing sound of water was loud as Nick blasted the garden with a hose.

'Nah, I won't,' he said. 'I'd like to, but later I might walk down the hill and go and see Marcelle. So I'll stick. Hey, catch a shark.'

'Yes, you go down there.' Janine held a stick of lipstick poised. 'And good luck. I expect a full report.'

Henry laughed, a sound that was more like a hiccup.

'Yeah, no worries.' He stepped back, clearing his toes

from the path of the car. 'See ya, guys.'

'Yeah, see ya, Henry.' Trot raised a thumb and drove out.

Henry wandered down to stand beside Nick. The sun was hot on Henry's back and below, across the river mouth, the beach was a strip of gold, the dunes and ti-tree behind less a colour than a texture. Henry thought of the girls, *any* girls, who'd be down there already, on their towels, absorbing the heat.

'Janine's cute.' Nick fired a silver bullet of water at a passing wattlebird. 'And Trot's a good bloke. I thought he might've been a bit of a bogan when he first turned up, but he's not. He's all right.'

Henry curled his toes over timber edging. For a moment he felt like he was at the centre of a whole lot of things; that the power of the place, the people around him, the thing with Marcelle, the Andy Lansell-Janine story, and the up-coming year, were all at work on him. Life was *happening* to him, it felt like, and happening to him in a way it hadn't before. Things were coming at him, more of them and in more complicated ways, and it felt all right – most of it, anyway.

'That's all you're gettin', plants,' Nick said, retreating across the driveway to pile the hose by the tap. 'Suck it up, guys.'

Henry followed. 'I think I'll go and see Marcelle. Before it gets too hot. I might shoot down there now, then meet you guys back here, and we'll go down to the beach. All right?'

Nick picked up a handful of the brown-black mulch that had been heaped around the garden.

'Good stuff, this,' he said, looking at it. 'From a scientific point of view. Doubt there's much of a buck in it, though.' He tossed it away. 'Okay. Get on your bike and we'll see you later.'

★ ★ ★

Henry knocked, the door feeling flimsy as cardboard. He waited, looking down, hearing footsteps, seeing that the mat had printed on it, *For Sandy Feet*. Whoever he is, Henry thought.

'Is that you, Henry?' It was Marcelle, her voice muffled, slightly wary.

'It is I,' Henry said. 'So, do you wanna buy a vacuum cleaner or not?'

The door opened, Marcelle in a shirt and skirt, not looking absolutely thrilled to see him, which Henry did not think was a sign of unlimited possibilities. She stepped back, red sneakers catching Henry's eye.

'Come in. Angie's just gone down to get some tomatoes. D'you want a coffee?'

Henry went inside. Through an open door he saw a black suitcase. The place smelled clean and the ocean, visible through sliding glass doors that opened onto a small balcony, was a distant melancholy blue.

'Yeah, a coffee'd be good.' He followed Marcelle into the kitchen. 'It's a beautiful day.'

Marcelle filled a kettle. 'That's what you said yesterday.'

Henry leant against the kitchen bench, thinking that the patterned skirt that Marcelle wore looked Balinese. Asian, anyway. He liked it. And with the sneakers. How did girls do it? Make themselves so tempting without a second thought.

'Please don't go home,' he said.

Marcelle turned the kettle on, in slow-motion Henry thought, then she stood against the bench opposite, arms-crossed and for a while they looked at each other without speaking.

'You only want me to stay,' she said eventually, 'so that *you* won't be upset that you've upset *me*. You don't want me to stay because of us. You just don't want to be responsible for wrecking things.'

Henry guessed what she had said was partly true, but only partly. He didn't want her to go.

'I *just* don't want you to go,' he said, unable to mount any other sort a defence. 'I *do* want you to stay.'

The mood of the apartment was unsettling. Henry was acutely aware of open doors to other rooms, a mirror, the deep silence of the flat like the oppressive atmosphere of a midday soap opera, the sea at the corner of his eyes as neutral a presence as Litmus paper. He felt like an actor and that everything he said was like lines from a script.

Marcelle moved away from the kitchen bench. Henry wondered if she might be about to cry. The silence of the place was driving him crazy. He heard footsteps on the outside stairs.

'That'll be Angie,' Marcelle said. Henry saw a silvery brightness in her eyes. 'All right? So what about we meet you guys down the beach this afternoon at two or something? At the wooden ramp. I don't want to talk about this now. I haven't made up my mind about what I'm going to do.'

'Yeah, okay, sure. That'd be good.' Henry uncrossed his arms. 'We'll be there. At two, by the ramp.'

There was a knock on the door. 'Mar-*celle*. You in there? Come on, girl. Arse to the door, sweetheart. I'm loaded down here like an African elephant.'

'Coming, *dearie*.' Marcelle turned away from Henry. 'We have an early morning visitor, Ange. It's Henry.' She went to the door and opened it, sunlight laying down a rectangle of light on the pale green carpet.

'Oh, *that* Henry.' Angie came into the kitchen, acknowledged him with a look, and lifted the bags onto the bench. 'Don't you go upsetting her now,' she said, 'or I'll hit you with a leek.' She pulled out a pale green vegetable and brandished it.

'Save it for the soup,' he said, 'I was just going. So, we'll see you guys at the beach, then?'

'Not if we see you first.' Angie opened the fridge. 'Joke,' she added, leek in hand, and managed to scowl and smile at him simultaneously.

Marcelle stood by the door as Henry went out.

'All right,' she said. 'Bye now. Thank you for flying Qantas.'

Outside, Henry was dazzled by sunshine. He went down the steps slowly, guessing that he didn't feel so bad. He felt things had taken a turn for the better. Today, at least, he thought, she wasn't crying. Close to it, maybe. But not quite.

Henry made a coffee, took out Andy's diary, and sat down in front of the wide windows in the lounge room.

'See if you can spill coffee on it,' Nick said, walking past, carrying a *Sports Illustrated* magazine. 'That'd make you popular.' He showed Henry a centrespread that featured a girl in a yellow bikini. 'Got any of these in there, brother? Or should I say *those*.'

Nick swept the magazine away before Henry could get a good look at it.

'It'll only ruin your concentration, sport. Get back to your brain food.'

'Already has.' Henry decided what Nick had said about spilling coffee wasn't stupid and moved the cup. He opened the diary toward the end and started to read.

On the night of May the twenty-eighth, 1918, Henry read, Andy Lansell had gone up to the front line, evidently carrying supplies, but the diary entry was so brief and matter-of-fact Henry knew that he was going to have to use his imagination if he was going to make any sense at all of the words, or the place.

Got back from carry to front line 3 a.m.. Odd up there. Quiet (tonight). Flares and star shells. Smell is quite choice. Made two trips tonight. One bloke knocked.

On the twenty-ninth of May, Andy had written,

Porridge (so-called) for breakfast. Put to work late morning unloading wire and pickets. Inspection tomorrow by brass. Will carry again tonight. Funny to think it is almost summer here, nearly winter at home. Guns booming.

Henry, still holding the diary, looked out of the windows, trying to picture this place in France or Flanders or wherever Andy was, but the brash summer colours of the beach knocked away any images he could come up with. It was only when he went back to reading with no expectation of action-packed writing or intricate detail, did he begin to think he might be starting to understand Andy at all.

Andy was a cautious writer, Henry reckoned, but not because he was a particularly cautious guy. He was saving his energy. Keeping his head clear, accepting the relatively minor things because the major were still to come. To write about anything in detail would be a waste of strength. The diary was in code. No, *code* was the wrong word. Henry decided Andy Lansell was writing in a kind of a *dialect.*

Andy was never going to write what he *really* thought, or what he had *really* seen or done, or perhaps even what had really happened. That's not what guys did, then or now. Or not many guys. Andy would be honour-bound to keep the whole thing low-key. To write too much would be far worse than writing too little. And perhaps one of the more important reasons he even kept the diary was that Cecelia had given it to him in the first place.

Henry doubted Andy was the type of guy who would go out and buy a diary himself. It was out of a sense of duty to Cecelia, he reckoned, that kept Andy writing. Or it was initially. And it was a sense of duty, Henry admitted, that kept Henry Lyon going as well. Or, often it was.

Henry read on through June and July of 1918, as Andy and his mates from Strattford, Bob and Darcy, moved up through the system of supply and reserve trenches until they were on the front line again. The way the entries were written hardly altered. Even the reporting of a mate from the battalion getting sniped through the ear was dealt with in one line.

Obviously, Andy was thinking and feeling far more than he was writing. Henry reckoned ninety-nine percent of guys there would have done the same. The whole thing seemed to come down to self-control, and it struck Henry that perhaps Andy was using the diary as a way to increase this control – that perhaps by recording all incidents as matter-of-factly as he had, he was laying down a foundation so that even worse situations could be handled when and if they happened.

In the middle of July of 1918, Andy had written,

Visited by strong German raiding party. Heard much shouting etc. Boys saw them off. Call that one a draw. What goes on here is quite unbelievable at times. Our boys are equal to any. You don't want to cross them.

Henry shut the diary. He couldn't imagine how he'd go fighting off a German raiding party. He doubted he'd ever get over it, even if he did survive. But surely not every person over there was born a wild and desperate fighter? How did the normal guys cope with it? Maybe you simply had to rise to the occasion, Henry thought, or let yourself get killed.

Henry and Marcelle walked along the beach away from town, their bare feet hardly leaving a print on the hard low-tide sand.

'I think, Henry . . .' Marcelle did not look at him. She looked along the sweep of beach to where the houses of another small town dotted the hills. 'Look, I think we'd better face the fact that we're due for a break. You know what I mean? I'm going to go home on the bus with Angie in a couple of days. I'm sorry, Henry, but I am.' Now she did look at him. 'I mean, we like each other, but that's not enough, is it? It isn't, I don't think.'

Henry knew he had no choice but to nod. The sadness that he'd had with him as soon as he and Marcelle had begun to walk, strengthened. It seemed to have invaded him, the whole day, the beach, the water, the sky, the feel of the wind on his face. Even the bloody sand dunes had a moody, desolate look to them.

'All right.' That's all he could think to say. 'All right. If you think so. If you think you have to go. But why don't –' He could think of nothing to add.

Marcelle stopped, her sarong blowing against her calves, her hands to hair to keep it off her face.

'Henry, look –' she moved around as if the words she was weighing up were shifting dangerously 'this is *not* all about you *not* spending time with me and that stuff. It's just that it's, the *whole* thing's not working out, is it? If it was I wouldn't have carried on about you doing things and you wouldn't be feeling guilty about all the stuff that you do. That's not the real problem. It's just us, all right?'

Henry knew he was hearing the truth.

'Yeah, all right.' He was unable to summon up anything else to say.

Marcelle stopped walking. 'Stop saying all right, will you? Look –'

'You stop saying look, then,' Henry replied automatically. 'All right?'

Marcelle let her face relax into a smile. She stopped to draw an arabesque in the sand with her toe. She'd never been a big walker.

'We should've done better,' she said. 'But, you know, we tried.'

Already Henry was missing her. He could see her with ultra-clarity and knew that she was a beautiful girl – and he had lost her because he was an idiot. White shirt, blue sarong, bare feet, belly button, blowing hair, good-looking. You won't be so lucky next time, he thought. You fluked this one and now you've blown it. He saw that she had painted her toenails pink and it made him laugh, then it made him jealous. He hated the thought of someone else being with her. He also didn't like how he was seeing himself – as kind of a low-life selfish bastard who was already thinking of what he was going to miss out on.

'If I threw myself down on the sand right here, right now,' he said, 'and kissed your feet, would that make any difference, d'you think?'

'It might,' Marcelle conceded. 'But it's probably more likely to make me laugh. Or kick you.'

'Maybe I won't then.' Henry looked at her, his head tipped a bit to one side. 'I like your toenails.'

'They're a holiday thing.' Marcelle cut a line back toward herself in the sand, using her arched foot like a little plough.

Henry stood, hands on hips. 'So –' he said. 'So.' Looking at her, the sarong clinging to her legs, he wanted to get hold of her hands, kiss her, go to bed with her, apologise, promise – but he knew she'd seen what he didn't want to see, and said what he wouldn't have said for years. He felt weak and devious.

'Let's walk back,' he said. 'I don't think I want to be with me anymore, either.'

July 9. 1917.
Flanders.

Into it now just about. Troops and guns everywhere. Wreckage by the roads. There's a few civilians roaming about. They look worried. So are we! Guns are thunderous some nights. Weather dry.

Andy's first impression of the supply area was as if a huge dull-coloured circus had pulled into town and taken over, although none of the bomb-blasted villages along the Menin road would ever be, he thought, in any need or state to host a circus again. Through the ghost city of Ypres the troops had marched, the soaring ruins magnificent still, rising over the men, seeming to trap silence and great volumes of blue air, although whole walls and roofs were gone and all of her citizens, leaving the place to exist like an unfinished monument to the unfinished war. Andy felt dwarfed by the towering wreckage and was relieved to march away, although he carried with him the feeling that he was not truly marching away from anything.

Past horse lines the boys tramped, past ammunition and supply dumps, past men in vests doing road work, past stacks of sweet-smelling timber, past horse teams patiently waiting, hitched to muddy limbers loaded with barbed wire, duckboards, picks and shovels, and crates that Andy figured held rifles – and on they marched until four in the afternoon when they reached an area below a small treeless ridge and were ordered to stop.

Brick farmhouses and sheds, partly destroyed by shellfire, stood in unfenced ground, pasture grown wild where it wasn't scarred by dirt and clay thrown out by men or explosions and left to settle like unmarked, untended, graves. The wind, smelling of salt and marshland, blew hard, dragging a sound from the place like the rustling of sheets or shrouds or sails. A captain, with a perfectly clipped moustache, ordered the men off the road and into a cobbled courtyard where rotting hay, rubble, and the now-white carcasses of lime-covered cattle had been dragged into a corner.

'Just lovely,' Darcy said, surveying the heap. 'Isn't it? Just bloody lovely.'

Captain Ellery, against a backdrop of broken wall, waited until the men had formed roughly in front of him before addressing them, his voice carrying loud and clear into the ranks on the numbing wind.

'We're here for the next day or so.' He waved a brass-tipped swagger stick at the farmhouse and surrounds. 'Then we'll be on up into a quiet sector to get a feel for things in the line, perhaps some carrying duties, and that's about all I can tell you today. Right. Get inside out of the cold and get settled. Hot food will be brought up. You're travelling well, men. We expect fine things of you. The diggers are well known up here for their unstinting efforts. Remember that.'

Darcy, pack hanging off one shoulder, turned toward the big brick barn.

'I had a footy coach talked like that. Except Spud tended to spit a lot more.'

The soldiers moved off, Andy noting that the sound of heavy guns, still dulled by distance, had intensified and rolled more fully, as if the only purpose of the sound was to reinforce the message that so far only chance had kept them apart.

'Are those guns ours or theirs, Captain Ellery?' Darcy asked, his path and the captain's crossing.

Captain Ellery stopped, boots and belt immaculate, polished to a depth of shine Andy had seen only on the best English saddles. The Captain, whose only outward sign of his eight months on the Western Front was a slight but ever-present tremor in his hands, was even taller than Bob Pike.

'They're all ours,' he said, his face composed of symmetrical planes that met at a nose that had been comprehensively broken and curved like a river. 'Every one of them. It's going to be a walk-over, Private Garrett. We'll stroll across, wander in, and sit right down. A day at the races, followed by a night at the opera, I should say.'

'Glad to hear it, sir.' Darcy snapped off a salute. 'I'll sleep a lot better for knowing that, Captain.'

Captain Ellery held his swagger stick flexed between his hands. Andy could see it vibrating like a diviner's rod.

'Yes, Private. I've also often found that bullshit works wonders in stressful situations.' He walked away, hobnails grating.

Andy followed Bob and Darcy into one of the barns, stored his rifle, took off his kit, unrolled his blanket onto mouldy straw and lay down, listening to the wind and watching tatters of grey cloth that someone had months or years ago nailed over the windows. The letters in his pack had been handed over and he had written another to his parents, telling them about Frances-Jane, blushing with humiliation as he had put down the words. Never before had he done something so wrong, so sure to bring dishonour on himself, and his family. And now, since Emily had died, leaving him as the only child and the family's one big hope, it could only make things harder and worse. Over and over he had cursed himself for being weak, for being stupid, for being dishonest, and even now, months later, he often woke hoping that the dance, the night, the whole thing, was a dream.

'We're goin' out to get this famous grub.' Darcy stood beside Bob who was trimming a fingernail with a pocket knife. 'Ya comin'? Because the rumour is that these lazy bunch of bastards won't bring ya tea in bed.'

Andy knew the longer he lay down the harder it would be to get up, but what he'd been thinking about had taken more of his energy than the ten-mile march. He sat, brushing straw off his tunic, but he didn't stand.

'Yeah, I'll see ya out there. I'll be there in a minute.'

Bob shut his knife and dropped it into a pocket.

'We'll save ya a bit of chocolate cake. Or do ya want the pavlova?'

Andy watched them go, then pushed himself back to lean against the wall. Looking up, the roof strung with cobwebs, he wondered what Frances-Jane was going to do, who she had told, and how she was coping – because if it was bad for him it was going to be a lot worse for her. He was over here, well hidden, but she was right there in the middle of all and everything. Unless she had taken off – which he could imagine her doing, and kind of hoped that she had, wild, blonde-headed Frances, heading for Melbourne, or for Bendigo where she had said she had a sister. And then in turn he thought of Cecelia, because he could never think of one girl without thinking of the other.

Cecelia was lost to him, he knew she was, his rights to dream of her given up; he was sure she would never again accept him in thought or in person, that as soon as she had read his letter she would be gone from him as surely as if he was to get himself shot tomorrow morning. There was no chance of any other outcome. He had lost the life he had hoped to have, and it was no one's fault but his own.

'Andy-boy.' Bob come back into the barn, scooping into a silver mess tin with a bent spoon. 'Grub's up. Not too flash, but not too bad.' He looked for somewhere to sit, found a wooden box, and kicked it over. 'Ya better get ya snout in before the trough's empty. Darcy's leadin' the charge. He's like a bloody bag with a hole in it.'

'I'll wait for the crowd to die down.' Andy tightened his collar against a draught diving down the back of his neck. '*Jesus* – ' he felt like spitting, but didn't. 'Yer know I've really bloody done it. I should be, I dunno, whipped.'

Bob put his mess tin down, took his hat off, and brushed back his hair with his fingers.

'Speakin' of that,' he said, 'because I have been givin' your, ah, indiscretion, some thought – I believe it's like this, mate.' Bob wiped his nose, then reclaimed his tea. 'Well, it's not like *this*.' He showed

Andy the muddy-looking stew. 'As this is pox. But I was thinking that compared to what's going on down the road here, you know, the war, well, what you've done is not the worst thing known to mankind, is it?' Bob stopped the spoon halfway to his mouth. 'It's bad, mate, but there's worse. It ain't the end of the road.'

Andy, hungry now, watched Bob eat. He could hear the boys outside in the grub line. He stood and brushed straw off his pants. A mouse scampered off between blankets.

'Yeah, but the thing is, Bobby –' he shook his head as if he was trying to dislodge the past, 'it's just *one* bloody mistake that I can't fix. I *can't* fix it. There's just *nothin'* I can do from over here.'

Bob plucked a strand of something from his stew and flicked it away.

'Yeah, but eh, it's not like you bloody killed anyone, is it?' Bob stopped, his spoon halfway to his mouth. 'Jesus, Mother and Mary, Lansell, it's kind of the bloody opposite. Look, I'll marry the girl meself. I will. It'll work out one way or the bloody other. Maybe not what you thought it would be, but it'll be all right.'

Andy scratched at a hot itch at the back of his neck. He hoped he didn't have lice, but guessed that he probably did.

'I've already offered to marry her,' he said. 'God knows what'll happen now. If I get out of this thing here I'll probably be shot as soon as I set foot in bloody Strattford anyway.'

Bob wiped gravy off his chin. 'More likely here, I would say.' He picked a scrap of meat from between his teeth. 'But Jesus, stop *worryin'*, mate. You get out of this and *then* you can start. In fact, it'll be a pleasure to do so and I'll join in. Go get somethin' to eat. The army'll shoot ya for starvin yourself otherwise. And get rid of the fuckin' horse face. That's my job.'

Andy summoned a grin as if it was something owed.

'Yeah, ya right. Better get in before Darcy sells my lot to a local pig.'

nineteen

The boys sailed late in the afternoon in moderate winds, the sun lighting up the waves as if from underneath. Henry hit everything as fast and as hard as he could, his take-offs turning into long jumps that he landed without fault, the hot buzz of joy replacing the dismal feelings of the afternoon walk with Marcelle. In one way, he guessed that he had wanted to end it with her. Like, it wasn't as if he didn't see any other girls he liked, because he did. He saw them every-day. On the other hand, he wondered if he actually did love her. Sometimes it felt like it, and then sometimes he was sure that he didn't. So, where did that leave him? He didn't know.

With speed, Henry swung through turns, coming out of them balanced and in control to leave the beach behind, or the shelving depths where the swells swept in to rise and self-destruct in avalanches of noise and foam. There was nothing else like this, he thought. Nothing.

After a shower, Henry put on clean jeans and shirt, took out Andy's diary again and read for another ten minutes. Now, Henry read, in July of 1917, Andy Lansell had been to the front – 'a quiet sector', he'd described it as, although he'd also recorded that sixteen men had been wounded and three killed by shell fire.

Henry stopped to think. He tried to imagine Nick and Marcus suddenly being killed in a similar situation – and then, with no time to think, he would have had to go on, like Andy had. Keep going on into battle – and then on, into other battles with more and more people being killed and wounded all around you. It was impossible to imagine.

But Henry did try to imagine this out-dated world where the guys sailed away in ships, were put in trains, marched to trenches dug with shovels, got into them, and existed. He'd looked at a few books at school, had seen photographs of horses carrying stuff along rough roads, men charging with bayonets, aeroplanes that were made from wood and wire, and Germans wearing helmets with spikes. It hadn't seemed real, but it was starting to seem more real now.

On TV he'd seen blurry black-and-white footage of soldiers going forward at a nonchalant trot, the whole thing looking too much like a Charlie Chaplin sequence to be taken seriously. And although Henry had watched the Charlie Chaplin soldiers sliding back into the trench as they were shot, or bayoneting each other, some with real moving faces, he realised that the Charlie Chaplin sequences were not the real thing at all – that the real thing had never been caught by camera, that the real thing was plainly too big, too loud, too wide, too unfathomable, and too other-worldly, for film.

Only someone who had been there, Henry reckoned, could know what it was really like. Only someone like Andy who had seen the thing rise in full colour to hang huge and immoveable over history, a guy who had helped make the thing, could know – in his head – what it was. Yet this little book, Henry knew, was a speck of dust blown from the thing itself. He opened it to a random page, September 17 1917, Andy's hand-writing neat, steady, and real.

All ready to go up to the lines tomorrow. Big plans in place over the next couple of weeks. Passchendaele. Nun's Wood. Polygon Wood. Belvaarde Ridge. It's the high ground we're after. Doubt Fritzy will be too pleased about giving it up.

Henry read on. The war went on.

July 26 1917,
Ypres, Flanders,
Happy Valley Trench.

In support trenches. It is a world of its own. Trenches everywhere. Endless miles of them with names and signposts. Dug-outs to sleep in. Settling in. Firing constant now. Never a dull moment.

Andy turned, the wind blowing hard on the side of his face, to see that the farmhouse and barns where the company had sheltered were far behind and becoming less clear, like a cluster of old, pleasant memories. The land around rose to a few low ridges, some bare, some wooded, yet more of it was flat like a board for a game to be played out on, puffs of distant grey and white smoke drifting across it like balloons broken loose from distant moorings. The soldiers talked excitedly.

'Shell bursts,' someone said with authority. 'There ya go, boys. Bloody shell bursts.'

'Really?' Darcy didn't bother to keep his voice down. 'I thought it was just some French friggin' farmer burnin' off the bloody blackberries. Just wait till I tell the Sergeant.' Darcy craned forward, looking through the ranks of men. '*Sergeant!* There's someone down 'ere says that that smoke is shell bursts. Is that true? Because if it is – ' Darcy walked on, 'someone could get hurt if they're not bloody careful.'

Andy grinned. Crossing the country, at least two miles off, he could see a series of zigzagging lines of trenches that ran roughly parallel, like cracks in the earth. A feeling, jagged like the trenches, cut sharply through his head, through the inner terrain, it felt like, of his brain. He was here. The trenches. Ten thousand miles they'd come. Six months it'd taken. And now they were here.

'A couple of miles on, men,' said Captain Ellery, halting the company on a quiet part of the road, 'we will enter the supports and depending on what is happening over the next weeks, we may or may nor make our way up through the system to the reserve trenches or the front line. This is a quiet sector, as you can hear. At the moment. And hopefully it will stay that way. Although I can issue no guarantees on that score. A bullet through the ear is still a bullet through the ear.'

Andy, preparing to march on, saw the Captain take tight hold of his stick with two hands, as if by controlling his tremors, he could eradicate them. The columns of men began to move, Andy listening to the sounds of the guns that seemed to come rolling down a distant valley. In areas on both sides of the road, sheltered by the shallow rise and fall of the ground, were soldiers and equipment, a few isolated artillery batteries hidden under camouflaged netting. The smell of cooking was strong, but not strong enough to mask an element of marshy foulness that clung to the air.

'Someone's been spreadin' the blood and bone a bit thick,' Bob said. 'By the smell of it.'

The company went on, making way for ambulances, lorries, and horse teams heading to the back areas where hospitals and supply dumps were placed beyond, mostly, the reach of the enemy artillery. On either side of the road were smashed limbers and gun carriages, the ground pock-marked with craters, and here and there the flat corpses of long-dead horses, some still in their traces.

'A cheery old place we find ourselves in,' Bob said. 'As we tramp along with a song in our hearts.'

'And a fart in our trousers,' Darcy added. 'Just for good measure.'

Andy saw a rider on a decent horse approach Captain Ellery, dismount, then point across country to where three or four fortified holes were dug into a bank, facing away from the German line. The dark entrances to the dugouts were strengthened and protected by pillars of sandbags, the ceilings supported by less-than-impressive timbers, and like splintered bones, the smashed trunks of trees stood out in front.

'All it needs is a nice new letterbox.' Darcy squinted across the destroyed ground. 'And I'd be quite prepared to move in, but as it is –'

Andy heard a scorching, streaking sound in the sky, a monstrous whistling that turned into a screaming wail that ended in an explosion of such force he fell to his knees, his head ringing, the ground shuddering, everything lost in noise and stinging earth. In front of him he saw one of the boys in the company fall full-length, still holding his rifle, one shoulder and his head replaced by an instant vivid burst of crimson and white, the sound of the shell seeming to be still crashing back and forth as the earth shivered.

Andy got up. The place still looked the same, the sky was blue, Bob and Darcy were getting up next to him, the wreckage beside the road was no more wrecked, the dugouts still stood, he was still in one piece – but the soldier on the ground lay full length and straight, blood pouring from his neck like water from a culvert. Smoke rose innocently from a crater that could've quite neatly housed an upright piano.

'All right, men.' Captain Ellery's voice hung in the air. Andy wondered if he was talking very slowly. It sounded like it. 'We'll get away from here and head for the dugouts. Four of you come forward and bring Boyd. And perhaps one brave man to bring his — no, I will bring it. You men, off the road. Go. Get to the dugouts and file in.'

The company, except for a small group standing around the Captain, moved away from the road and toward the dugouts. Forty yards away, Andy saw that curls of smoke still rose from the freshly churned dirt and the harsh stink of high explosive filled his nose. With the others, he walked over a track made of joined timber slabs, seeing that a number of the faces and tunics of the boys were dotted with blood and small pieces of flesh like the rind of some sort of strange fruit. He felt numb. He would've liked to sit down in the sun somewhere and recover, or at least think things through.

'Eh, you blokes over there.' Darcy spoke in a strangely quiet way that Andy thought was odd. 'Hey, Billy and fuckin' Stacky. Wipe ya faces. Here, use this.' He pulled a handkerchief from his trouser pocket, cut through the mob of walking soldiers, and held it out.

'Piss off, Darce.' Billy Poulton fended Darcy off. 'What d'ya think ya doin'? You're not me bloody mother. Jesus, it's only bloody mud. Piss off, will ya. No, don't. Give us a smoke, ya tight arse.'

Darcy fished his cigarettes out, extracted a smoke for Billy, then held the open tin out to the soldiers filing past.

'God bless you, my son,' Darcy said to each, the boys grinning, muttering thanks, lighting up as they moved on. 'And me not even a Catholic. Good gracious me. Father Ryan would be proud.'

twenty

The lights in the lounge room, diamond-edged, met the darkness at the windows, both land and sea invisible until Henry pressed his hands to the glass. He could imagine sharks cruising down in the depths. Looking off to his right, he could see the town, a cascade of lights reaching down to and ringing the inlet. For the one hundredth time that night he wondered what Marcelle would be doing. Out to dinner with Angie, he guessed, the both of them dressed-up and looking great. He felt the sting of jealousy and a counter-stroke of self-blame.

'We'll head back tomorrow,' Trot said, picking out a few Cheezels from a packet before handing it on to Nick. 'It's been great, guys. Thanks. But I gotta bit of shit to do at home and stuff.'

Janine, curled in an armchair, was barefoot as usual, and wore a tight T-shirt and a denim skirt. She picked up a Cheezel by poking her little finger into it.

'Yeah, like what, Trot? Wash the car?'

Trot considered. 'Yeah, there's that.'

The five of them sat in a rough circle, the coffee table in the middle, a few beers on it and a bottle of Coke like a black rocket. No one said much, the effects of the day lingering like warmth rising from the ground. The TV was on, chattering inanely to itself.

'I'd better get you the diary, then,' Henry said to Janine. 'Or Miss Hainsworth might come looking for me.'

Janine unfolded her legs so that she could reach the table where her drink stood.

'Have you finished it?'

'No, not quite.'

'Keep it until you go home.' Janine picked up her glass. 'Drop it in on your way through. I'll be at the motel. If I'm not, leave it in an envelope and Grace'll look after it. You might as well finish it.'

Henry got the feeling it was an instruction rather than an offer.

'Yeah?' He came back to his chair and sat down. 'All right.'

'But if I see you in town wearin' a slouch hat,' Trot said, 'you'll be in deep shit. Now who's comin' outside for a smoke?'

'Yeah, I might.' Marcus pushed himself up. 'Elite athlete that I am.'

Henry thought about going home, and what he would do in the six or seven weeks until uni started. Probably try and get some work at the old man's factory, he thought, since he wouldn't be seeing Marcelle. He felt a body blow. Your own fault, he told himself. Your own fault.

'Did you ever see that movie, *Psycho*, Janine?' Nick picked up his beer. 'You know, the chick getting stabbed through the motel shower curtain? The music? *Squink! Squink!*'

Janine added Coke to her drink. 'What, was she attacked by a mouse?'

Henry laughed and found himself trying not to look at the curved line where her calves met, her legs folded sideways together in the chair. He liked her self-containment. She seemed to be at ease pretty much all of the time and in most situations, and he wondered, vaguely, if that's what Andy Lansell had been like. In fact, Henry realised, when Andy was killed he couldn't have been much older than Janine was now.

'Speaking of that diary.' Nick sat, beer poised, as if he might offer a toast. 'My great-grandfather was in that war. Except that he was on the other side. You know, the dirty Germans.' Nick laughed. 'Sorry about that, folks. You know, it's okay, though. We lost.'

Janine stretched, elbows out, her hands open like stars.

'Oh, that's all right, Nick. It was a long time ago. And I wasn't even there.'

Henry took out the diary before getting undressed and decided he would read just a single entry to see what would come up, a kind of a Russian Roulette thing. With two hands, using his thumbs to part the pages, he focused on the first date that caught his attention.

Henry saw that on August 8, 1918, Andy Lansell appeared to have split the day up into four parts.

Darcy's birthday. Go forward in half an hour. Feel a bit jittery. Hope to do well. There's a million blokes here.

Resting by a hedge somewhere in a field beyond Villers-Brett. The day goes on. Bloody hungry.

In a different paddock. Still bloody hungry.

Still hungry. Bloody thirsty now.

Henry re-read the entries, then he looked down the page. There was only one more entry made in Andy's handwriting, then someone else had written neatly in similar grey lead pencil,

On this day, the 9th of August, 1918, Private Andrew Richard Lansell, volunteer soldier of the AIF, died at Villers-Bretonneux Field Hospital, France, of wounds received in battle. He was one of the best. He always was, and he always will be.

The entry was signed, as far as Henry could make out, by Darcy Garrett, and after it there were only blank pages.

Henry sat for a while holding the diary. A couple of times he looked at what Darcy had written, the way he had quietly recorded Andy's death. It didn't seem right that a young guy like Andy Lansell should be killed in a war twenty thousand kilometres away from home, but that's what had happened. And in the end, Henry knew, the war had been won and no war had ever been won without anyone dying.

Henry wondered what Andy had seen, the day before he died, that was so incredible. *There's a million blokes here.* Even now it would be interesting to go to France; to stand on the ground where the battles had been fought, to be where Andy and his mates had actually been. Not that he could, of course. Or not for a long time. Henry Lyon had stuff to do at home that could not be put off, but that was life. His life, anyway, for the next few years.

July 17 1917.
Flanders.

It's an underground world here. Or in the ground anyway. Big dugout we're in, with steps and everything. Getting used to this life. Boys joke around. Homesick for the farm and the horses, but we push on with the job.

Andy sat on his groundsheet on the floor of the dugout, the place unevenly lit by the light of a few hurricane lanterns. Within the smoky smell, he reckoned he could pick out the cold odour of mud, the warmer, more reassuring smell of dirty clothes and bodies, and the ground-dwelling mealy smell of rats. The dugout was large and reinforced, although the walls seemed to waver, less than solid in the waxing, waning, light of the lamps.

'Poor old Boydy,' Bob said, staring up at the timber and tin sheet ceiling. 'Bloody gettin' yer head knocked off first day in. He was a good shot, too. Ripper had him down for sniper duty.'

Darcy examined his hands, dirty from the burial detail.

'Yeah, better get a couple back for him, eh? Gees, the dirt round here's shit.' He picked off scabs of dried earth. 'It's like diggin' friggin' mashed potato, pardon the poetry.'

Andy could still hear the guns, the sound of them like something seeping out of the walls, a far-off heavy booming. He realised he was scared now, all of the time. It didn't affect how he talked or acted, but he could feel it, as if his body had been tightened a few turns, the screws beginning to bite. Just to see the churned dirt, like shit-coloured mashed potato, as Darcy had said, was enough to do it. It was sick ground, all right; it wept blood, rust, gas, shit, wire, steel, poisoned water, and it stunk.

And even now, with hardly a shell coming over, there was an oppressive sense of menace, similar but far worse than that first whiff of bushfire smoke on the hottest day of summer. Andy could feel real fear coiled deep in his flesh, dormant but stirring, and how he would deal with it, or how it would reveal itself, he didn't know.

'Carryin' up to the supports tomorrer night, Rip reckons.' Darcy lit a cigarette that he had botted back. 'Should be a bit of fun. Geez, ya should'a seen poor old Captain Ellery when we put Boydy in this mornin'. Dropped the bloody bible in the hole. Had to fish it out with a shovel. Still, no worse for wear. The Captain that is. The good book was a bit crook, but.' Darcy picked tobacco off his tongue. 'He's a bit shaky, the boss, but he won't let it get to him.'

Suddenly, the loud, idiot clanging of gongs flew into the dugout, swarming like a flock of bats. The boys looked at each other, then dived for their packs, elbows flying as they dragged free their gas masks, pulling them on, the underground shelter becoming a lair for goggle-eyed monsters.

'Gas!' someone was yelling. 'Gas! Fuckin' gas!'

Andy, mask on, stood with the rest of the boys, waiting and wondering, the lot of them an uneasy herd of freaks with green canvas heads, holding their rifles. The mask stank, Andy's world seeming to have shrunk, becoming darker and more evil as if the horror of what he'd got himself into was being compressed and held against his face. Someone was trying to kill him with poison gas. He could hear the flat 'phut' of the exploding shells and he knew, the thought sliding smoothly into his head, that he would welcome the chance to kill this enemy. It would require physical effort, maybe, but no thought.

'Sorry about the fart, boys.' Darcy's voice was muffled. 'But there's no need to carry on to this degree.'

Andy laughed into the stifling greenish stink. This was the strangest day, he reckoned, that he'd ever lived through.

twenty-one

Henry, Nick, and Marcus walked back into the house, the sound of Trot's car fading into the first couple of bends of the road.

'They come, they go.' Nick gave a little sigh. 'And once again it's just the originals. So what's the plan for the day, boys?'

'Ah, the beach?' Marcus stamped his bare feet on the mat. 'Just for something completely different.'

Henry knew, without having to look down to the windsock by the river, that there was nowhere enough wind for sailboarding. The water below them, sheltered by the hill, was glassy, the waves at the surf beach had little power.

'No wind,' Nick said. 'But there's some snorkelling gear in the laundry. Should be enough for everyone. Melissa's boyfriend left his behind and we can always buy shit if we're short. Whaddaya reckon? Be perfect at the moment. Like swimming in a pool. We can just drop in off the rocks by the wharf. There's a couple of hand spears somewhere. Vote?'

'Do it,' said Henry, liking the idea. 'But I gotta see the girls off later at the bus.' His mood flattened; it seemed Marcelle was going further and further away from him in some way, every day.

'No problem,' Marcus said.

'You'll be right, Hank.' Nick hit him lightly on the arm. 'We'll look after ya. Take you out. Pay for a hooker or something.'

Henry laughed and followed the boys into the house.

'One thing,' Marcus said, as he watched Nick going through the laundry cupboards, 'is that I *definitely* must have a spear. And those black and yellow flippers there, Nick. I want those. Because if they don't attract a shark, nothin' will.'

The water, green-blue, rose and fell against the rocks as if the sea had the slowest of slow heartbeats. Henry, wet-suited, his mask and snorkel pushed back on his forehead, dragged his flippers on. Nick, as usual, fiddled around, complaining.

'These masks are crap on your hair,' he said. 'But anyway, here goes.' Fish-faced, he nodded toward the water. 'One in, all in.'

Henry clambered to the edge, bent at the knees then plunged forward, hands up to his mask. For a moment he trod water, cleared his snorkel, then went under, his initial uneasiness disappearing as the bubbles cleared and the world that he was now in came into focus. Specks of mica glittered in the rocks, shells as delicately whorled as fingertips clung, and fringes of brown and green weed swayed in endless chorus lines. He looked around and saw Nick and Marcus, holding a handspear each.

Henry flippered along, occasionally looking out into the

sombre curtain of foggy green. He tried not to think of a White Pointer coming through it, mouth wide open in an idiot leer. It was easy, he reckoned, to disregard sharks when you were on dry land, but not so easy when you were paddling around in their backyard.

Henry swam over weed beds that thinned as the water got deeper. There wasn't much to see in the way of fish, although a few Toadies hung around, seemingly confident that their ugliness and inedibility guaranteed their safety. Henry cruised toward the river channel, thinking that he might see some Flathead in the sand, but instead he reared back when a black stingray exploded away.

To calm himself, Henry trod water, seeing Marcus was well out. At the river mouth he noticed a white launch motoring slowly for the open sea. The boat's bows pushed out a small, lazy wave, the skipper taking no chances in the narrow confines of the river – but once the bar was safely negotiated Henry knew he'd hit the gas for the run out – where Marcus was, low in the water like a sodden black log. Henry took off his mask.

'Hey, Marcus!' he yelled. '*Hey!*'

Marcus took no notice. For a few seconds, Henry did nothing, then he flung his mask and snorkel out onto the rocks, and started to swim hard for the channel, flippers driving.

Henry was a good swimmer; he hadn't trained for years, but he was fit and tall and already he was moving fast. He stopped to yell again, saw the boat was nearing the sand bar, stuck his head back under and ploughed on, a good thirty metres to go. Fear pushed him, he stroked harder, ignoring pain, dragging his hands back through the water and hoping that Marcus would hear the props of the boat and look up, and start waving. Again Henry pulled up, saw Marcus was still snorkelling, and so he yelled again, the boat planing now as the driver accelerated in deeper water.

'*Marcus!*' Henry felt something give in his throat. '*Marcus!*' There was no time left to swim. Henry, like a Seaworld dolphin, propelled himself as high out of the water as he could, to wave and yell at the launch. 'Hey!' yelled. '*Eh!*'

Suddenly, where Marcus had been, Henry saw black and yellows flippers as Marcus duck dived. Henry did the same, kicking and stroking down into the deeper water. He could hear the boat, fear spiralling as it passed, fear diminishing as it moved away. Surfacing, he saw Marcus ten metres away, mask up, his face shiny with water.

'Holy bloody hell,' he said. 'Fuck me.' Wearily he began to swim over. 'Why didn't ya tell me I was in the bloody shipping lane? And I lost Nick's spear as well. And I ain't divin' back down there to get it. No way. Too deep.'

'Me, either.' Henry looked up and down the channel, saw that the only boat in view was the launch, now moving out past the wharf. 'Hey, I *was* yellin' at you, ya deaf bastard,' he added. 'And loud.'

Marcus flicked water from his eyes. 'Yeah, well, I didn't hear ya until I put me head up, because I thought the bloody boat was a plane going into the airport. So I guess you think I owe you a beer now?'

'They would've missed us anyway.' Henry was reasonably sure about that. 'They turn here to head out deeper.' He pointed vaguely. 'Anyhow, I might go in.' His arms and legs felt heavy, but the sea was supporting him like a big cold couch. 'Comin'?'

'Yeah.' Marcus looked back over his shoulder. 'Pity about the spear, but stuff it. How much d'you reckon they're worth?'

Henry had no idea. 'Don't worry about it. Nick won't. It wasn't his, I don't think.' The sun felt good on his face and in front of him the scrubby cliffs rose out of the sea. He lay back and began to propel himself toward the rocks. Above him there were wisps of cloud edged with rainbow colours. 'Nice day,' he said. 'Couldn't be any better really.'

Henry put Marcelle's suitcase with all the other bags. People in summer clothes milled around, the smell of fish and chips drifted, mingling with the smell of diesel fumes from the bus. Angie offered Henry a Jaffa, which he declined.

'Okay, Henry.' Marcelle put her hands on his shoulders. 'I guess I'll be hearing from you back home. We'll talk then, all right?'

Henry was aware of Angie moving away. Saying goodbye in public was only slightly less embarrassing than having an argument. This was like a combination of both, he thought, except worse.

'Yeah, I'll ring you as soon as I get back.' He kissed her quickly on the lips, his hands fleetingly on her sides. He tried to create a smile. 'Enjoy the trip.'

Angie drifted back, Jaffas rattling. 'See you, Henry. Say goodbye to the boys. And drive home safely.'

'Yeah, I will.' He tried to appear nonchalant. 'See you, Marcelle.'

'Yes, Henry.' She hugged a white woollen sweater she had in readiness for the bus ride. 'Bye. I think we'd better go.'

Henry watched them get on, move down the aisle, and sit. Marcelle waved once, then the bus was pulling out, engine loud, headlights on, a big, silver oblong moving off down the main street. For a few seconds, Henry stood where he was, then walked away down the path around the inlet. The water was black and silver. It looked like smoked glass.

So. She was gone, and she was gone because he had not treated her very well – although he doubted anyone else would've noticed, except Marcelle and himself. But that was enough, quite obviously.

On a carry up to the front tonight. Can't say the boys not excited. Getting used to living underground. The smells are interesting. Funny to think of the hundreds of thousands of men in this game. Had a cold. Poms shot a deserter today. You'd think gaol would be better.

The night, to Andy, seemed to be full of phantoms and if they weren't phantoms, then they were soldiers who were not like soldiers of the day. He could feel them in their hundreds as his company carried barbed wire and ammunition up the road toward the trenches. Sometimes he glimpsed them, crouched and shadowy, or heard them utter disjointed words not meant for him until he realised that he had become one of them, involved in the immense, hurried, night-time business of the war.

In the distance, a flare shot up, bloomed, and drifted like a furiously burning star over land as featureless as the ocean. A machine gun rattled, tacking a fine thread of noise across the deep booming of heavy artillery. A few desultory rifle shots added a minor diversion.

'Bloody cracker night,' Darcy muttered, lugging wire. 'Penny bungers and sky rockets all round. Get yer two bob's worth here all right.'

The flash-crash-crash of guns lit up the horizon. Andy could hear shouting, lost and unknown, an echo perhaps, but eerily unreal and inhuman, the fighting unimaginable. The land around them was black, unseen, with an aura of menace, and now they were moving down into it, a guide leading them through a ruined house to a shallow trench that zigzagged away from the road and the tinkle and stamping of horse teams.

Men muttered low greetings from dugouts, Andy's nose

registering different smells, thick, meaty, and gaseous, as he stumbled along behind Bob, earth and sandbagged walls rising comfortingly over his head.

'That's the way, fellers. Good on ya, boys.' A figure stood in the mouth of a dugout, cigarette glowing to show sucking cheeks and the brim of a helmet. 'Nothin' much comin' over tonight. He's busy out mendin' and gardenin'. You'll be home on a pig's back. '

'Tag along,' Darcy said. 'No worries.'

There was quiet laughter. 'Already been, mate, don't you bloody worry about that.'

Andy went on, sweating and thirsty, blindly following as the trench twisted and turned. At muddy intersections, signposts were driven, pointing this way and that, but the guide moved unerringly through the system that had quickly stripped Andy of any sense of direction.

'He's like a bat, this little bloke,' Darcy said. 'I can't see fuck-all, but he's noodlin' along like a bloody ferret. We'll probably end up in bloody Berlin.'

'Ballarat,' Bob muttered. 'With an ounce of luck.'

'Stinks,' someone said. 'Jesus. That *pongs*.'

It was a smell like no other Andy had ever encountered; heavily putrid like rotting cow, but stale and on a far greater scale, as if it had been accumulating for weeks, ceaselessly rotting down like a foul sinking cloud. He could feel it clinging in his throat and reckoned if he rubbed two fingers together he'd feel slime. Bob turned, his face invisible.

'Front line in five minutes. Pass it on. No noise at all.'

Andy relayed the message and walked on carefully, wire cradled, a scrap of wood between the barbs and his chest, his back aching. The place they were in felt different. The trench walls were close, enclosing silence, although the place was really never silent at all. Distant noise stiffened the darkness, as did the stink that dwelt everywhere, a smell so thick Andy could imagine it engulfing the muffled coughing, the clink of metal, and the squeaking of what he guessed were rats. He struggled on, sweat sliding, hearing shells burst miles away, perhaps on Hellfire Corner, or wherever the Germans thought material or men might be coming up.

Andy was told to dump the wire. Gratefully, he did so, his knuckles encountering something protruding from the ground. He recoiled instantly, as if he'd been stung, recognising that he'd touched some part of a partially buried body, perhaps an elbow or a knee.

'Oh, don't worry about old Klaus,' whispered one of the front-line privates, a boy about Andy's age but significantly smaller. 'He's a mate. Been on our side for bloody months now.' The soldier grinned. 'Thanks for the fuckin' wire. We want bloody stacks of it.'

Andy nodded and felt a sensation move through his limbs, strange and lingering, not unlike a type of satisfaction. Something significant had just happened to him. He was no longer scared of the dead. The dead were dead. They were just dead. German or friendly, whoever, whatever, they were just dead.

'What's it like up here?' he asked the private, whose compact face was briefly visible as he lit a cigarette. 'Bit rough?'

'Smoke?' The soldier offered an open tin. Around them, the rest of Andy's company rested, squatting, smoking, drinking from water bottles. 'Rough? Here?' He slid the tin away. 'Shit, no. But when a stunt's on, mate, I hope I won't be within five hundred miles of the place. This joint's beautiful. The boys across the road are a bunch of poofs. They don't do nothin'. It's bonzer. Where ya from?'

'Strattford,' Andy answered. 'Victoria. The bush.'

The private inhaled hard. 'Oh, yeah. We're all South Aussies 'ere. I'm from Gawler. Never heard of it, eh? It's by the bloody beach.' He laughed. 'Well, I better get on with it.' He eased to his feet. 'Eh, you wanna have a look over the top of the bags? Bloody night school, eh? The Mechanics Institute.'

'Is that allowed?' Andy felt like a kid. He stood up. 'Yeah, I'd like to. What about the other fellers?'

The private smoked hard. 'Sure. Get 'em over 'ere. All quiet, though.'

At Andy's request, two figures separated themselves reluctantly from the trench wall.

'Yeah, what?' Darcy was eating something that smelled like sausage. 'We're supposed to be bloody restin'. I'm not goin' on a raid, if that's what ya got in mind. I gotta note from me bloody mum.'

'Listen to this bloke.' Andy pointed. 'Do what he says.'

'Over 'ere, boys.' The private took them out of the bay to the front of the trench. 'Hop up.' He patted a step about hip high. 'Now no smokes nor rowdy songs, eh. Or you'll lose your loaf and I ain't fuckin' jokin'.'

Andy climbed up onto the firestep to stand elbow to elbow with Darcy. The blackness pressed, Andy unable to see anything beyond belts of barbed wire wrapped in thick skeins around steel stakes. The open air felt colder, the wind blowing fitfully from no one direction. Above the rumble of guns, Andy could hear the breeze hissing lightly through the wire. He felt madly exposed, his head ripe as a pumpkin for any machine gunner who cared to take a second or two to rake the tops of the bags.

''ang on a tick.' The boy from Gawler climbed down. 'Stay 'ere. I'll be back.'

The boys, who had been joined by five or six others, nervously peered out into no-man's-land. A couple of hundred yards across there, Andy thought, were the Germans. I could walk over there right now and jump down into their trench and it would be like a foreign country – correction – it *would* be a foreign country.

The mystery of the opposing trench, the presence of the unseen enemy, held the uneasy fascination of a ghost story. Looking to the south, Andy saw stabs of orange fire that were out of synch with the rumble of artillery, and he thought, disconnectedly, that the trench he was in ran all the way to bloody Switzerland.

The private returned, carrying a bulky pistol. Nimbly, he hopped up between Andy and Darcy.

'The boss says it's all right,' he said. 'Just the one. Now when she goes up, don't move.' He aimed the pistol at the sky and fired, sending a big spark speeding upwards as if going over a hill. With a '*fittt*,' it exploded and a great wash of green light descended, lighting up flat ground that was ragged with grass, humps, holes, and unidentifiable rubbish. 'We run out of white ones,' the boy added. 'Pity. They go longer than the greenies. The red ones are nice, too.'

Andy stared at the expanse of rough secretive ground, on the one hand willing the flare to float on and on, dispensing its misty green glow, on the other, desperately wishing for darkness. Then the world was black, as if someone had put a hand over his eyes.

'And there you 'ave it, boys.' The private climbed down. 'Now 'op down in case Fritzy decides to send a few daisy-cutters over. He's got us ranged down to a T.'

The boys scrambled down, their relief exploding in stifled laughter, the lot of them ducking as a machine gun opened up and bullets smacked into the sandbags like pelting rain.

'Ah, tit for tat,' the boy said. 'Stick along a fence, the dog barks. Righteeo, fellers, go easy, eh? Don't do nothin' I wouldn't.'

Ripper appeared from a dugout, unmistakable even in the dark, shouldering aside the air.

'I 'ope that was informative.' He took a slow drag of a tiny cigarette. 'Now I think it's time we wandered off to see what else they got planned for us. Because I'm sure it will be somethin'.'

In a line, the boys headed back, collectively stopping like a frightened grub when shells whistled over to land, crumping and thumping in quick succession.

'Probin' for ammo dumps,' Ripper said. 'Nothin' like a few incendiaries to warm the pies.'

The boys went on, moving quickly through the calm orange light of a fire, then ducking as a salvo of shells hurtled overhead to slam into the ground two hundred yards away. As he crouched,

Andy felt a fine, subtle set of shockwaves come up through his boots.

'There are certain places in this world,' Bob Pike murmured, pushing himself upright, 'where it would probably be better not to find yourself standing.'

twenty-two

At eight o'clock in the morning, three days after the girls had left, Henry drove around the inlet, across the bridge, and out past the airport. He glimpsed again the black grids of exposed oyster leases, then they were lost behind trees, as the road turned away from the water and toward the bush. Next stop Strattford.

Henry parked his car midway between a takeaway food place and the Rosewood Motel. He took the diary from the glove box, pocketed it, and was thinking about buying a milkshake before seeing Janine when he heard his name being called. He turned and saw Miss Hainsworth standing in the shade of a florist's veranda, poised over an aluminium walking stick, regarding him with a short-sighted but direct stare.

'Henry Lyon.' She said his name as if he was someone who annoyed her. 'The boy from Melbourne.'

Henry was well aware of the diary in his shirt pocket. Did

Miss Hainsworth know that Janine had leant him the bloody thing? He had no idea and he hoped he wasn't about to find out.

'Hi, Miss Hainsworth.' He took a few steps toward the old lady, who was as fragile-looking as the dried flower arrangements in the shop window behind her. 'I'm on my way back to Melbourne. I just stopped to get a milkshake and see, um, Janine, for a minute.' He pointed down the road to the red and white sign of the Rosewood Motel. 'At her work.'

'Yes, it is a warm enough morning for a cool drink.' Miss Hainsworth granted him that. 'So, you are seeing Janine? Yes, she is a very good girl, Janine. I like her, yet for her sake, I wish she would leave this place. I do not want her to stay here like I have done. The opportunities for a girl like her are severely limited in a backwater like this.'

All Henry could do was nod. 'Yeah, I guess so. It's, um, a small town.' He glanced along the main road, feeling that the place had no depth to it beyond the shops, the park, and a small industrial estate.

'Although going away also has its risks.' Miss Hainsworth's gaze did not waver. 'Would you not agree?'

Henry agreed. 'Especially to a war.' Suddenly he wanted to let Miss Hainsworth know that he hadn't ignored her story of Andy Lansell, that he hadn't just been mouthing the words in the pub that night. 'Like the one that Andy Lansell went to. It must have been terrible.' If she sees the diary, he thought, she'll call the bloody cops.

'It was terrible beyond understanding.' Miss Hainsworth looked past Henry, as if he was obstructing her view of the past. 'And people did many terrible things in the name of it, as well as conveniently using it as an excuse for poor behaviour.' She focussed on Henry again. 'There was an amount of scandal here before *and* after Andrew Lansell left, and it affected me directly, I must say. I won't go into it, but it concerned a girl, as it often does – yet, it was also a very long time ago and the people involved were certainly very young.'

Henry nodded and tried hard to maintain a look of ignorance. Miss Hainsworth continued to look at him closely, as if she was trying to ascertain what he knew about, well, Henry thought, everything.

'But by the time I had seen fit to forgive,' Miss Hainsworth continued, 'it was too late. And so I lost not only Andrew, but any chance to make contact with the only person on this earth who was directly of his blood. And that has been the one great regret of my life – that I did not meet Andrew Lansell's child.' Cecelia ran frail fingers across her brow. 'And that was a mistake that I cannot unmake, Mr Lyon. It is something that I have to live and die with.'

Henry nodded, not sure what else to do. He tried hard to think of something to say that would not incriminate anyone.

'It was a real pity Andrew got killed,' he said, and added, on safer ground he thought, 'it'd be really interesting to go to France and see where they fought the battles and stuff, those guys. I'd like to do that one day.'

Miss Hainsworth nodded. Henry could see that the hand that gripped her walking stick looked to be more bone than flesh.

'Yes,' she said, 'I would like Janine to go one day, too. She would appreciate it. And Graham, he would benefit from it as well. So. Who knows? It may happen. Goodbye, Henry Lyon. Enjoy your milkshake.'

'I will, Miss Hainsworth.' Henry's mind was spinning. 'It's been nice to meet you again. And I did go out and see Andy's tree in the Avenue of Honour that day.'

'I know.' Miss Hainsworth shuffled off. 'I saw you. I was out that way myself.'

★ ★ ★

Henry sat in the shade, sunglasses on, drank his milkshake, and tried to analyse the facts of the conversation he had just had with Miss Hainsworth. She hadn't, he didn't think, actually admitted that she knew Andy Lansell was Janine's great-grandfather – but she certainly had not made it clear that she didn't know, either. So what had she said? Only that Janine and Trot, and himself, would benefit from going to France to see where the battles were fought; and that a scandal of some sort had occurred, and that war was a bad thing. Which was certainly a lot different to saying that she knew Janine Walker was Andy Lansell's great-granddaughter.

So, should he tell Janine what he *figured* Miss H *might* have said? Or did he simply hand over the diary and then get going? He'd hand over the diary and get going. After all, he wasn't *really* sure that Miss Hainsworth had told him any hard facts at all. Henry crumpled the milkshake cup, stood, and looked around for a bin.

Obviously he would say nothing, or very little to Janine, because the trouble that could be caused by him giving the wrong information would be, no doubt about it, his fault.

July 26 1917.
Gorse Trench, Ypres, Flanders.

Up to the front line tonight to relieve. Got the wind up, but Ripper will make sure of the rum ration, so boys are happy. Devastation all round here. Wouldn't know what the real world looks like any more. Hopefully we'll go right out of the lines after our stint up the sharp end. Chaplain came around today and blessed us all.

From a sky invisible in the darkness, rain fell onto the trenches, hissing and pattering, rivulets of mud running down the walls, the trench bottom a series of ponds rising and joining to cover the wooden duckboards the soldiers walked on. Andy, in his cape, stood on the firestep on sentry duty, so cold that his joints seemed to have seized like ancient bolts. In a dugout in the rear wall, Darcy and Bob slept, the entrance to the hole covered with canvas.

I'm in the front line, Andy thought. I'm in the bloody front line in the Wipers salient. The words ran through his head. Front line. Wipers salient. Front line. Wipers salient. And now that Andy knew exactly what the 'salient' was — a few miles of English-held ground that poked out into German territory like a hernia — the word held a sinister ring as well as a dire meaning. Here, the Germans held the higher ground on three sides, their artillery calibrated to rain shells into the trenches whenever they chose.

The darkness Andy looked out into seemed, at times, like part of a show. Green and white flares, close and far, rose and died along the line, illuminating the falling rain more than the strange, infinitely dangerous strip of no-man's-land. In the drifting white light of a magnesium flare, Andy saw his hands were pale as bones, as alien-looking as the well-oiled rifle that he held.

The night, with its booming artillery, flares and rain, seemed to live, writhing sometimes, twisted by light and sound, then it would lie down, inert as if it was exhausted or wounded or had drawn back to crouch, poised, the two armies within it, in their ant lines, labouring.

Andy thought of Strattford, its nights hushed and harmless, part of a childhood dream where he wished he was, bare-headed, unarmed, just standing, breathing, under a starred night sky that reached down to the dark rim of the hills.

In no-man's-land, right now, he knew there were men working, German and Allied, attending to their wire, estimating enemy positions and strength, crawling close to the others' positions, working around, over, and with the rotting dead, yet like the dead they were silent. And when he was sent out he would go, and come back if he was lucky, like the other men, filthy, exhausted, cut by wire, or made sick by pockets of poison gas that lingered in holes, with nothing to say of what he had seen or done or touched.

Andy looked to the front, his boots sucking and slurping in deepening mud. He rolled his shoulders as if he could shrug off the weight of rain, but the weight remained, and his body was filled with vague pains that flickered and fused. To his left and right, for as far as he could see, flares floated through air whitened by rain and now, suddenly, was split by the sound of a heavy shell.

Crouching, Andy pressed himself into the sticky wall, ducked his head into his chest, and was hit by a force that blew every thought, word, reflex, and response from his body. For a moment he was nothing, totally blasted out of himself, and he only knew that he had gone when he returned to his senses to find himself in the bottom of the trench, someone shouting in his ear, the blackness stinking of smoke and deep earth, the adjacent fire bay now part of a long hole populated with men crawling hopelessly in the light of a flare hanging like a judgemental star.

'The firestep!' Iron claws hauled him up, a voice like tearing tin grated in his ear. 'Man the fuckin' firestep!'

Andy climbed to the lip of the trench, crouched there, somehow still holding his rifle, looking blindly forward, the flash and ear-splitting boom of another shell rocking the ground, obliterating noise with noise, plastering the world with mud and metal. A flare went up, showing no-man's-land to be blank earth, rain tipping into it from a black sky that seemed to support some towering mid-air structure divided into lanes for the shells to come screaming down and hit like crashing trains, to cover an attack by black figures.

But there was no attack, just shells drilling the sky, explosions, and the chaos of the trench which he could not enter, as he was the sentry, the sentry, the man who could not move. Explosions stamped along the front, giant flaring footfalls, dying, rapidly superseded by the next, batteries of artillery on both sides pounding, the neutral sky conducting the shells, conveying the sounds, allowing the flares to hang, and the rain to fall.

Andy, up to his knees in collapsing clay wall, looked into the trench, seeing shadowy figures labouring with shovels like mad builders, or crouched like trainers over fallen players, or working together like factory hands feeding belts into a childishly chattering machine gun. Or standing watch as he was, like a boxer waiting to be felled – hearing – whenever there was a pause in the shelling, the shouting of maniacs and the crying of injured things, and smelling the almost welcome human smell of vomit, the warm stink triggering school memories of fragrant sawdust, quiet sickrooms, of lying down alone in peace, the world outside bright, peppered with the sound of children playing.

'I am the sentry,' Andy repeated, a prayer for strength. 'I am the sentry.' And although he expected at any moment to see Germans rise from the ground, huge in drenched black tunics, bayonets fixed, none broke through the cracking air to lunge – and then the shelling stopped, leaving only the understory of small arms fire and shouting, the darkness seeming to regain its elasticity, to shrink back on both sides as if it was pulling the front lines apart, a few flares falling to earth like spent insects as the sizzle of rain and the disembodied gunfire and screaming went on.

Andy heard Bob's voice, and hearing him, was lifted by exultation.

'*Bobby-boy.*' He looked for a moment down into the dark guts of the trench, and recognised a toiling figure. 'Hey, Bobby-boy. Jesus, Bobby-boy.'

'Andy, mate.' The figure came closer. 'Christ. Sentry of the century.' Bob breathed deeply, as if he might start crying, as if he had been. 'Stay where y'are, digger. We'll get some sandbags up to yer in a minute. Jesus Christ, what a fuckin' mess. We gotta fix this. I think Darce's been taken back wounded. Just stay where yer are.

There's bits of blokes down here that I don't even know who they belong to. It's just gone mad, mate. Fuckin' mad.'

For the next thirty hours, Andy stayed where he was, stepping on dead and wounded men whose bodies shifted under his feet like sacks of sodden grain until, finally, he, like the rest left standing, stumbled back through the darkness, through the skin of the earth, as blind and mindless as a worm. Arriving at dawn at the bare bones of a town, he slept in a shed, beyond dreaming, leaving the unreal, the unbelievable, and the impossible, to be dealt with by those still holding the line.

twenty-three

Henry looked up at the pearly glow of the streetlight, dialled, then walked a few calming steps as he waited for the thing to ring.

'Come on, Marcelle,' he muttered. 'Be there.'

As if to plan, soap-opera perfect, Marcelle answered.

'Hello, Henry,' she said calmly. 'I'm sorry, but you'd better make this quick because I've got to go out.'

'Oh, okay.' Henry had no idea how to deal with such a statement. In the space of a few seconds he felt furious, sad, lost, and insulted. 'Yeah, all right,' he said, 'have a nice night, then.' He ended the call, instantly regretting it, but knowing with clarity and plunging regret, that it was more than just the phone call that was over.

Henry stood with his father on the steps at the rear of the warehouse of Hoestler Chemicals. The yard, filled with a few rusty shipping containers, piles of smashed packing and assorted rubbish, was large enough to accommodate a second warehouse complex that actually was on the drawing board. Wiry grass grew around, through, and over just about everything. Along the fence it had twisted itself upwards for a metre and a half.

'Big job, Henry.' Walt crossed his arms, sending creases running up to the shoulders of his shirt. 'Maintenance used to keep it up, but now it's the last thing on Clive's list. You up to it, mate?' Henry's dad liked using the word, 'mate,' although with his faded Canadian accent Henry was not convinced that he should. 'There's a self-drive mower and safety gear – you gotta wear all that – and tools locked up in one of the containers. So if you want to give it a go I'll get Clive to bring down the keys.'

Henry did not consider not giving it a go. He didn't think the yard looked too bad; not if he had a week or so to do it in. If he could take his time, he thought it would actually be pretty easy, although hot.

'You'll have to get a big dump bin in for the junk,' Henry said. 'Like, not one of those little ones that Mum gets. A big one, like builders use.' Henry could imagine it sitting right there on the concrete drive, yellow, dinted, and empty.

Walt looked pleased. He smiled heavily, standing by the white metal rail like the captain of a ship.

'Sure. I'll get Clive to order one and then bring you down what you'll need to get started. Don't knock yourself out. You got money for the lunch shop? And there's a tap just down here.' Walt pointed. 'Let it run for a while to get the rust out. Okay, see yer, Henry.'

Henry walked out into the yard, the bitter-sweet smell of spray paint drifting from across the road, grass sawing at his socks. For a while he poked around, working out how best to attack the mess. Turning, he saw Clive on the steps, his bleached white hair standing out against the concrete wall. Henry walked back.

'So you're the gardener, then.' Clive lit a cigarette, appearing to savour both the smoke and the chance of being outside. He came, in no hurry, down the steps. 'Just be careful handlin'' any old plastic barrels and crap. The Germans are great at labelling hazardous shit, but the boys here are hopeless once they chuck it out.' Clive unlocked a shipping container. 'Anythin' with a skull and crossbones on, like don't drink.' He left the keys hanging and Henry followed him into the stale, steely heat.

Henry carried, wheeled, mowed, hacked at, dug out, pulled down, and generally laboured at the back of the warehouse for a week. He didn't find the barrels of hazardous chemicals that Clive had mentioned, but he did fill two seven-metre dump bins with everything from old packing cases to a broken barbecue. At lunchtime, he sat in the shade against the wall and contemplated the yard, its aura of contamination gone.

The place looked something like a heavy-duty playground; empty blue and black plastic barrels neatly corralled, the shipping containers like industrial cubbies, and wooden pallets and cable drums like part of an obstacle course. Under a crate, he'd found an old cricket bat, its handle smoothed with yellow tape. He had not thrown it away, but instead had leant it against the wall next to his chair, sometimes using it to hit stones across the railway line.

Hearing the warehouse door, Henry cranked his head around. An older guy, a storeman, who Henry knew vaguely, stood on the landing, weighed down by paint cans.

'Ah, the yard is looking much bedder,' the storeman said. 'You do a good job. And in this heat.'

Henry stood up, trying to remember the guy's name. Gus? Gerry? Jack? *Gerry*. Gerry Von somebody – a German who'd been here since the day Walt had started, and probably ten years before that. Gerry had worked, Henry remembered, for Hoestler in Germany.

'Yeah, it's looking a bit better now.' Henry squinted into the heat. 'That grass grows like crazy.'

Gerry inclined his head. 'Oh, yes, in Germany the long grass and garbage would never be allowed. Hoestler over there, ah, very *organised*. Hoestler here a liddle bit different. Bedder, in some ways.' Carefully, he came down the steps, put down his two cans, and stood pushing at the small of his back. 'Ah-ha, Henry, I see you have found our cricket bat.' He went to the wall and picked it up. 'The grass became too long for us to play. We could certainly play again now.' He took a small, careful, swing. 'You could perhaps mow us a pitch between the containers there?'

'Sure,' said Henry. That would be a better job than stripping grass from the fence. 'I'll do it this afternoon.'

Gerry leant on the bat. 'Once I hit the ball over the fence and *over* the railway line there.' He smiled at Henry, his face inflating a little. 'It was given out, but it was a damn good shot for an old bloke.'

Henry had already mentally marked a place between the containers where he would put the pitch. And he would make a sign and hammer it in. The HCG, he'd call it. The Hoestler Cricket Ground. A passenger train rattled rhythmically past.

'All the way up the bush that line goes,' Gerry said. 'Sale, Bairnsdale, Claybank. It would be nice to be on it, I think.'

Henry agreed. 'Does it go to Strattford?' The question popped up for no good reason that he could think of.

'Yes, I think Strattford is on that line somewhere. Anyway, you see this dirty thinners?' The storeman lifted the cans. 'I pour it on the weeds to keep them down, but they do not die. Or only for a little while. Pretty remarkable, eh? They grow back even though you'd think the ground would be poisoned for years.'

'Yeah, it's tough stuff.' Henry prepared to start the mower. 'Okay, Gerry, stand clear.' He took up the slack on the starter cord. 'The Hoestler Cricket Ground is about to open for business.'

July 29 1917.
Battalion huts, Ypres, Flanders.

Day off. Feel a bit knocked-up, but will recover shortly. Go into the village later. Spend a few quid!

Bob and Andy sat at a table in the front room of a small brick house that had been turned into a cafe. They drank tea, taking it in turns to politely pour it into mugs from a stained green and white teapot as big as a football. The place was filled with soldiers and the soldiers had filled it with a brotherly stink of steamy warmth, cigarettes, dirty clothes, and subdued vitality that occasionally broke into laughter and shouting.

Andy had never felt as welcome in any other place in his life. This place was like a club, the only requirement for membership was that you had been up, or were going, to the front line. If any man had asked him for a few bob he would've given it. In this place, he thought, as long as he didn't have to leave, everything would be all right.

'Darce'll be back in bloody England,' Bob said. 'Good on him. I hope his leg hurts like buggery. They'll get him back here, though, wouldn't yer think? In a while. A broken leg ain't much. Shit, yer can get that playin' tiggy.' Bob rubbed his nose. 'Or when half of Flanders falls on ya. He was lucky. We were lucky. I mean, like you and I. The other blokes . . .'

Andy's chair creaked as he stretched his legs out. His mind felt strange and small, like an empty box. He could not really make himself think of anything much at all. All he knew was that he felt good in this place, and that he did not want to move, or leave it. It was beautiful just to sit and feel warm tea go down and see an apple tree outside the window. The time in the line was like remembering sickness – no, madness. There was a division in his head, in himself; there was Andy Lansell before he went into the line, and there was Andy Lansell after he came out.

'We'll get stuck into the wine after this.' Bob pushed his cheek out as if he had a toffee wedged between his teeth. 'I'll take a punt it'll taste like piss, but I think we owe it to ourselves to get plastered. Pardon the P's.'

Andy nodded, knowing that drinking wouldn't bury the last few days where it couldn't be found, but it would further smooth it over for a while. The front, what really happened there, would not be spoken about in here. That was why the soldiers came.

'Yeah, a few hundred glasses'd be all right.' Andy put his arms behind his head with a feeling of utter luxury. 'I'm just gunna stop here until they kick me out.' He looked outside at the grey day, a few spots of rain not troubling the many strolling soldiers and few citizens that passed up and down the cobbled road. There was mud everywhere, brought into the place on boots, wheels, and hooves, but it was slowly drying out. 'Good day for a kick of the footy.' It was like a Strattford winter's afternoon, and he could clearly imagine a football, tomato-sauce red, spinning, to slap hard and welcome into his hands.

That's what he felt like doing. Kicking a bloody football, preferably back on the Stratty oval, just him and the boys, no game, no spectators, just the attendant scribbly-trunked gums that surrounded the ground.

Bob propped one leg across the other, his boot dirty and misshapen.

'So, cobber. You got any letters from home lately? Any, ah, news?'

Andy laughed, surprising himself. He also lifted a boot, sitting it across his knee.

'Ah, no. I mean, well yeah, the bun's in the oven, but the letters I wrote won't have made it back yet. But when they do I reckon there'll be a fair bit of, ah, discussion to be heard in the main street of a Sat'dee morning.'

'Yep, feathers'll be flyin'.' Bob checked the level of tea in the pot. 'For a while. But ah, fuck it, eh?' He unfolded his long legs. 'Hey, do they pay you more if you got kids? You know, that could be a bit handy. To keep the ball rolling back home. I mean, it won't change nothin', but it wouldn't hurt, either.'

Andy watched the dark-eyed, dark-haired daughter of the woman of the house pouring wine into glasses from a big jar. You're beautiful, he thought, not looking at her face but at the whole of her. He removed his gaze, but felt uplifted.

'Yeah, I'll make sure Frances-Jane gets some,' he said. 'But money means nothin' to Cecelia. She'll just want me shot.'

'Ah, bullshit, mate.' Lately, Bob's long face seemed better suited to severity. 'She bloody would not. Shit, don't even say that.' He bounced a fist off Andy's knee. 'She might perhaps want your old feller wounded in action, but she wouldn't want you not to come back.'

Andy was not convinced. 'She's bloody hard when she's crossed, mate. Like granite. Now let's get a drink. I'll go.' Andy stood, somehow still feeling all right. 'Wait here.'

'Talked me into it.' Bob dropped a wad of dirty-looking French francs on the table. 'And get some chips and eggs. Plenty, boy, *plenty*.'

Andy left Bob's money behind and made his way to the bar, stopping for a moment by the fire, realising then and there that he was thinking of the baby in a very different way than he had a week or so ago. It held a value for him now, some kind of value beyond its present circumstances. And he suspected, warily, that the longer he was over here and the more he saw and did, the more this baby would mean.

Something was happening to him. He was changing. He knew about flesh and blood. Too much, he knew. He and a million others had seen what no one should see. He could not un-see it. That was the problem and that was the truth. He was not like he was and never would be again. He would not ever be able to look at people in the same way, knowing what they could do to each other, and what could be done to them. His baby, whole and unhurt, growing, was a most precious thing. And to hell with anyone who might say or think different.

Standing at the bar, he could not help thinking of – no, dreaming more like it – of Frances-Jane, of Frances-Jane taking off her lilac blouse in the moonlight. Inadvertently, he smiled, shook his head, and smiled down at floorboards gouged and muddied by hob-nailed boots. A couple of diggers made way for him.

'Jesus, mate, what are you so happy about?' asked a soldier with raw black cuts all over his face. 'Y'ain't even got a bloody drink yet.'

Andy pulled out money. Still he smiled. It was like the warmth of remembered sun.

'I was thinkin' about tits, actually,' he said, 'to tell ya the truth.' He laughed, felt the laugh go right through him. 'I was ten thousand bloody miles away makin' a dog of meself.'

The soldier leant on the bar as if he had to consider fully and carefully what Andy had said. Andy could see his hands were also cut, black stitches holding together what looked like knife wounds.

'Gor lumme,' the digger said ruefully to his mate. 'Jesus. Tits, Ralphy. Why didn't I think a that? Here we was, thinkin' about bloody *football*. I must be off me scone.' He turned to the room and held up a glass of pale red wine. 'Boys. I propose a toast to tits. And may we soon all be well in amongst 'em. Amen.'

Andy raised his glass. There seemed no reason in the world not to.

twenty-four

Henry spent half his time at Hoestler Chemicals outside, doing general maintenance, and half his time inside, helping dispatch chemical samples requested by Hoestler offices Australia-wide. At lunchtimes, if it wasn't blisteringly hot, he played cricket on the HCG, a casual game with rules that evolved daily.

Outside, his shadow compacted, Henry squatted at the tap and rinsed out paint brushes. A train clattered past, as shiny as if it had just been washed, and seeing it Henry thought of Strattford and Janine. He wondered what it would be like living in a town like Stratty, knowing everybody and everybody knowing you – and your history – well, knowing *some* of your history. Henry whipped the brushes, flinging water.

He wondered if Janine would ever tell Miss Hainsworth her story. It was the truth, and Miss Hainsworth would be pretty keen on hearing the truth, Henry reckoned, no matter what it was. In fact, he guessed Miss H had a *right* to know – to not tell her would be almost the same as lying.

Henry put the brushes down and thought about ringing Janine. For a minute he sat in the shade, looking at the train line, imagining it running all the way up to Strattford. Through the factories and 'burbs it would go, out into paddocks; over bridges; alongside tracks and roads; until eventually, with never a single break, it'd reach Strattford. Henry poked in the number of the Rosewood, only to be told by a woman called Grace that Janine had not come into work that day.

'Are you a friend of hers?'

Henry glanced at a few high thin bars of bright cloud that reminded him of neon tubes.

'Ah, yes,' he said. 'I am. I just rang to ask her something. It's okay. I'll ring back another time. Will she be in tomorrow?' Henry waited out a pause in the conversation.

'Do you know Graham Trotter, her boyfriend?'

'Ah, yes, I do.' Henry wondered where all this was leading. It seemed a bit strange, but nevertheless, he guessed he'd see it through. 'Yeah, he helped me when my car broke down in Strattford. That's when I met Janine.'

The next pause was longer. Henry waited.

'Well, I guess I can tell you,' the woman said, 'that Graham's been killed in a car accident and that is why Janine is not in today. She's at home. So shall I leave a message that you rang, or will you ring her there? I'm sorry to have to tell you in such a – such a sudden way. It's a terrible thing. I can hardly believe it.'

Henry couldn't speak. He heard the words and he could picture Trot clearly, alive, but he couldn't process what he was being told. This fact he'd been told could, he supposed, quite well be true, but he couldn't accept it. Not straight out like this. He couldn't write Trot off, well, this instant, without a fight. He couldn't accept it at all. Henry realised he had not said a word for a long time.

'I can't believe it,' he said. 'Did you say a car accident? Gees, I can't believe that. Trot was a good driver.' Henry was conscious of how he sounded. He forced himself to start making sense. 'Could you please just leave Janine a message that I rang? My name's Henry Lyon and I'm from Melbourne. Janine'll know who. She's got my number. Thanks.' Henry ended the call and sat staring through the grey haze of cyclone-wire fences.

Trot was dead. Dead. The word, although Henry had not said it out loud, began to take on some form, as if it was solidifying. He'd never had to deal with the word, or the world like this before. Trot was *dead*. He was gone. *Now*. Gone.

Henry sat, hands draped, the silver case of his watch glittering at the corner of his eye. He felt weak and infinitely clueless.

'Shit,' he muttered. 'Fuck.' But the word *dead* was so far beyond the power of swearing that he wished he hadn't even opened his mouth.

He did want to speak to Janine, though. If he spoke to her he felt he might learn something, get somewhere with the reality of what had happened. He could picture Trot's car crashed, on its side in long yellow grass, the bottom of it crudely exposed, maybe its roof crumpled around a gum tree – he did not allow himself to imagine any further.

'Get up,' he said, and he did.

Directory assistance would have Janine's home number. Strattford was not a big place. He'd ring her when he got home.

Henry sat on his bed, looked out into the backyard, and watched Minnie the Golden Retriever padding around, a few sparrows hopping after her. He dialled Janine's number, and was told by a person he assumed was Janine's dad, that she would come to the phone in a few moments. Henry waited, feeling lost, and when Janine answered all he could think was that she sounded tired.

'I'm glad you rang, Henry,' she said. 'I was going to ring you. But I didn't get around to it. Gracie told me you called. I dunno, I'm just not able to do anything. I've been looking out the window for two days.'

Henry nodded, looking out his own window, watching the sparrows searching around Minnie's bowl for crumbs.

'I know. I mean, I can't believe it.' Henry wondered if what he was saying was only going to make things worse. 'I mean, I didn't really know Trot all that well, but you know, I liked him. A lot.' Henry was intent on telling the truth. 'He was a good guy. He helped me out a heap. You know, I'm really sorry, Janine.'

'I don't even think he was speeding,' she said, vaguely. 'I mean, I know he did sometimes, but evidently a guy on a tractor had dropped one of those really big round hay bales on a corner, and when Trot tried to swerve around it, he went off the road. At least he was in his car. He loved that bloody thing. I'm sure he thought it would've got him out of anything, but it didn't.'

'Yeah.' Henry nodded. 'Yeah, if it was possible, Trot would've made it, but I guess it just wasn't. He could drive and that car was a good car.'

'People said he shouldn't have had it.' Janine's voice did not falter, but it seemed to have a distant quality to it. 'But it was all he ever wanted. It made him happy. Hang on. I've got to blow my nose.'

Henry heard a tissue being torn from a box and some nose blowing.

'God, there, that's better.' Janine's voice sounded stronger. 'The funeral's this Wednesday. Do you think you could come? I mean, I know it's a long way and you're probably working and things, but – I mean, if you can't, that's fine but –'

'No, I'll come.' Henry hadn't even thought about there being a funeral. 'I'll be there. I'll borrow the car or catch the train or something. I'll be there. I liked Trot. I'll be there for sure.'

Janine cleared her throat. 'Thanks, Henry. That's very nice of you. You know, he said a couple of times how he liked you. You two would've been good for each other. Anyway, I guess that wasn't meant to happen. Or not like it might've. Henry, I've gotta go, but I'll ring you with all the times and stuff, okay? Thanks for the call. I'll talk to you soon. Bye.'

Henry put the phone down. It was strange, he thought, how a town he'd never heard of a month ago and people he'd never met, had become part of his life. One thing led to another, all right. Outside, he saw the day was fading. There were no rules that guaranteed you anything, he thought. But there were things you *had* to do, as if there were rules. And going to Strattford was one of them.

---

*September 19 1917,
Passchendaele, Flanders.*

Go over tomorrow morning. Thousands of heavy guns in place. Hope to scrape through. Thinking thoughts of home. This is a big stunt.

The barrage of artillery fire was so far beyond noise Andy did not know what it was. It was as if the sky was a black river of endlessly roaring sound that reached down into the earth to catch the massed troops in its eddies and whirlpools, the sound taking their breath and their voices, pressure waves driving tears from their eyes, and pummelling their chests and heads.

In front and behind, the flickering glow of the guns did not rise or diminish, but held position over the Allied and German lines like two opposing orange and black storms rippling along the horizon.

Andy stood loaded down like a pack animal, head bowed, holding his rifle, swaying against other soldiers. He felt numb, his senses crushed by the noise and concussions of explosions, not even looking up when the earth shook as shells fell down the line, the ground bucking, the troops stumbling into each other, gripping each other's shoulders, rifles clutched, faces barely visible in the darkness. And then, at the first lightening of the sky, at a signal from Captain Ellery, Andy with Bob, and the rest of the battalion climbed out of the trench and began to walk, slip, skid, run, and crawl forward.

The ground Andy was crossing in the drizzling dawn was like the surface of a smoky brown planet, countless thousands of craters and holes linking up, the bodies of men spread over it as if they'd been cast there in a single sweep by a huge and careless hand. Bullets whipped by, a man to his left cannoned back into him and fell, and ahead, like a sweeping, smashing curtain, the shells of the Allied barrage rained directly onto the German front lines, the sound not for one second ever ceasing but flowing, rolling and roaring, folding back on itself, unfurling, leaping forward even louder, lit from above and below by thousands of flashes and explosions.

Again Andy fell, his pack driving him into the churned dirt that was rapidly turning into mud and again he got up, his short-handled shovel catching as he rose. Turning, he knocked it free, then turning back he saw, through drifting smoke, six or seven German soldiers retreating as fast as they could. Sighting on them, he fired, worked the bolt, fired again, and moved on, part of a thinning ragged line that wormed its way forward, using shell holes for cover, men rising up to fire and move. If he had hit anyone he could not tell.

Every few yards, Andy passed wounded and dead, some just killed, looking like large khaki sponges soaked with blood, pale limbs bared, muddied hands clasped, torsos spilling various bright bloody loads – yet there were other bodies long dead, withered and awful, some having been buried and blown up, white bones poking from grey and green cloth, white skulls amongst the trash and tangle of bombed barbed wire and equipment of what had once been a front line position. The wounded, apart from a few men he helped down into shell holes, he passed on by, leaving them to the stretcher bearers. His job lay ahead.

Crouching amongst a tangle of telephone wire, broken rifles, and breached woodwork, he wondered if this smashed ditch might be the objective his battalion had been set. It was, or had been, an enemy position. He could see and smell the difference; the air was more pungent but with less the stink of shit, and the trench had been well-built, with proper timberwork and plenty of re-inforced concrete.

Ripper appeared, as compact and determined as a Fox Terrier on a rat hunt. He pretended to shovel.

'Dig in!' he shouted. 'This is it. They've all fucked off! Dig in!'

The barrage was creeping away over German ground, its sound like cliffs collapsing, smoke rising like dust over the next line of enemy defences where fire was being concentrated in an all-out effort to crush a counter-attack from troops held in reserve. Andy could hear, lacing itself through the boom of artillery, the sharp stuttering of machine gun fire and the cracking of rifles as the German defenders sought to repel the attackers, hundreds of minor battles fought over the possession of ten-yard sections of trench, or patches of disputed ground.

Bullets snapped out of the smoky air as Andy, with hundreds of others, began to dig, throwing up mud and dirt in front to consolidate the battered position, sentries posted, the line being shelled in retaliation already.

Bodies pulped by shellfire were slung away, or left if too deeply buried, the sight of them hardly registering as Andy slaved at try-ing to make something out of the smashed trench, stopping once to drink, his thirst like something unnatural.

He prised a bent rifle from a dead infantryman and tossed it over the sloppy parapet. He dug around the body as if unearthing a log, levering an arm up, a leg, glancing at the white face that was pinched with pain and streaked with mud. For the soldier in grey, Andy felt nothing, although some remote part of him acknow-ledged the German as a fellow sufferer. That he could feel anything in the noise of the barrage, as he worked in a trench where sprays of blood dripped as the rain strengthened, he found interesting. I'm still in my brain, he thought. I'm still in my body. It was like a minor miracle, a miracle illuminated with a sense of elation; that he was able to stand this thing, to stay, to do his duty.

He freed the German's shoulder, a cupful of thickened black blood pouring forth as the head flopped, Andy seeing a wound across the back of the man's skull that could've been put there with an axe.

'*Bombers here!*' someone screamed from the next fire bay. '*Bombers here!* Here they fuckin' come!'

Men dropped their shovels, picked up rifles, or clawed for Mills bombs. A Lewis gun opened fire, soldiers ran to where the trench zigzagged, Andy with them, snatching up a haversack of grenades. In a section of trench somewhat intact, men crouched, jumping up to throw grenades, explosions smacking the air, filling the place with poisonous grey smoke from which came shouting and some kind of heavy animal screaming. Andy threw grenades, pulling the pins, lobbing the heavy little bombs forward in high arcs, attempting to drop them right on the heads of the unseen enemy.

'With me!' Ripper yelled into Andy's face and gestured with an automatic weapon he had taken possession of. 'Next corner!'

Andy went forward, slipping and sliding over muddy boards, stopping behind Ripper as he crouched. Bullets slapped into the opposite wall, punching splintery holes in the planks.

'Bounce a couple off the fuckin' wall!' Ripper shouted into his ear. 'Then we'll go 'round and clean 'em up.'

Andy pulled a bomb loose and hurled it, bouncing it off a boarded wall, the bomb disappearing then exploding. He bounced another and waited, flinching as bullets cracked and whined, his shoulders twisting as the grenade blew up. The gunfire stopped.

'Let's go!' Ripper took off, Andy following him around the corner into a cloud of blue smoke, Ripper's Lewis gun kicking.

Andy could see little, but kept going forward with his haversack of bombs, stumbling over bodies, and then they were in the clear. Again the Germans had fallen back, long belts of empty brass shells on the trench floor indicating where there had been a machine gun.

'Right, stay here.' Ripper nodded hard. 'I'll send more blokes up in a minute. All right?'

Andy crouched, the trench to his right blown wide apart, a dead Australian half-buried as if he had been caught in a mudslide, the sky above the body yawning dangerously wide, steel-grey, flogged by wind and rain. Moving back into a tiny dugout, Andy lay his haversack down, and arranged what bombs he had left. At any moment, he expected the Germans to come sweeping back and he would try to stop them, although alone he knew his chances were about nil.

He waited, fear swelling like a sickness, as vulnerable-feeling as if he was a bubble, the sky-high roar of artillery seeming to falter as if the river was slowing, then it came back in depth, a wave smashing forward from the other direction as the German guns began to fully rain shells on the front line they had lost.

There was nothing Andy could do but crouch and shake. He felt as if he was continually screaming, his bones seemed bent with tension, a feeling like a dam of blood at the back of his throat was about to spew out, the sound and concussions dashing more and more thoughts from his head until he relinquished the idea of fighting anybody or anything, tried to wrap himself up in his own arms, and breathed in the animal heat of his own moaning, the dugout shaking, lumps of dirt knocking him sideways.

For an unknown time he crouched, the trench walls rippling, slipping in, mud raining down, then there were men in the trench – Australians – from a battalion that was not his own. Someone knocked on the top of his helmet.

'Hey, matey!' He was being shouted at. 'Y'all right down there? Time to get up. We're the relief. Y'can fuck off now. Where are yer mates?'

Hands dug into his armpits, he was hauled up, his eyes drinking in the familiarity of Australian uniforms, faces, and weapons. He felt himself returning to himself, with no idea where he'd been, except that it was a corner so dark it did not bear thinking about.

'Down there.' Andy pointed, his whole arm shaking. 'I'm goin' back.'

The soldier nodded, his eyes blue and bloody.

'Good on ya. Don't forget ya bombs.'

Andy shoved his bombs back in the haversack, and stumbled back along the trench, rounding the corner where he had crouched with Ripper. A shell had scythed away a perfect crater, and what was left of whoever had been standing there had been thrown up out of the trench, the body somehow stripped of its tunic. Andy kept going and saw the boys digging, Bob and Ripper amongst them, the sergeant bat-like in a black rain cape. Three or four wounded men lay beyond, white-faced, under a tossed-together shelter of galvanised iron sheets. Ripper grinned.

'Yer done good! So who's up there now? Us or bloody them?'

'Us.' Andy put his haversack down and picked up his shovel, which was exactly where he had left it, wedged under the dead infantryman's shoulder. 'Plenty of 'em.' He began to work, feeling a seeping desperate tiredness.

Mud stuck to his boots in great glutinous brown globs, his tunic lay soaked over his shoulders like a frozen poultice, and the pounding artillery dulled his ability to think until he wasn't think-ing, he was only digging. Someone draped an arm across his back.

'Andy-boy. How yer goin'?'

Andy looked into Bob's face. His eyes seemed to have sunk down into their sockets, and were so glassy they'd changed colour, from blue to black. He looked ancient, but he was still Bob. Ancient Bob.

'All right, Bob.' Andy sucked in air. 'You?' Every word he had to shout.

'Alive.' Bob looked around, the trench more like a deep hole in mud. 'Well, we got this off 'em. For now. Ripper reckons we'll be reinforced, the others'll go on through to the next line, and we'll stick here. Which'll be pleasant, I'm sure.'

'Some are already in.' Andy pointed down the trench. 'The others've probably been held up. Jesus. Hear the machine guns.'

The sound of machine guns was continuous, but rose and fell in waves as guns stopped and started. Andy came up with an image of ropes of bullets flying, lost the thought, and was simply glad to see Bob and the few remaining men of the company. He took another quick look at the wounded in the murky shelter of tin, their faces hopeless, mud dripping onto them as if it was being poured.

'There's tucker around,' Bob said. 'The boys got a good haul. Geez, look at Ripper. You'd reckon he was on 'oliday. He wants to do everythin' before he has to go home.'

Ripper stood on a small firestep reinforced with broken boards. He held a long-barrelled German rifle with a telescopic sight, which he rested on a rolled rag, its muzzle out through a gap in the mud-filled sand bags.

'Better get rid of this.' Andy rested his shovel on the dead German's chest. 'All right?'

'Right.' Bob squatted, delicately put his hands in under the cuffs of the dead soldier's grey pants just above his jackboots, and freed both legs from the mud. 'We'll dump him in that crater. I don't wanna be standin' on his face for the next two days.'

Andy saw the German's bare calf muscles swing loose, white, and useless on the bone. Not a footballer then, he thought. Not much track work gone into them chicken legs. He got hold of the front of the wet tunic and hauled the torso upright, the head flopping forward with a weight that seemed far too great for what it was. Andy swapped his grip to the collar.

'Too heavy. Drag 'im.'

Bob obediently dropped the legs, and moved next to Andy, hands clenched as they began to slide the body back through the mud.

'And here's me –' Bob checked behind, 'who never even got into a fight at state school. Bloody unbelievable.'

The boys dumped the body into a hole already filling with water, and made their way back through mud thickened with paper, cans, splintered wood, and things unidentifiable slipping down from the ever-collapsing walls.

'Imagine what she'd be like up top,' Bob said. 'Imagine tryin' to go forward through this shit now.' He lifted a boot, the mud like brown jelly. 'You go down in this shit and you're done for. Oh God, here's trouble.' Bob looked up at sky the colour of a dirty shilling. 'A bloody Minnie.'

The piercing wail of the Minninwerfer cut through the rumble and boom of the bombardment. All along the trench, men crouched as the German shell gained speed and volume – and then hit, the explosion turning the air into something solid that smashed Andy backwards, the sound too loud to process through his ears, the bones in his head taking it like a kick. It seemed to go on and on until something fell on him with such weight his breath was gone and he was buried. He was in blackness, encased, suffocating, as good as dead until he was dragged out by the boots and lay gasping like a fish someone had smacked on the skull, staring up, unable to blink. He began to cough.

Around him were men and noises he could not understand.

His head was filled with pain that slid cold and silvery, penetrating right up into his ear canals and eyeballs. He felt himself vomit, the warmth and weight of it on his chin and neck before he rolled over to clear his mouth, retching into dirt that stunk of swamp and smoke. In his head, as he spat, words formed in the shimmering lake of pain to surface, and utter themselves.

'I want to go home,' he said, or if he didn't say it, he thought it – and it was all he did think. There was nothing else left in him but the desire to be home. He could not imagine home, he could not imagine any part of it in any shape or form, he just wanted to be there.

'One day,' someone said, and hands, unseen, sat him up and leant him back against the side of the trench. 'How d'ya feel? Shithouse, eh?'

Andy nodded. That he was being talked to was doing him good. The words were familiar, home words, and they were doing him good. The words were like the words said when you had gone down during a game, words designed to get you up and get you going. He took them into his head, his mind layering them like a pearl.

He was handed a canteen, the water clearing whatever was disgusting in his throat. He spat and looked. The Minnie had landed beyond the trench, but had still blown out the back wall, leaving a crater that a lounge room could be built in. He was hauled to his feet.

'This joint's a shit hole, all right' Walter Steeply said. 'And I used to think Collingwood was bad.' The soldier's eyes were as glassy as Bob's. 'Som'a the boys gone forward, some come back. And the sigs run a line out, but all we heard was they copped a pastin' all the fuckin' way. Still. Maybe we gotta show. Who knows?' He lifted a muddy hand. 'I'm goin' back up there. I'll see yers later, if God can be bothered.'

All Andy could do was nod, and, unable to think of anything more constructive to do, he looked around for his shovel, hoping its handle might be sticking out of the foot and a half of fresh dirt and clay that had filled the trench. There was no sign of it, or his rifle, or his pack.

'Hey, Andy.' Ripper struggled down the trench carrying the sniper's rifle. 'Since you got no shovel I got a little job for ya. There's a nice little possie where ya can do some damage.'

Andy followed Ripper back up the trench. The sounds of the battle were as endless and complex as the sounds of the sea, booming from miles away, but also, wherever he went, through the ringing in his ears, he sometimes could hear its smaller sounds: stretcher-bearers shouting, a shovel clanging, the wounded calling for water, the spattering of rain. Ripper showed him the position.

'Even got ya a sniper's plate.' Ripper winked. 'Right. Wipe ya hands and then I'll give ya a hand up.' He helped Andy up onto the step. 'Right. Rifle. Don't knock the scope.' He handed up the weapon and a jar of ammunition. 'And some lollies. Now see if ya can dong a few. It's dead on at four hundred yards, she's got one up the spout, and the trigger's a feather. Good luck.'

Andy pushed aside the tiny steel gate and poked the barrel of the rifle out. He leant forward against the trench wall that Ripper had covered with a German tunic and settled in, moving shoulders and elbows, and distributing his body weight evenly over his feet until he was steady. All he could see was mud and shell holes, a strange tingling sensation in his fingers as he traversed the battlefield with the telescopic sight.

In stark detail he saw a body in the mud, a splintered tree trunk, a lost rifle, another body, half a helmet, half a body, but between his trench and the next German position – if it still was a German position – nothing moved. If there were men out there, and there had to be, considering the thousands that had gone forward, all had gone to ground.

'Come on,' he muttered, coming upon another destroyed section of trench, belts of barbed wire ten and twenty yards across where it wasn't blown apart.

Something moved. Khaki green. Andy searched on, the ground

seeming to race through the sight as if it was flowing. Now he sighted a British machine-gun crew behind their black Vickers gun, boxes of belted ammunition at the ready. Most of the soldiers were smoking. The gun, aimed across the latest stretch of no-man's-land, was not firing – and then it was, blue smoke and a bright flicker of flame pouring out. Quickly Andy raised the scope beyond the trench to cover less broken ground that ran up to a wood of shredded trees. Here, there was movement. Running legs, fire from the trees, a squirming back, someone ducking into a shell hole.

Andy zeroed in on a running figure, uniform made dark by the rain, held the cross-hairs on the top of the coalscuttle helmet – allowing for the distance which he figured was probably beyond the rifle's range – and gently squeezed the trigger. The soldier dropped as if he had been shoved.

Andy was more surprised than shocked. There was something unbelievable about what he'd done, if he'd done it; and when he looked for the fallen soldier he could not find him, as if he had been taken away, or had never been hit, or had never been there at all. But there were more men running up the wide-open hill toward the wood, some with weapons, some without.

Uniforms flashed like cards; green, grey, green again. A shell burst, Andy flinched, and found by chance he'd sighted on a group of German infantry trying to climb, like boys caught in blackberries, back through their own wire entanglements, a cloud of dancing sparks around them as bullets struck wire and pickets.

Andy took aim at a heavily-built soldier and fired. Again and again he shot into the men, groping into the jar for slim gold rounds until a smashing blow to his forehead instantly removed every particle of the light of day, and it wasn't for hours – he had no idea how many – that he found himself as part of a crawling tide of men retreating over ground that had been shelled ten times over.

Retreating, he helped drag a wounded man from a hole brimming with water, and in turn was dragged free of the mud by others — and every so often he looked up into a sky that refused to lower its darkness, shells and wasp-bullets buzzing past in search of a warm home, a feeling of sickness in him so deep that it could not have been of the body.

In a crater, holding a found rifle, he tried to think of Cecelia and Frances-Jane, but all thoughts of them failed. He could not even name them. It was only the unborn baby that brought the tiniest gleam into his head, and that was, he knew, because it was the only sliver of him that had any chance of remaining in this world for any length of time. Where he was simply was not survivable. Or if it was this time, it would not be the next. In the gathering gloom, with other faceless men, Andy eventually waded out of a channel that led to a barn, where he slept a sleep that was unfathomable.

twenty-five

Henry stared out of the train window, waiting for paling fences to give way to cyclone wire, behind which he was confident he'd spot the Hoestler warehouse and his cricket pitch. The sun dodged from cloud to cloud, boom gates tolled in his ear, and the city seemed endless, but not mundane, because he felt that on the day of a funeral he owed it to someone, or something, to find value and interest in everything.

The train was not full. Most people sat with heads bent over books or hidden behind newspapers. At Henry's feet was his overnight bag. He would miss the afternoon train back to Melbourne and so would stay a night at the Strattford pub. And if he hadn't been worried about going to a funeral, and if he wasn't still trying to convince himself that Trot was dead, and if he wasn't dressed in clothes his mother had passed as respectable, he would've been enjoying the journey. Instead, he felt as if the trip was happening to him, that he was being swept along by events beyond his control.

Of course he could've chosen not to go to the funeral, like Nick and Marcus – not that he held their decision against them. He was the person who'd met Trot, he was the person who had invited Trot and Janine up to stay, he was Trot's friend. Or he had been for a short while, although he figured he was now Trot's friend forever.

In a way, Henry felt above grief. He was devastated by the fact that Trot had been killed, but the devastation he was experiencing was at a pretty objective level. He felt some guilt for not feeling worse, but he also figured it would've been a bit strange if he was being torn apart. Yes, he had liked Trot, but he hadn't really known him well. So, I'll be a bit like an observer today, he thought. I'll say nothing unless I'm asked, and I'll do nothing except try to be polite.

Cyclone fences appeared and then, briefly, the Hoestler warehouse. Henry was glad not to be there.

His dad had given him time off without question and his mum had been truly sympathetic, but stopped short of letting him have her car for two days, probably thinking it bad karma to send him off in a vehicle he could crash. So here he was on the train, quite liking it, and happy not to have to pay for the tank of juice the Volvo would've drunk to get to Strattford. Impatient, he wanted the houses to end and the bush to start.

Self-consciously, Henry joined the crowd outside the church, saying nothing to anyone, and spent most of his energy on keeping his hands out of his pockets. Three silver cars, including a hearse, were parked out on the road, and seemed to hold light from the sky. He looked for Janine and spotted her in a group of people just about to go in through glass double doors. There was no way he would talk to her now, so he attached himself to the edge of the crowd, and inched forward.

At the entrance, a middle-aged woman wearing black gloves handed him a copy of the service. She smiled sadly but quite warmly at him.

'Welcome,' she said. 'You can sit wherever you like.'

Henry found a seat at the back, his eyes drawn to the big wooden coffin that rested at the small altar, its lid draped with an Australian flag on which lay a folded football jumper, and a mound of mostly yellow flowers. Without warning, feelings of ultra-reality washed over Henry, some small, others powerful. Trot was in that coffin there. Trot was in that big shiny brown box, and in about an hour he would be buried deep under the ground.

Henry pictured him alive; Trot in the kitchen at Nick's house, just before he went fishing, eating cereal, big and hefty in the corner, wearing a flannelette shirt, his arms like those of a butcher. To steady himself, Henry looked around, guessing there would have to be close to three hundred people present. More maybe. Every seat was going to be taken. Standing room only in a minute. To make space, Henry moved up, stained glass windows rising over him, gold, red, and green. By the aisle near the front he could see Cecelia Hainsworth, and in the very front row he saw Janine in a black blouse and skirt, her hair held back by a black and gold headband.

She looked calm, Henry thought, and beautiful, and immediately told himself off for even thinking that. Around Henry, people spoke to each other in muted voices and men who looked like farmers shook hands. Quietly, an organ began to play and wordlessly, a priest dressed in white and gold – Henry guessed he was a priest – faced the congregation, arms held out.

'Welcome one and all,' he said. 'Let us pray.'

Henry was absorbed by the service, and although he did not sing audibly or pray, apart from murmuring 'Amen', he felt himself being carried along within it. Even the hymns he liked, following the words, thinking about the thoughts and ideas expressed in each. Kindness, caring, love, yes, it was all good and hopeful, and to hear and think about stuff like that in this situation, with Trot's polished coffin right there. Henry was surprised to feel somewhat calmed by it all.

Trot's father, an enormous man with wavy silver hair, spoke about Graham and talked about the things he did well with his hands, and the way he was a quiet and honest friend to many. The captain of Trot's football team, a guy called Trevor, spoke about Trot's strength and how Trot would come out of a pack with the ball tucked into his chest as if he was going to run home with it.

'He was a mighty bloke,' the captain of the Strattford Tigers said, whom Henry reckoned would also be absolutely unstoppable on a football field. His shoulders seemed to be trying to escape from his shiny black suit, his hands looked capable of bending steel. Henry could not imagine playing footy either with or against guys like that, and was in awe that Trot had been able to.

'But best of all,' the captain continued, 'Trot was a feller who spoke the truth, did the right thing, had plenty of courage, and I only wish he was gunna be around here because this town needs men like him.' The captain looked at the coffin. 'Trot, *Graham*, everyone here knows what your heart was like, mate. It was big and it was made of bloody gold, and we'll miss ya forever, mate. And that's all I can say. You were one of the best.'

Henry could hear people crying quietly, some helplessly, endlessly, it sounded. He didn't feel like crying. He felt a kind of sad, frustrated anger that Trot wasn't here anymore, and that by going he had let himself down, and had left a great big hole that was only ever going to be filled with sadness. With on open hand, the priest indicated that Janine should come forward.

Quietly, the back of her shoes shining, Janine took her place behind the wooden pulpit. The priest tilted the microphone down and stepped away. There was a rustle of paper as Janine smoothed a sheet, before looking around the congregation, acknowledging people with a nod that served as a general greeting to all.

Janine stared at her notes, her hair falling forward. Henry, like everyone else, waited.

'Of course,' she said, looking up, 'Graham would not have liked us talking about him behind his back like this.' She allowed a small smile. 'But bad luck, Trot, because there are lots of things I want to say.' Her voice was strong through the microphone. 'Graham – Trot – was a person of action who tended to do things rather than talk about them, although he was one of the most thoughtful people I've ever met.' Her blue eyes shone with something other than tears.

Henry leant forward to listen. Janine steadied the sheet of paper she held.

'When you're big like Trot is – was – out here in the country, you're supposed to act in certain ways and do certain things. And Trot did do those things, like play footy, work hard, and stand up for himself, and others, too. But Graham's physical strength was certainly not his only strength.' Janine took a measured breath.

'Trot had room in his heart for many people, and if someone was in trouble, he would help them. He was very courageous and that was not because he was so strong – it was because courage was something he believed in. And so do I. And I wish that when he had died –' Janine's voice faltered, she looked up at the ceiling, cleared her throat, and continued, 'it could've been doing something heroic rather than an awful accident, because that was the sort of person Graham was. He was bigger than what happened to him. Much bigger.'

Henry could see tears on her cheeks. With the side of a finger, she wiped them away.

'What Trot was best at was inside him.' Janine stopped to clear her throat. 'He was best at being a kind and generous person. He was best at helping other people to do well. He was gentle and he was funny, and I'll miss and love him always. But this town helped make Trot, and Trot helped make it. And this town's filled with good people and that's how I want Trot to live on.' Janine no longer looked at her notes.

'Trot can live on in the good things that people do around here – and if we can at least *try* to do good *strong* things, then some, or part of those good things, can be because of Trot, and then I won't feel that he's gone so far and that he's gone forever.' Janine smiled again, the smile surfacing slowly, as much an expression of pain as anything else. 'And when you hear the roar of some hotted-up V-8 Ford or Holden, don't think too harshly of the driver – probably on P-plates – because some of those guys who drive those cars are the best guys you could ever hope to meet.'

Henry saw a tear fall like a sequin. Janine looked at a spot above the church doors.

'I love you, Trot, and I miss you.' She lowered her gaze. 'And I thank everyone for being here today, because by seeing your faces I know that I will never be alone in missing Graham, and that in the end all that really does hold us all together is love and friendship. Goodbye Trot, I'll see you again in a while, I hope. But I'm not so sure, and that's what makes this so bad. Thank you, Graham. See you, mate. Goodbye.' Janine nodded at the coffin, wiped her eyes, gathered her notes and walked back to her seat, a hand reaching out to her as she sat down.

Suddenly, Henry was ready to be out of the place. He wanted to be away from that coffin and the stuff of the church.

He didn't want to stop thinking about Trot, but he wanted to do it in another place. Out in the fresh air, for instance.

Eventually, after watching Trot's coffin carried out high up on shoulders, he filed out slowly with everyone else, shook the hands that were offered to him and stood in the warmth of the breezy afternoon, wishing he'd brought his sunglasses. The day seemed long and shapeless. Henry felt tired, and wished that he could get home tonight, but the train was gone. He'd heard its whistle while he was in the church, and could picture it cutting away to the city through the dry brown country.

He felt a hand on his arm and turned. Janine stood there, her eyes red-rimmed and sparkly.

'Thanks for coming, Henry.' She smiled a little, which Henry accepted as gratefully as a gift. 'If you need a lift to the cemetery,' she said, 'I can organise it. But if you don't want to come, I can get my parents to pick you up after from the pub. There's going to be drinks and stuff at Trot's folks' house. You're welcome to everything, of course.'

Henry felt himself nodding.

'No, I'll come,' he said. 'To the cemetery. Yeah, a lift'd be good. That was a great talk you gave. It was one of the best things I've ever heard.'

Janine shrugged. She looked exhausted.

'Thanks.' She hardly seemed to see Henry. She put a hand up to her temple. 'But it seemed too short, you know, for what it was for. I'll get your lift, Henry. And talk to you later.'

Henry walked out of the cemetery in a daze. The finality of the burial was like a blow to the head. He couldn't quite believe what he'd seen, but he knew quite well, somewhere deeper, that he did believe it. He looked back at the mound of clay covered by a green sheet, then he looked away to the trees that formed a border between cemetery and farmland.

A gully wound along, a narrow creek at its bottom, the slopes patched with dry brown bracken, but in between there was green grass and gum trees filtering the sun with their fine leaves. Henry could see a track down there, worn by stock. The timeless appearance of the place made him think of Andy Lansell.

Later, he walked back along the main street to the pub. Cars passed, some with surfboards on roofs and bikes on racks. It would be nice to be heading up the coast, he thought, as he went into the hotel, stopping at his door to dig around for his key.

'You are a good boy for coming today, Henry Lyon. It did not surprise me to see you.'

Henry turned to see Miss Hainsworth in a black dress decorated with red flowers.

'I liked Graham,' was the only thing he could think to say. 'He was a really good guy.'

'I also liked Graham Trotter.' Miss Hainsworth granted Henry a curt nod. 'I was hard on him because I cared for him. But obviously I was not hard enough. He was a boy who would've done better eighty-five years ago with something heroic to do, as Janine said. Although I would not have wished that war on anyone.'

Henry guessed everything that Miss Hainsworth said was right.

'Janine let me read some of Andy's diary,' he said, feeling as if he was making an admission rather than a statement. 'It was really interesting. I mean, I was really careful with it. He was a brave guy, Andrew. And his mates. They all were, to go over there, and do what they did.'

Miss Hainsworth stood, breathing steadily, her hand on the doorknob for support. Henry tried to ascertain if she was angry, but he found it hard to identify any emotion in her old face. She gripped her silver stick tightly.

'Yes, it would be a mistake,' she said slowly, 'to think that the things that people have done before us have nothing to do with us now. I do know, of course, Janine Walker's connection with Andrew, but more importantly I am pleased to see that she is a good and strong person. I am really –' Miss Hainsworth rattled the doorknob, 'still quite on the ball, Henry Lyon. Anyone who knew Andrew could quite plainly see Janine has the Lansell eyes. As does her mother, Rosemary.' Miss Hainsworth seemed amused. 'Anyway, life is interesting. Good night.' And she was gone, leaving Henry with the impression that although she had not smiled, she might as well have.

In the morning, Henry packed, then went to the station to check what time the train for Melbourne departed. One thirty-three p.m. precisely, he was told by the stationmaster, who wore a fob watch with a gold chain. Henry thanked him.

'Could I walk up the platform?' he asked. 'Just for a look?' He liked everything about the old station.

It was made of brown brick, each wall featuring a diamond pattern of bricks of a lighter colour, its slate roof splotched with pale green lichen. Swallows flitted past the ticket office and in the dark spaces under the eaves.

'Not a problem.' The stationmaster lifted his ticket window a bit higher. 'Yeah, she's a nice little place. My grandfather worked here, you know. Before he went off to the First World War. I found his initials carved on the bench in the parcels room. They gave him a job when he got back, although he came back with only one arm.'

'Oh, right,' Henry said. 'That was good. That he got the job, I mean.'

Henry walked out through the gate and up the platform. Already heat was rising from the gravel and from a line of gums across the railway lines he could hear cicadas. Sitting on a seat by a small dry garden, he put his feet out, and contemplated his sneakers. He had the feeling that it would not be right for him to see Janine today. Why, he was not sure, he just had the feeling that he shouldn't.

He pulled out his phone, checked his messages, found nothing and then, unable to provide himself with a reason why he shouldn't ring Marcelle, he dialled her number. He needed to talk to someone about the last few days, but she wasn't home, and he didn't leave a message.

It was pleasant sitting, the sun not yet too hot. Henry let it loosen him and allowed the events of the last couple of days to settle. He looked beyond the end of the platform and along the tracks, the rock ballast shimmering, the line disappearing into a distant blue gap like a tunnel. How did it happen that he was here? Well, it just did; it was all just a random matter of seconds and circumstances. If he'd driven on for ten minutes back in January he would never have met Trot, Janine and Miss Hainsworth, and he would never have heard the Andy Lansell story.

Henry reckoned right now, the way the day was, if he thought hard enough he could just about conjure Andy and his mates out of the thin summer air. If he could just slide back through the seconds and the days, he could summon them up like an image brought back on a screen, and they would walk out onto the platform, in uniform, the year 1917. He looked, but only the station master was there, pottering with a steel watering can.

'Do it,' Henry muttered, opened his phone, brought up Janine's number, and rang it. Her mother answered, whom he'd spoken to at the funeral. She remembered him.

'Yes, Henry,' she said. 'She's here. I'll just go and get her for you.'

Henry waited, and then to the best of his ability, he told Janine what Miss Hainsworth had told him the night before.

'She said she's known for a long time about you being Andy's great-granddaughter. She said you've got the Lansell eyes. She said your mum has them as well. She didn't seem upset about it − at all.' Henry found himself talking into silence. 'Like, I think she really likes you. I mean, she does. She said so. And so do I.' Henry blushed, gritted his teeth. 'And that's the news. Though she said some other stuff about Trot. I mean, how she liked him. But I'll tell you it all another day, all right? You okay? I mean . . .'

'Ah, yeah,' Janine said. 'I'm okay. God, Henry, you're like someone who everyone tells everything to. It's your talent.'

Henry thought she sounded annoyed, but he didn't accept that she was really annoyed *with* him, as such. He heard her sigh.

'*More* stuff for me to think about,' she said. '*And* what I'll do about it. I mean, I'll do something, but not yet. One day. I'll ring you. Thanks for coming. Say hello to everyone. Goodbye, Henry. See ya.'

'Yeah, bye, Janine.' Henry didn't want the conversation to end with this lost-in-space feel to it, but he didn't know what to say to avoid it. 'I'll talk to you soon,' he added, ended the call, feeling lonely, and in a place he did not belong.

He got up, walked back up the platform, and went out through the gate, the stationmaster looking up through the wire grill. Henry saw the steel plate screwed into the counter was polished from years of people's hands tendering money and taking tickets.

'You'll be back then,' the railway man said.

'No, I don't think so.' Henry felt sour enough to want to let someone, *anyone*, know he'd had enough of Strattford − before realising what he was being told. 'Oh, yeah, you're right.' He raised a finger as if awarding a point. 'I will be. This afternoon. I forgot. For the train.' He didn't feel like smiling, but he did anyway. 'Yeah, one thirty-three. See ya. It's a nice station.'

'And more people come back to it than leave,' the railway man said. 'It's a funny little town like that. You'll see.'

Henry doubted it.

September 26 1917,
Camerons Huts, Ypres, Flanders.

The boys have done great things. This place must go down in history. It is a muddy hell that could never be equalled for hardship and slaughter. Polygon Wood. Passchendaele. Broodseinde. I will work at forgetting those places until the day I die.

'And back to the circus we go.' Bob hoisted the wooden duckboard onto his shoulder, blue-silver moonlight running along the wooden edge. 'I've heard the clowns are very good. Bit hard to see them in this light, but there's all sorts of novelty acts. One-wheeled bicycles and acrobats. Bloody jugglers and effing knife throwers.'

Andy lifted his duckboard, liking the feel of the rough-sawn timber. It wasn't too heavy and he was much happier with a one-man job. Sharing a box of ammo, stumbling through the mud, trying to hang onto a handle, would be an absolute bastard. Hefting his load he felt as if he might be on his way out to a shed, or a fence, to do something at home – except he didn't usually work at midnight at home.

'I actually hope the show's not on,' he said, and saw, miles to the south, the soft orange glow of artillery firing as if to bring down the moon that rode through clouds of the same colour. 'But I reckon that'd be too much to ask.'

Ripper's voice came out of the darkness.

'Orright boys, all set? Off we go. Hi ho, hi ho. Jesus, I wish

I was 'ome in bed. Now, heads down. I want yers all back for breakfast.'

The line of men went up the road, through a brick pile that had been a village, out the other side, and entered a shallow ditch in single file. Andy tramped on obediently, boots skidding in mud, his feet hurting already. His hands were cold but he could feel the welcome warmth of exertion as a thickening layer. His breath fogged and he was as aware of stars as he was of the flat, wide-open ground all around.

'When's that stork comin' to your place, Andy?' Bob asked. 'Must be pretty soon now. We've been away from home for, geez, I dunno, has to be nine months. You could be a dad by now.'

'I must be,' Andy said. 'I guess.'

Bob stopped, swapped his load to the other shoulder, resumed walking. 'I'm pleased, you know. I mean, not that you're in trouble and all that, but there's gunna be a little Lansell runnin' around.' He nodded, his helmet slipping a fraction. He pushed it back. 'I don't give a fuck what anybody back home says, mate. It's the best thing any of us 'ave ever done and might ever do. I think about it all the time. I'm its godfather. Darce, too, although he doesn't know it yet, but he will when he gets back, the bludger. Geez, I hope the kid has your brown eyes, Lanse.'

Andy snorted a laugh. 'Yeah, you drop-kick. Still, it's probably gunna need all the friends it can get. So you're on. Don't be stingy with the presents.'

Lately, Andy had felt that there was a new part to himself, or of himself. It had something to do with his heart. This new part actually felt like it was there, in his heart, a pocket or space for this kid, for what it meant — because what it meant now was very different to what it might have meant if he had been at home in the same situation. The things that he had seen and done here had changed everything. A child was like a sacred thing, even if grown men here were nothing like it. His baby, out of marriage, to the wrong girl, he had accepted. If there was blame to be laid it was only his and even that idea he was beginning to disregard. Yes, blame he would accept, but not shame. Stick that.

Here, shameful things happened. Here, on the orders of men ten miles behind the lines, troops attacked in waves and died in piles. Here, there were bodies that had lain unburied for two years. Here, he'd picked up pieces of fellers to be buried in a hessian bag. How could the birth of a baby back home be shameful compared to all that? It couldn't be.

'I'd teach the kid to ride.' Andy brushed against roots that poked out of the side of the trench like severed limbs. 'Maybe that's about the only thing I *could* teach it.'

Bob plodded on. 'Geez, brighten up, misery guts. You don't think people'll be happy to see yer when yer get home? They'll be all over yer. You'll be a bloody good dad. Let alone what you've done out here. See? Good character.' Bob laughed. 'Well, reasonable, anyway.'

As the carrying party went on, the boys talked less and struggled more. The mud was deeper and cold. It gripped boots and calves, numbing feet and legs, although Andy was sweating. Overhead, the occasional dry whistling of spent bullets could be heard and the foul belly smell of the battlefield was with them, heavy in the trench as if it sought the lowest ground to lie in. Andy, like the others, followed blindly, a guide somewhere up ahead twisting and turning through the earthen system that was home to men whose presence was less than real, the trenches and dugouts more like pre-prepared graves than places of rest.

Sometimes, under the mud, he stepped on things that had shape, or moved or gave, but he refused to acknowledge what they might be, and dutifully kept on going. Ahead he saw Ripper, like a carpenter with his duckboard artfully balanced, waiting by a dugout to pat each man on the shoulder as they passed.

'Only five hundred miles to go,' he said. 'Be there by Christmas.'

There was more activity in all the trenches now. Men moved up and back, carrying or returning after a carry. Occasionally, wounded were taken past and once in a sap dug off the main trench, Andy saw a raiding party preparing, their faces blackened, holding clubs and weapons, their uniforms stripped of all badges and identification. They looked like the damned, he thought, and was glad to not be going out with them. He'd seen raiders return, tunics black with blood, cradling their slashed arms and hands, with nothing to say of what they had seen or done.

Reaching a communication trench about a hundred yards from the front line, the soldiers, with relief, stacked their duckboards on other duckboards already disappearing into the mud.

'Siddown for a minute, fellers,' Ripper said. 'I just gotta go see the Capitaine then we'll be out of 'ere and home on a pig's back. Bloody shoo-in, boys.'

Andy and Bob sat, listening to the rumbling and grumbling of artillery. Occasionally, the trench was lit by the radiant light from a flare, the walls in places as rough as a creek bank and piled with wreckage, wire, and unidentifiable rubbish. For a few seconds, the soldiers' faces were moon-coloured, their hands and fingers like grubs in the semi-light, then everyone disappeared as darkness swiftly resumed its rightful place.

Tonight, Andy could feel his fear skipping lightly along his intestines to the sound of the guns. It was like a spark, or what he imagined electric current might look like. It was like a fairy or a sprite using his guts as a dance floor and the guns as an orchestra. Andy did not try to banish it. He let it dance, knowing that it would anyway, as long as he was up here, as long as he could hear the batteries thundering.

Ripper came back, crouched down. 'We got another little job to do, boys.' He leant against the wall of the trench. 'Nothin' big. We just gotta take a casualty back. Their youngest kid got knocked this afternoon and the Captain doesn't want to bury him up here, which is fair enough I s'pose, so I said yeah. A couple of you blokes just grab a duckboard, eh. Come on.' Ripper stood. 'Good boys. And it'll get us out of comin' back up here tonight. Fuckin' bargain. '

Four soldiers were dispatched to bring the body down. A duckboard was pulled off the stack, the blanketed soldier lashed to it. A smashed hand was tucked in.

'You three –' Ripper addressed Andy, Bob, and another private standing closest. 'Get a hold, boys, and see how we go with four for a start. Might have to go back to two dependin' on the mud and shit. Right. Lift. How's that? Bloody awkward, I know.' Ripper nodded. 'Still. Not so shockin'. Off we go.'

In the dark, the dead soldier was merely a shape under a blanket and although the task was shared between four, the body seemed to possess far more than its fair share of weight. Constantly, Andy knocked elbows with Ripper, slid in the mud, banged his outside hand and shoulder on the trench wall.

'Gees, young feller,' Ripper said to the corpse, 'we're doin' our best for ya, matey, but you ain't makin' it all that bloody easy.'

'Ah, he's all right.' Bob spoke evenly. 'It's not too bad. We'll just proceed slowly.'

The dead soldier's head swayed loosely next to Andy's left hand, sometimes knocking into his wrist. He could feel the nose. Andy focused on the boy's swaying boots and the twists and turns of the trench until time and distance were concepts lost in the labyrinth as the company made its slow way back, the mud frosted silvery in the moonlight, lending it a slightly festive glow.

The soldier's head bumped the outside of Andy's wrist, the weight of it hefty, the feel of it hard but not rock-hard, more like fresh-sawn timber, still sappy and giving, but lifeless. It dripped steadily, but Andy was unable to wipe his knuckles.

'There'll be a cuppa tea when we get back,' Ripper said. 'Some tucker and a sleep. Right. Swap over.'

Andy handed over to another soldier and trudged along behind. He did not consciously think about the boy on the duckboard, but the presence of the dead, all the dead, was like a dark sea within and so obviously vast, so obviously immoveable and unchangeable, that he could do nothing but accept it as something he would always gaze upon or gaze over, no matter what he did or where he was. The dead he'd seen were countless; the enemy like rubbish at worst, or at best, human, but the dead Australians were like a piece of himself — not a piece removed, but a portion of grief added.

Andy knew he'd seen too much; that even if the whole thing stopped now he'd seen far too much and he knew too much. It wasn't what he'd done. That was duty. That was his job. It wasn't even exactly what the Germans had done, because everyone was doing the same thing. It was what the whole thing was, and what the whole thing was was a vacuum that took hope as well as life, and in its place left knowledge that was filthy and foul, and that would always be filthy and foul.

'Darce'll be back soon,' Bob said. 'Bad luck for him. I bet he's wishin' they'd had to lop off a few toes. You could put up with that easy enough for a long ride home on a ship full of nurses.'

Ripper turned, his face striped with moonlight. 'Well, the *good* news is, we're goin' out of the lines for a while. Or so I heard. Trainin' for some stunt. Hopefully not back here. But don't tell anyone I told yers, because it ain't official.'

'Touch wood,' someone said. 'Touch bloody wood.'

Hands reached out to touch the duckboard.

'Ah, *that's* better,' someone said. 'I can bloody walk now. Mud? There's no mud. Gees, I dunno what all you blokes were complainin' about.'

Half an hour later, the section had made it back to the shelter of the battalion's barn. The men carrying the body stopped short of the door.

'Just leave it against the wall,' Ripper said. 'Not where anyone can trip over it. Look after it in the mornin'. Go get ya grub, boys. Good work.'

The body was lowered.

'See yer, chum,' Ripper said, and patted the blanketed form. 'Sleep tight, cobber. We know you done your best.'

Andy went to go into the hut, then stopped, unable to help himself from comparing the utter stillness of the body to the horizon that flickered and flared with what seemed like life.

'Hey, Andy-boy.' A figure appeared in the dark. 'How'ya goin', mate?'

'*Darce*.' Andy could make out his thin face as he lit a cigarette over cupped hands. 'How's ya bloody leg? How are ya?'

Darcy walked over. 'Too fuckin' good, unfortunately.' He shook Andy's hand tightly. 'So here I am. Back here with you bastards. What's the story with dead blokes outside the bloody hotel? I dunno whether I'm too keen on that.'

Andy had forgotten about the body. He glanced back, the body a black lump. 'Oh, yeah, just a kid we brought back from the line. So what was it like in dear old Blighty?'

Even in the dark, Andy could see Darcy's smile.

'She's a bloody ripper, mate. Treat ya like royalty. And by the way, there's a letter waitin' for ya in London. In the bloody hurry to get to the station I bloody forgot it. I'm real sorry. But you blokes are due to go on leave, accordin' to my books, so I'll give ya the address. I think it's from Frances-Jane, Andy-boy, to tell yer the truth.' Darcy nodded once, formally.

'It probably is.' Andy was too tired to think. 'Ah, well. Whatever's in it won't change now, eh? Couldn't be any worse than this shit, anyway.' The cuff of his tunic was sodden with mucus or blood. It was just another thing. Just another thing.

'Good point.' Darcy dug into his pockets. 'Still. Here. Wrap ya laughin' gear around this. Chocolate. Get stuck in. And I got that much rum in me pack if the boat'd gone down I would'a sunk like a bloody brick.'

twenty-six

Henry liked walking through the city. If he was with Marcus, they talked and laughed all the way down to the railway station. If he was alone, Henry cruised through the crowds, feeling light and agile, although his backpack was solidly loaded with books. Marcelle, he knew, worked in Collins Street, high up in an office block that cut itself into the sky like a square grey mountain.

He thought about her a lot. Once, they had had coffee together in a cafe near her office. She had asked him, to fill an awkward silence, if he was seeing anyone. Hundreds, he'd said. She had tapped him on the hand with a sugar straw, smiled, as if for old time's sake, then told him she had to get back to work.

They had walked down Collins Street together, Henry in possession of a sadness that stemmed from the feeling that he might not ever see her again. He had watched her cross the street, elegant in black, her coat hem lifting in the breeze. She had not looked back.

October 6 1917,
London.

Arrived late, picked up new uniform and pay. Had a bloody hot bath! It's lovely here. The people very welcoming and no shortage of places to go and sights to see. Visit Darcy's friends tomorrow. It's not quiet, but it is bloody peaceful.

In London, Andy was filled with a perpetual sense of joy. As soon as he woke, felt clean sheets, and worked out where he was, he was instantly cheerful. It felt like he'd just drunk two glasses of champagne, except that his head was clear, and his senses were sharp. He felt younger. He wondered if he didn't actually feel like someone else.

The city, after France and Flanders, seemed like a parade. The colours were complete, the buildings intact, the people obliviously taking their lives for granted. Walking through it, Andy breathed deeply, and with heartfelt gratitude savoured the sights, sounds, smells, and the innocent rhythm. To look at women was a gift. He wanted to laugh out loud. It was beautiful to be under a sky innocent of threat.

'I don't think these people have quite got a handle on what's goin' on over there,' Bob said, as they made their way up a damp street of narrow brick houses, the smell of coal smoke in the air. 'Still. How could yer, eh? From over this side of the ditch.'

'Couldn't.' Andy was not unaware of the pride he felt in his uniform, what he had done, and what he had come through. He was a digger and the diggers were great. 'They ought'a make a series of postcards for 'em. Here I am at the dressing station, Mrs Smith, having my arm cut off.' He laughed. 'Here I am in a muddy hole shittin' myself.'

'And here we are,' Bob said, opening inward a small iron gate that led to the front door of a narrow brick house. 'At number twenty-nine. *Entre-vous, meine freunde.* I hope they're ready for this.'

Andy followed, waiting hat in hand at the door, worry penetrating his gut. Inside was the letter from Frances-Jane.

'Remember, sport,' Bob said, polishing his boots on the back of his leggings, 'in the great and overall scheme of things, mate, whatever it is it can't be that effing bad.'

The door was opened by a young woman with pale, elaborately plaited hair. She smiled brightly.

'Oh, do come in.' She put out her hands to the boys. 'I'm Esther Stanton. And you must be Bob and you must be Andy.' She couldn't seem to stop smiling. 'Come in. Darcy's told me *all* about you two. Are you both well?'

'Couldn't be better.' Bob climbed the two steps and wiped his boots on a new-looking doormat. 'Ready for anything.'

Andy followed Bob into a sitting room, aware of the clean, slightly antiseptic smell of camphor. A coal fire burned in a grate, above was it a large mirror, and a mantelpiece on which sat two letters. He could see his name written on one in large, well-formed letters.

'Mother's in the kitchen,' Esther said breathlessly. 'Getting the tea. I shall go and help her in a minute. Please do sit.'

Andy sat in a velvet-covered chair with a curved wooden back, Bob in a frilled armchair. Esther went to the mantelpiece, picked up Andy's letter, and brought it shyly to him.

'This came for you. But in the hurry to get Darcy to the station it was left behind. I'm very sorry.' She clasped her hands. '*All* the way from Australia. Imagine that. From right *across* the world!'

'Just a-bloody-bout,' Bob said. 'Pardon the French.'

Esther turned, almost a dance step. Andy looked at her ankles, neat in black stockings.

'I shall go and help mother with the tea.' She looked quickly at the boys. 'Please make yourselves at home. It's so very nice to have you here.'

'And for us.' Bob beamed, his hat on his knee. 'You're very kind, Esther. And I'm sure Andy'll be able to say somethin' for himself just as soon as he's read that letter. He's got a one track mind, the poor kid.'

Esther stopped at the doorway. 'Andy, there's a little study down the hall if you would like some privacy —'

Andy laughed. It all seemed *too* civilised.

'Nah, I'll be fine here. That is, unless you mind me —?'

Esther took a step away. 'Of course I *don't* mind! I hope it's full of good news.' And she was gone, with a swish of her skirt.

Andy tore into the envelope. 'So do I.'

'Good luck.' Bob stuck his legs out and admired his new boots. 'Could be triplets.'

Andy read quickly, skimming the first few sentences until he found what he was looking for.

'I've got a *daughter,*' he said quietly, the room suddenly strange-looking, as if he just woken up in it, as if he had never seen it before. 'How's that, Bobby? How's that, eh?' He held the letter up, he put it down. 'Her name's Eliza and she's got blue eyes.' Andy couldn't shift the lump in his throat. 'A daughter.'

He felt remarkable. Amazed. Dazed. Not unhappy at all; perhaps he felt happier than he ever had, although he wasn't sure. He had a daughter. Jesus. Well. He returned Bob's handshake, but was unable to muster much strength.

'Well, that's bloody great news.' Bob's grin would not buckle. 'That's bloody *beautiful* news!' He sat down. 'See?' he whispered loudly. 'Who gives a fuck, eh? It'll be all right in the end, mate. Won't it? It will be. I promise. I *guarantee* it.'

Andy swallowed. He felt different. Permanently altered, already. He nodded, not looking at Bob, but at the stripes of wallpaper.

'Yeah,' he said. 'Yeah, I guess it is good news. I guess it is.'

Newly etched lines added ferocity to Bob's smile. He loosed off a big wink.

'You've got a *kid*, mate!' He twirled his hat in his finger. 'She's *half* you! Mate, we've gotta go get pie-eyed as soon as possible. And not with pies, neither.'

Andy found it hard to listen. He had a daughter. Eliza. With blue eyes. It had happened – almost three months ago, to be exact. His daughter was in the world. She was a long a way away, but she was in the world, right now.

'*Shit*, I wish I was home.' He slapped his leg, an ineffectual gesture. 'I bloody *should* be.' To be home, to see his baby, that's all he wanted to do. And do it *now*.

If he could be, nothing else could touch him. The boys knew how he'd done over here. He'd fought and now he'd had enough of fighting, but who hadn't?

Esther came in pushing a wooden trolley laden with tea things, and biscuits and cakes. She was followed by a large woman whose navy blue bulk filled the doorway. Andy was in no doubt it was Esther's mother.

'Welcome to our home, dear boys,' she said, a double string of pearls rattling in the valley between her bosoms. 'And may God deliver you safely home when this whole ghastly thing is over.'

Andy and Bob stood.

'I'll drink to that.' Bob bumped his chair with the back of a knee. 'But before they send us back, we're off to Scotland. Me and Andy are catchin' the train up there tomorrer for a bit of a look around. And by the time we get back to France, with a bit of luck the whole show'll be over, and we can bugger off home once and for all. Pardon the French.'

Andy felt the first waves of shock receding. He could see straight, for one thing. That was a help.

'It's very nice of you to invite us,' he said. 'You've got no idea how wonderful it is just to be here. In a lovely house. With people.'

''Ere 'ere,' said Bob. 'And if I might fill me a cup I'd like to pro- pose a toast to you, Mrs Stanton, and your lovely daughter, Esther. I kid you not when I say it's like bein' in the company of two angels.' Andy saw Bob wink at Esther who hurriedly went to work on the cups and saucers. 'God save the King!' he added. 'And all the boys doin' England's work out there in the trenches.'

'And God protect them,' Esther added. 'Against those dirty, awful, German Huns.'

twenty-seven

Henry was on his way to the kitchen with dirty coffee cups when the phone rang. He answered it, and promptly hung a U-turn when he discovered it was Janine. Returning to his room he sat.

'Sorry it's taken me so long to get around to ringing you, Henry,' she said, 'but I'm still a bit out of it really, I guess. Although I have spoken to Miss Hainsworth. It's all sorted out, or nearly. It's been interesting, believe me.'

'Yeah, I bet.' Henry hoped this was not a stupid thing to say. 'Ah, what'd she say?'

'Got a minute? Like ten?'

'Plenty.' Henry rocked back in his chair.

'All right. Andy Lansell, right?' Janine's voice was steady. 'Well, when he was in the war he wrote and told Cecelia about this Frances-Jane being pregnant. So Cecelia, of course, called off the engagement. Then Frances-Jane went off to live in Bendigo. Then, when Andy's mates came back to Strattford when the war was finished, they kind of looked after her and the baby, although she didn't marry one of them, or anything. They basically just sent her money and stuff from Stratty. One worked at the railway station here. Darcy Garrett, and the other guy was Bob, although I don't know what his other name was.'

'I remember them from the diary,' Henry said. 'Did Darcy lose an arm or something?'

'Yeah, he did. Anyway, to cut a long story short, Cecelia found it all out from Darcy. I think she scared him more than the Germans did. Right, so she regrets not trying to forgive Andy, and she regrets not trying to ever see his daughter – who was my grandma – she died like forty years ago. So, anyway, Cecelia has made me an offer, Henry. She says it might go part way to fixing up the past.'

Henry sucked on a pen. 'What sort of an offer?'

'She wants me to go to France to visit Andy's grave and to see the places where he was. She wants to give me an air ticket. Not to say she's sorry, I don't think. She called it a scholarship. She says she just wants me to get out of here for a while, see the place, and learn some things. And to go for her, because she says she can't go herself.'

An assignment Henry had up on his computer faded to black. He sat up straight in his chair.

'So are you gunna go? I mean, it's a good offer. What do your parents say?'

'Well, they're leaving it up to me.' Janine took an audible breath. 'I must say, though, that I'm pretty tempted. It's very generous of her. I think I will go. Both to go, and to get away, you know? I need a break. I mean, I've got some of my own money. She said if I wouldn't allow her to pay she'd be insulted. Like, that's her way of – I dunno, doing things. Balancing things up.'

'It'd be a great trip.' Henry was sure about that. 'It'd be fantastic. I mean, France. Wow.'

There was a pause. Henry could hear nothing, but sensed something. He waited.

'So why don't you come, Henry? No strings attached. You could.'

Henry rocked back in his chair and nearly tipped over. The possibility of the trip swirled. Could he go? Really?

'Well, yeah, I guess I *could* go.' He wasn't sure if he believed this. 'But I mean, like when would you –'

'Oh, later in the year, I guess.' Janine's voice was stronger, alloyed with humour. 'November or December or something. I haven't worked it out. I haven't even agreed to it yet. I'll understand if you can't, Henry. I'm not an idiot.'

'Yeah, no, I know.' The idea had lodged in Henry's head. He was in the grip of its possibilities. He did have the money from his work at the factory. Maybe it was possible. 'Look, I'll have to think about it. Give me a bit of time and I'll ring you back, okay?'

'Sure, Henry. Whenever.' Janine laughed, the first time Henry could remember hearing her do so since Trot died. 'You know, it would be good if you could.'

'Yeah, no, it would.' Henry's head was thumping. 'I'll ring you in a couple of days, Janine. No, would a week be okay? I'll ring you then.'

'Whatever, Henry.' Janine laughed again. 'And don't stress. It's just that, you know, who knows? It would be good if you could. Bye, Henry.'

Henry put the phone down. He couldn't go. No way. There were just too many things against it. There was uni, there was the money side, there was the Janine-Trot thing, and his parents . . . and? And what? Plenty. Plenty of things.

Marcus put his beer down on the bar. Henry sipped his pot, waiting to hear what he had to say. The Exford, a grubby pub close to the university, held only a few drinkers. The sound of the city traffic made its way in through the grimy glass doors as if it was swapping places with the musty, fried-food smell making its escape.

'Well, it'd definitely be somethin' else, all right.' Marcus scratched the knee of his jeans, exposing the collapsing leather of an old cowboy boot. 'But you couldn't cut uni, could you? And like, so what would the deal be with . . . you know, with Janine, if you went?'

'Yeah, well that's it, isn't it?' Henry could see himself in the mirror behind the bar. He reckoned he looked worried. 'I don't really know. But I mean with Trot gone –' He couldn't say what he was feeling. He didn't know what he *was* feeling. 'It's complicated.'

Marcus ripped open a packet of beer nuts.

'Yeah, it's that for sure. But it was pretty much like five months ago or somethin' that he got killed, wasn't it?' Marcus shrugged. 'I mean, you mightn't be going until the end of the year, so you'd be in the clear there, I reckon. I mean I know that sounds harsh, but . . .'

In Henry's head feelings circled, became confused.

'It's difficult,' he said. 'But I mean, well, I do like her.' He wasn't one hundred percent sure what he meant by that. 'I do.'

'Okay, so that being the case,' Marcus pushed the nuts along to Henry, 'you'll just have to put that legally-trained brain of yours into action.' He dusted salt off his hands. 'And come up with the right course of action. Just don't ask me for advice. Because I'm only a bloody builder, and I wouldn't know.'

October 8 1917.
Edinburgh, Scotland.

Train to Scotland. Feel a bit light-headed with everything to tell the truth.

Enjoying ourselves. Scenery very pleasing. Imagine it to be very cold in winter. It's cold now. We are eating a lot of shortbread.

Andy ran a hand along the cold steel of the cannon's polished barrel. The wind was sharp, forced vertically upwards by the castle's massive wall, bringing with it the smell of the sea. He could not lose the worrying sensation of standing right out in the open, his body exposed to a great sweep of land and buildings. It was not possible to ignore the urge to put something between himself and non-existent snipers.

'I think the Germans should re-arm with these old bangers.' Bob examined the cannon's breech. 'I'd be a lot happier. I reckon a bloke with a decent bat could probably hit 'em right back over Fritzy's head.' He gazed out across the city's roofs and roadways. 'Where are we again? Glasgow or Edinburgh? It's not bloody Dublin is it, I know that much.'

Andy laughed, because he knew Bob was serious. He moved into the lee of the tower's battlements and felt a lot better.

'Edinburgh, mate. That's what the sign at the station said.'

'So this'd be the Edinburgh castle, then.' Bob pulled a face. 'And a very nice castle it is, too. So where's the pub?'

Andy pushed his chin into his collar. The wind was sharp. He looked off between the stone battlements.

'I'm tippin' it'd be down there somewhere. Let's bugger off.' He set off for the steps, feeling a diffuse warmth as he thought of Frances-Jane and the baby. *Eliza.* He could hardly imagine a baby, let alone imagine his own. He'd never paid attention to one for more than ten seconds in his life; but he could picture Frances-Jane *holding* a baby. 'Bobby,' he said, 'maybe I can get a photograph sent over?'

'Shit, yeah.' Bob rattled down a few steps. 'Get several.' He rattled a couple more. 'Get a hundred.'

Exiting the castle, they came out into parkland, the stone buildings of Edinburgh a cold golden colour, with sharp roofs, towers, and spires rising.

'Geez, now where are we?' Bob stopped. 'I wouldn't have gone up that bloody pile if I knew it was so far back to the bar.'

Andy pushed him in the back. 'Nah, High Street, mate. There. We're nearly out of it already.'

The boys walked on in sunshine that was not warm but welcome, the sky pale, streaked with clouds like lazy brush strokes.

'I quite like Miss Esther.' Bob thrust his hands deep into his greatcoat pockets. 'A lot. She cooks a nice cake, and besides, I think she's quite keen on old Bobby-boy. She told me I had very *manly* hands.' Bob held them out limply, like a dog begging. 'Whadda ya reckon?'

'I reckon you'll get a kick in the nuts,' Andy said, 'if you stand with 'em out like that, mate. You look like a bloody Cocker Spaniel.'

Bob put his hands away. 'When we get back to London I'm gunna ask her out for tea — *avec moi*. We'll have a night there before we have to go back over, won't we? I think it would be the gentlemanly thing to do. Plus, I don't want to put the moz on us, but I think all *opportunities*, if that's the right word, should be *seized*. At this point.' He stopped to sniff. 'Pub.' He pointed. 'We're in there already.'

The boys walked into the small hotel, its white-framed windows recessed in stone, wisps of smoke coming from clusters of chimney pots. A barman in a white apron wiped ashtrays.

'Afternoon, boys.' He stopped what he was doing. 'And welcome to the cold old hole we fondly know as Auld Reekie. Sit yourselves down and would you like a whisky? And maybe a little scone or some stovies? The girl's cookin' out the back and aye, she's not so bloody bad at it, either.'

Bob lifted a bar stool out for Andy and took one for himself.

'Bloody oath, mate.' Bob sat as if on a horse. 'We'll have everythin'. And it's nice to be here. So how ya goin' yaself?'

'Ah, fine.' The barman, red cheeked and big-nosed, set up three glasses and poured whiskey the colour of wheat. 'And might God go with ya all the way, and come back all the way with ya again.'

'Cheers.' Andy drank, the whisky smarting in his throat. He put his glass down and folded his arms on the bar. 'The Scotch boys are brave,' he said. 'They're wild men. They go in hard. We like 'em.'

The barman added a decent splash of whisky to all three glasses, although Andy's and Bob's were not empty.

'Be no braver than yourselves, from what I've heard.'

Bob cleared his throat and dragged his stool in close to the bar.

'We do our best under difficult circumstances.' He took a decent sip. 'The Hun are the main sticking point, I find, in our push for victory.'

Andy smiled, feeling immeasurable warmth for his mate. Bob had a liking for the truth, as he saw it. Andy had no use for anything else.

'Hullo, hullo, hullo.' Bob inclined his head to the doorway. 'Eyes left, Lansell. Skirt arriving in *tight* formation.' Bob got off his stool as two young women came into the pub, accompanied by a few tumbling leaves. 'Morning, ladies.' He picked his slouch hat up off the bar and raised it. 'Would you like a wee drink to warm yourselves up from the inside out? I can recommend it. And of course it would be our pleasure to provide it, compliments of the Australian Infantry Force, on leave from *la belle* France, as we are.'

The girls, in dresses slightly shorter and tighter than Andy had seen in England, wore wide crimson hats and black gloves and held their umbrellas tips-to-the-floor. He stood, thinking that they might be sisters. Twins, perhaps. Their eyes were blue, and their hair was black and curled. They smiled independently.

'We accept, thank you very much.' The girl who had not shut the door waited for the other to turn. 'Although we've only really come in here to escape that bitter wind.'

'And the tea rooms two doors up not open?' murmured the barman as he took down glasses. 'If ye would like to retire to one of me tables, ladies and gents, I'll serve ye over there. It's a mite more comfortable closer to the fire which I shall bank up, since that wind does seem to have not abated one wee bit.'

'*That's* a grand idea.' Bob returned his stool to the bar. 'Andy, you bring the drinks, and I shall seat the ladies *right* next to that window *right* there.'

The barman poured more whiskeys and left the bottle.

'And I shall take two shilling off one of you lads, if I may. And the afternoon can proceed into the sunset with all sails set.'

Andy paid up and took the drinks to the table. The girls' hair, curly and dark, bounced coyly at a length just below their shoulders, and when they sat he tried not to watch their every move with obvious intent. He put the drinks down and turned on his best smile, which felt ridiculous, lop-sided, and un-practised.

'We like Glasgow,' he said. 'It's a real nice place. We just went up the castle. It was, ah, magnificent.'

The girls laughed, one removing a black glove to expose a hand so delicately veined it appeared to have been decorated.

'Glasgow?' she said. 'Glasgow's a tip, but this is Edinburgh, and so that's why the girls are nice and the whiskey's good. If ye was in Glasgow ye'd be drinkin' wi a gang of stinkin' sailors, not lasses like us, who know their way around, and like to welcome boys like ye from so far away.' She smiled, showing crooked teeth.

Andy relaxed, returned her bold look, and raised his glass.

'Well, that's great news. Cheers. Here's to Edinburgh and to you two.' He looked at them, their faces uplifted and unlined, the pale light of the fading day catching in their eyes, and he could see beauty in them as if he had never known what beauty was before. *Women.*

Bob leant forward, pushing salt and pepper shakers aside.

'And I'll let yers into a little secret, ladies. Scottish girls are a lot better-lookin' than Aussie girls, if you two are anythin' to go by, aren't they, Andy?'

'Certainly.' Andy felt a knee brush his. 'And I'd like to stay here forever.' Which was not entirely untruthful. He would've liked to stay anywhere that was not France – or at least until the Germans had gone home.

'Amen to that and one half.' Bob drank, and slapped down the little glass. 'And if one drink was good then two, three, or four, must be better!'

twenty-eight

Henry sat on the train, heading for uni, and looked down over the roofs of the inner suburbs. Old churches, old pubs, and old houses stood resolutely between crowds of new shops, new houses, and apartments. On a corner, beneath the railway line, he spotted a feed and produce store complete with bales of hay and bags of firewood outside. A sign proclaimed the place to be run by the Murphy Bros, who had evidently established the business in 1901. Henry doubted if there were any of the Murphy Brothers still there.

Still. It wasn't that hard to imagine the place a hundred years ago. Subtract a few cars and add a few horses. Lose a few pairs of hipsters and find a few long skirts. He could call on Miss Hainsworth as an expert witness, since she'd been there – well, she'd been in Strattford, but what the hell.

History was basically one day turning into the next, Henry thought. Things only changed slowly, but change they did. One night Andy Lansell was heading into Melbourne for the war, eight-five years later Henry Lyon had travelled the very same train line to Strattford. And there was Janine – with the blue Lansell eyes, living in town, her great-grandfather dead and buried twenty thousand k away. The thing was like a big web, Henry figured; interconnected and ever-widening, the strands becoming thinner and finer the further you moved away from the centre, but they still held.

So how much did he like Janine? Well, a lot, he was sure. There was like a sort of a power coming from her: a fierceness, a kind of a determination without any clear focus. He didn't think he'd met any girl like her. Looking out of the train, his chin propped on his hand, he decided that it might be possible for him to go to France. It *was* possible. The idea affected him like a drug. Yes, it was possible.

October 9 1917,
Edinburgh, Scotland

Head down to London tomorrow. Edinburgh is a most spectacular city with many points of historical interest, including some fine hotels! It is my hope in vain that we might not have to go back to France, but it will be good to rejoin the boys. Now we are off to the pub!

Andy found himself in a tiny room in a tiny house. He sat on a chair, Sheena sat on the narrow single bed, a small wooden wash-stand between them serving as a table for their drinks. Through a quarter-pane window, Andy could see a square of blue-black sky, a few stars visible.

He studied them, distant sparks, impossible to understand. He looked at his hat on a peg, the bronze badge of the Rising Sun catching the soft light of the two lamps that lit the room. He looked at Sheena and smiled, and she responded with a smile of her own.

'Are ye all right, Andy? Ye lookin' quite thoughtful over there.'

He nodded. 'Yeah, I'm fine. It's just nice to be somewhere quiet.'

Around him, things did not seem to make their usual sense. The jug and basin that Sheena had taken off the washstand and put in the corner seemed significant. The bed, with its pale green bedspread and white pillow, and he and Sheena facing each other was like a formally composed scene from a painting or a play.

'I do feel kind of odd,' he admitted. The room was so small it was box-like, but Andy found it comforting rather than claustrophobic. 'It must be bein' so far up in the world. You know, seein' that me and Bobby are from right down the other end.'

'Do ye want to leave?' Sheena, without her hat, coat, and gloves, looked younger and more intense, her eyes dominating her finely featured, almost pinched, face. 'Ye can have half ye money back if ye do. I'm not gunna force ye into anything, eh? I could'ne anyway, that sort'a thing.' She smiled, as if she was estimating what sort of person Andy really was. 'D'ye want a ciggie? Or a drink?'

'No, thanks. No, I don't.' Andy shook his head. 'I don't want to go, either.' He moved a hand, noticing that it too looked unfamiliar, harder and more angular than he remembered it. 'It's lovely here.' He sat with his hands on his thighs like a schoolboy. 'This is the happiest I've been for a long time.'

'I'm glad.' Sheena picked an errant thread from her dress. 'It must be bloody awful over where ye are. I wish it would end. Ye could all go home. It's a long way where ye all come from.'

Andy absorbed her sympathy. That she understood, that she *tried* to understand, was a kind of love.

'Goin' home,' he said. 'Most of the time it seems too much to hope for. And that you'll put the moz on yerself.' An image of the trenches rose like nausea; he could see the place, the sky rimmed with artillery blooming black-orange like monstrous flowers, he could feel the slamming of the guns. 'You've got no idea how *big* it is over there.' He lifted his hand, an ineffectual gesture. 'I can't explain it. It's like its own world.' Andy felt too insignificant to even bear the idea. 'It goes on forever. It's like it is forever. I dunno how it can end. It's just too bloody big. You know, what can you do? There's nothin'.'

Sheena shifted the washstand back to its position beneath a mirror, but did not replace the jug and basin. She took hold of his arm.

'Come and sit next to me. On the bed. It's a nice wee bed, as good as gold. Ye'll feel better there.'

Andy sat next to her, the pressure of her linked hands around his arm warm and sisterly. She smelled of rose water, he thought. She smelled like she felt; soft, safe, welcoming, feminine, real, and close, the opposite to fear and memory.

There was no possibility of him leaving this place for the darkness. In this room he felt safe and alive. Home was too distant, too beautiful to be considered. Where he was and what he was doing was real, although it was counter to what he had always considered possible in Andy Lansell's life. But now he welcomed it without question or criticism.

'I understand this,' he said, when he did not mean to say anything. He looked at the girl who was his age, or maybe a year or two older, although age meant nothing. '*This.*' He moved a hand around. 'You and your room are like the opposite to where me and Bobby are. This is like –' he thought hard, so that the girl might know. 'Like *light*. Yeah, it's like light.' This idea was right. He felt it was. 'The good things are like light.' He tried to think of what *type* of light. 'Yeah, like say, sunlight. Morning, afternoon, you know. And you, too. Like light.' He touched her hand, the thought expanding. 'Home is like light. That sort of –' He shrugged. 'Light.'

He did not mention the baby because she was inexplicable and unimaginable, so star-like, so other-worldly, that only he, Darcy, and Bob, and the frontline boys could understand because they had seen the opposite. The baby was beyond light, beyond words – she was like the goodness left in the boys' souls after they had walked from the battlefield. The baby was like the joy of men who'd been told they did not have to go forward that day. The baby was like seeing the sky and knowing you had the next hour. The baby was life without question.

twenty-nine

Henry sipped coffee, the froth cooled by the wind to a flattened sour layer. He tried not to think of Janine in terms of how much he liked her, and failed. He liked her a lot. He did. That much was simple and obvious and there was nothing wrong with it. He couldn't help it, could he? No, but there was something wrong with liking her *too* much. She was still, in a way, Trot's girlfriend, and she would be for a while. He knew it, he guessed everyone in Stratty knew it, and he figured Janine would know it, too.

But *she* had asked him to go to France with her. So she must've felt that it was all right. Otherwise, she would not have asked him. That had to be true. But truly – really – how could he have ever thought he could go? Come on. It wasn't exactly the sort of thing he should do. And the one main reason why he shouldn't do it was that Janine was still Trot's girlfriend.

In fact that was the only *real* reason. The other reasons: uni, his parents' concerns, the money, the reasons for the trip, could all be got around. He did want to go. He did want to visit Andy's grave and see the place. It meant something to him and his reasons were real, honourable, and truthful. And that he liked Janine was not wrong, but at this point it wasn't exactly right, either. Trot was stopping him. Poor old bloody Trot.

Henry finished his coffee, the wind an ugly breeze that brought dust, papers, and a few rattling foam cups. So, where to from here? Home and work, he supposed. In typical Henry Lyon style.

Henry knew that he had a good attitude to work; all sorts of work, really. Sometimes it bothered him, knowing that there was this expectation within himself, and this expectation of him. Henry Lyon was a *smart* kid, a *good* guy – Henry Lyon was easy to teach and coach, a percentage player. Sometimes, like now, it shitted him because the more you walked the walk of the good guy, the more you had to walk it, even if the path got narrower and harder to follow as you got older because there were more things to deal with.

If you'd done the expected thing all your life, then the expected thing was what you'd be doing for the rest of your life. But step off the path just once – hey, get pissed and throw up in the bathroom – and immediately everyone thinks you've gone insane. My God, Henry, you know better than that. Henry, what *were* you thinking?

Henry surveyed his computer, his slew of books, folders and pens. It looked like the stuff had been dropped in an air raid. His room was a *place* of study. It was like a solitary confinement cell for the mind. A single bed, a wardrobe, a window, and a desk like an aircraft carrier. Man, he had *two* reading lamps. He could study *ambidextrously*! He was a living, breathing, junior lawyer-in-the-making!

Henry pushed his chair back and stuck his sneakers up on

the desk. Still, it wasn't a bad thing to be, a person who did the work. He didn't know where the drive came from – his parents probably – but he'd always had it. It was like a sense of duty. He was a serious young insect and he couldn't change that, even if he really wanted to, which he didn't. He wanted to do the work. Or some work, anyway.

What he wanted was for people to realise that sometimes he might not want to do what *they* thought he should do. You did, after all, owe allegiance to yourself and your ideas. That only made sense. In fact, it might be the one thought in the world that did. So, if he weighed everything up and felt that he should go to France with Janine, then he would go – well, he *might*, anyway. Wasn't it his *right* to decide?

Henry reckoned Andy Lansell was also a person who had done the work – not that it was possible to pin-point how exactly he'd arrived at this conclusion, but he was sure it was true – and the war had been part *of* the work. Henry admired Andy. He more than admired him. Henry knew that Andy had accepted the work and got killed doing it. Andy could have *not* gone. Lots of guys didn't, but it seemed obvious Andy had never considered the option.

Well, back to it. Henry dragged his sneakers off the desk. The year was flying, there were exams coming, and the idea was to pass them, for one reason or another.

October 10 1917,
Train to London.

Heading back to London today. Very nice train. Missing Edinburgh already although we have just left. Weather gloomy. Bob and I are not! Got a couple of days leave left.

'I wouldn't mind if this train turned around,' Andy said. 'Or even ran off the bloody rails. Considering the pastin' the Germans have been handin' out down at Amiens. They break through, we're gone.' He watched misty rain falling into a green and bracken-brown valley. The train crossed a stream. 'It's nice out there, eh? Although the bloody weather's a bit like Omeo in the middle of winter.' He settled back. 'Still. I could stay for a while. Build a little cottage with a fireplace and drink whussky.'

'No wood, mate.' Bob squinted out through a wet window. 'You'd freeze your binoculars off.' He dragged a handkerchief out and blew his nose. 'But anyway, maybe you're worryin' too much. 'Sposedly the boys are being pulled from up north, so 'opefully we'll be just hangin' around, gettin' numbers back up with reinforcements.' Bob winked. 'Nice girls, eh?'

Andy nodded, considering how to answer, in deference to the middle-aged civilian couple in the compartment.

'Yeah, lovely.' He guessed he felt guilt, but guilt over sex was not something he was prepared to devote much time to any more. 'And all fully paid for.' He raised his eyebrows for Bob's benefit, and again looked out the window, the train slowing as it climbed, the engine visible five carriages ahead on the bend, scarfed with smoke, pistons flashing silver.

He'd changed. It was not hard to see why. Maybe he was weak. Maybe he was. He'd done the wrong thing with Frances-Jane, he'd done the wrong thing again last night, and Jesus, he'd probably do it again next week if he got the chance. It was wrong, but it was not that wrong. For Christ's sake, he'd done his duty here, more than some, less than others, and that he'd come off the straight and narrow hardly mattered. Or it hardly mattered to him. To others, he knew it might matter a lot. But they were at home and they didn't know. He remembered what he'd said about light. It was true.

'You boys seen a bit, then?' their fellow male passenger asked, the checks on his tie the same ruddy rural colour as his cheeks. 'It's a bit rough all over, we hear. The Germans seem quite determined. But your boys have been doing well.'

Andy had heard that the Australians had taken objectives in Flanders, but what he had read and what was possibly the truth, were two different things.

'Good on 'em,' Bob said promptly. 'I left instructions.'

Andy did not raise his head from where it was propped.

'I know what your instructions'd be, Pike,' he said. 'Stay in the pub till stumps, have a good hard think, decide it's all too hard, then trot off back home.'

Bob's face, as usual, was ingrained with humour.

'Not true.' He shrugged formally into his tunic. 'I said that *after* stumps, those who wanted to kick on with the fight were quite welcome to do so, as long as their noise did not wake those other boys who wanted to sleep.'

Andy didn't bother to comment further. He certainly had nothing to say to the bloke in the suit.

'So you're heading back, then?' the man asked. 'All hands to the helm, I expect.'

Bob coughed up a laugh. 'Not if we can help it, mate. Wild horses couldn't drag us.'

Andy felt a measure of good humour. Bob, encouraged further, turned to the couple, the middle-aged woman smiling at him in a benign way, hands folded over a black bag.

'I gotta say –' Bob, with an audience, was energised, 'there is gunna *have* to be an almighty stunt put on very shortly, otherwise we are gunna get done like a dinner. But with the Yanks, Canadians, us, your boys, the frogs, and whoever else isn't busy on the day, they'll make a huge push and *our* plan –' Bob inclined his head toward Andy, 'is that Lance General Lansell and myself, Archduke Pike, are to be as far away from this as possible. Preferably in a little tea room in Ballarat or Bendigo.'

The woman, in a thick skirt, granted Bob a most courteous smile.

'I hope it happens just as you say.'

Bob accepted her wishes with equal measure.

'Madam,' he said, '*nothing* can go wrong.' He waved a hand dismissively. 'Our planning is meticulous. Our troops are first-class. The enemy is over-confident. And one more thing –' Bob consulted his watch. 'The bar's open.' He stood, straightening his tunic. 'So if you'll excuse us, the General and I are off to take some refreshment. Unless you care to join us?'

'No, no, it's all right.' The man in the tweed suit took out a worn wallet, selected a note, and held it up. 'But I'd like to buy ye a drink anyway. For good luck and a safe journey.'

Bob took the money. 'That's bloody nice of yer. Don't worry, we'll spend it wisely. We'll bring yer back a scone. Cheers.'

Andy dragged open the door. 'I'll do my best to keep him up there for as long as I can.' He felt his animosity toward the couple fading. They were a bit like his parents. 'But it won't be easy. He'll often take a whole teapot to himself.'

Andy followed Bob, the windows rattling like machine guns, the passing fields summoning thoughts of home and the horses, the thoughts letting loose feelings that were like the rings of a tree, a complex record of many, many things. And the only thing that went beyond them, he reckoned, was his body's instinctive hold on life.

He followed Bob, not even bothering to acknowledge how inextricably they were caught up in what they had volunteered for. There was no choice but to go on, no legitimate exit unless it was offered by the war, because the war controlled everything. The war was a monster, a machine, a chain reaction, something in perpetual motion – and it was only the thing that could release him, either as one of the dead, wounded, captured or insane men cast aside into the wake of a ship that could not stop.

What *could* stop it? Andy thought gloomily. Both armies just kept on coming up with more men. You couldn't kill every one. You'd never get there. Men would just keep on coming, filing into the trenches to take their position in the line – and they could keep on coming forever and the war would keep on killing them forever, and they would keep on coming, killing and dying, and filing in, because that was the way it was. Who was going to end it? Who could? Not the armies, not the generals.

Bob waited at the doorway. Andy could hear the sound of the train as it raced along.

'Bar's up here.' Bob opened the door, a blast of cold air and noise hitting them. 'Gees, we're movin' along all right.' He had to shout. 'Ya don't realise, do ya?'

The train seemed to be flying. Through cracks in the crossover, Andy could see the lines and ballast passing in a blur. The train was like something that was part of the whole thing. It was taking them back there as fast as it could bloody go. He felt like shooting the driver.

'Prefer to bloody walk,' he shouted. 'What's the big hurry?'

'Me date with Esther, mate.' Bob flourished a pound note. 'Back me in, sport. I'm on a lucky streak.'

thirty

Henry's mum interrupted his stacking of firewood by bringing him the phone in the backyard.

'It's Marcelle,' she said, her face not changing expression.

Henry took the phone and sat on the wood.

'Hey, Marcelle,' he said, and felt somehow as if he was suddenly breathing more than just air. Pure oxygen, maybe. Things around him seemed bright and clear. 'How are you going?'

'Oh, really good,' she said cheerfully. 'I've moved into a little house in Fitzroy with Angie-baby. So do you want to come down and have a look? Just for old time's sake. I mean, I know we probably shouldn't, but I was just thinking I didn't want to not see you ever again. I mean it'd just be for coffee, Henry. We could go down to Brunswick Street, if you like.'

'Yeah, sure.' Henry stood up at the bumbling approach of the dog. 'When?' He patted Minnie's big gold head.

'How about now?' Marcelle laughed. 'Or is this not a good idea?'

Henry blinked. 'No, no, it's fine.' He set off for the back door, Minnie snuffling at his hand. 'I'll just see if I can get the car. It should be cool. Mum's got some carpet-guy comin' around or something.' What the hell, he thought. He'd go with the flow, as risky as that might be. Whatever happened, it had to be more exciting than stacking wood.

Marcelle's hair draped as she fixed an emerald earring into place. Henry helpfully shifted empty coffee cups for the waitress, a black-haired girl with a silver stud in her tongue.

'Here.' Marcelle handed him a creased copy of *Black and White* magazine. 'Have a 'zine. Be cool.'

Henry opened the magazine and saw a naked woman photographed so close-up her skin was an undulating land-scape of tiny goosebumps.

'This one's only in black and white,' he said, closing it. 'It's a dud.'

Marcelle awarded him a smile. 'So funny you are.' She turned to check out what was on the blackboard menu. 'So, Henry, how have you been? And what've you been doing for the last six months of your life?'

Henry drove home, enduring a loneliness that had begun the minute he had walked out of Marcelle's house. In truth, the feeling had started as soon as he and she had got out of bed, but now, alone, it twisted through guilt, regret, and a brash-ness he did not believe in.

'She rang *me*,' he muttered, and changed radio station although he hadn't identified what song was playing. 'Not my fault.'

So what did it all mean? Were they back together? Did he

owe her anything? Did she have any power over him? Or him over her? You should *not* have gone, he told himself. But the temptation had been too great. He *liked* her. And it wasn't as if he hadn't savoured every second of it – even if he was aware of an element of sadness as soon as they had started to kiss.

So now what? Exactly.

Marcelle had said that she hadn't planned it, and he believed her. But he *could've* said no. Or *she* should've, but neither of them did, so it was a mutual thing – and that at least was good, because, not that he was any great expert, sex always seemed to have repercussions of one type or another.

Henry accelerated through an amber traffic light. You idiot, he thought. Slow down.

January 14 1918.
Amiens, France.

Training exercises again today. Bombing school yesterday. Will probably go back into line in next week or so. Things seem to be gathering speed. Germans massing divisions in the Somme. Full dance cards for everybody I would say.

Andy, Darcy, and Bob lounged in the shallow trench their company had dug in the middle of a field that ran down to a stream. Rifles leant, muzzles sheathed, bayonets, more grey than silver, lightly pricking the skin of the earth. Andy rested with his feet on his pack and squinted into the cloud-decorated sky. The top halves of a row of poplar trees were visible, leaves fluttering, lulling him into a laziness of such heaviness he felt he might simply sink into the dirt. There was no sign or sound of the tanks that were supposed to form part of the exercise. Andy was relieved. He was happy right where he was.

He thought about Cecelia, Frances-Jane, and the baby, but was so doped by the sun he could hardly differentiate between them. If only he could go home, he thought, but the thought was hardly a thought – it was more like an element in his blood, something permanently within him – and in everyone else in the bloody trench, too.

Cigarette smoke drifted, mingling with the smell of food, men, and freshly-exposed dirt. A meadow lark on tiny winnowing wings, as if it had been sent as a joke, threw its song far and wide. Words, fragments of words, were in the air, Andy gathering some, ignoring most. Today, he thought, the world seemed to have righted itself to spin as smoothly as it used to.

'At least someone likes me,' Darcy muttered as he cracked lice he was catching in his undershirt. 'These little brown bastards.'

Bob, arms crossed, sat, leaning back into the trench wall.

'If *this* could only go on forever. Listen. Whadda ya hear?' He cocked his head. 'Bloody nothin', except a French Kookaburra. And no guns and no tanks. Beautiful.'

'I could live here,' Andy said. The sun shone a golden blood-red through his closed eyelids. 'Just like this. Put on the kettle will ya, Darce? Get out the bickies.'

'Fritzy will.' Darcy wiped his fingers in the dirt, then went back to the hunt. 'And he's gunna bring our tucker over. And some lovely blonde girls with big tits.' Darcy worked with the concentration of a seamstress, talking merely to embroider the air. 'Of *course* we'll be good to 'em, kamerad. Of course we will. What d'ya think we are? Monsters?'

Andy absorbed the day, feeling the warmth of the sun on the backs of his hands, his head, and cheekbones.

'We came,' he murmured, 'we saw, we slept. Hooray for us. We are the mighty ANZAC. Call us when you need us. We're always alert.'

'Between the hours of ten and two.' Bob surveyed the area behind the trench. 'Just ring the bell.'

'And if no one answers –' Darcy flicked the remains of dead lice off his nails, 'you can take it we're not bloody interested and go and see someone else who might be.'

'I've heard the Germans are quite war-like,' Bob said. 'Just turn 'em around and send 'em back. I'm sure they could defeat themselves if they really tried. Especially in the dark.'

Andy, hearing the distant growl of big motors, sat up.

'Shit, here's trouble.' He stood, feeling dizzy and weak.

Bob joined him, looking out over the back of the trench. Six or seven grey tanks emerged from trees.

'Coming like Christmas,' Bob muttered. 'And about as fast. Geez, they're ugly bastards. But at least they're big.'

The tanks crawled like giant grey snails.

'Well, they look all right.' Darcy reassembled his tunic. 'On that hard ground.' He blew out cigarette smoke as if it was poison. 'Let's hope they don't get bogged and have the shit blown out of 'em like last time. As well as the poor bastards who went in with 'em.'

'Wouldn't mind walkin' in behind one,' Andy said. 'That could have its advantages.'

The trench was lined with men watching. Black plumes of exhaust-smoke rose above the tanks like battle standards.

'Yeah, it could be quite nice back there in the shade.' Bob spat, as if that might help him see more clearly. 'Bloody hurt if they run over ya foot, though.'

'Gee, now there's a half a thought for a sweet trip home.' Darcy flicked his cigarette butt. 'And here comes *Sergeant*. Oh, goody.'

Ripper stopped on the edge of the trench, hands in pockets. 'So what do we all think of His Majesty's land ships, eh? We got the big size just for you blokes.'

'Oh, they're *marvellous*, Serge.' Darcy waved his hands around as if he was strewing confetti. 'Yeah, I'm sure there's not *one* high explosive shell on the *whole* German front that could even put a *dint* in one.' Darcy took out a scrunched-up white paper bag from his pocket and took a black and white lolly out of it. 'So what do they do when they fall in a hole? Put up two big floppy ears and pretend they're a rabbit? Ya wanna Bullesye, Rip?' He held out the bag.

Ripper took one. 'I'll bet ya a pound to a pinch,' he said, 'that you'll be stickin' as close to 'em as a baby to its mother's tit.' He pointed to the east as he sucked on the sweet. 'Over there it's paddocks, mate, not liquid manure. The whole thing's comin' to a point, if you ask me.' He paused, in thought or hope. 'Now, you blokes, two sections between each tank. Form up now. Rifles and packs. Let 'em go through on the ramps then we're out after 'em. And don't choke on ya lollies, kids. Pick up ya gear and get ready.'

The boys loaded up, standing unsteadily, watching the tanks grinding over the field, bearing numbers and colours as if they were in a race. On good ground, Andy reckoned, as Ripper had said, they might just be all right. But in a big stunt, absolutely *nothing* on earth was unstoppable.

In battle he'd felt time stop. It might have been ticking on by down the road, or in England, or back home, but in a battle he would swear that seconds, minutes, hours of his life had been bombed right out of existence. In a battle, forces were unleashed that were beyond imagination; that he understood, and even if tanks were monstrous, thoughtless machines, that would not stop them from being pounded beyond recognition.

'At least they're movin',' Darcy said. 'Shit, you couldn't miss 'em if they stood still.'

Ripper jumped into the trench as the tanks clanked closer, dark clods dropping off their tracks. Andy could feel the ground vibrating, the noise a deep, deafening roar.

'Anyone ever hear me say things were gunna be perfect?' Ripper had to shout. 'No! But if we *do* attack with 'em, next time there'll be bloody *hundreds* of the buggers, so get used to the idea. Because this is the year that's gunna make us or fuckin' break us. We're gunna be in and outta the line like no bastard's business.'

thirty-one

Henry sat at the kitchen table, endeavouring, with one of his mother's needles, to dig out a splinter from his index finger. Marg stood at the sink, holding a coffee plunger she had just washed.

'Did you have a good morning with Marcelle?' She put the plunger aside and wiped her hands. 'How is she? We haven't seen her for a while.'

Henry didn't look up. 'Yeah, she's good. She lives in Fitzroy with Angie now. They rented a house.' He knew Marg would've liked more information, but he was not about to give it. His mum liked Marcelle.

Marg walked away from the sink, Henry guessing she might be on her way out, since she wore shoes instead of her old tennis runners.

'And Janine rang at lunchtime,' she said. 'There's a note and number on the pad. I'm going out to see Jenna Conlan so I'll be taking the car. There are rolls in the freezer. All right? See you, Henry. Good luck with the surgery.' Henry heard her walk out into the hallway and take her keys from the hook.

'Where's the phone pad?' he called out, holding the needle to his finger as if it was a pen to paper. 'Where's the phone?'

'By the fridge.' His mother's voice was distant. 'Bye. I'm going.'

Henry heard the deadlock self-righteously return to its place. For a while, he sat thinking about Janine and Marcelle. Thinking about them was like hearing the first few bars of two songs he liked. He felt his mood widen in one direction, he felt it swing and expand in the other. Blushing, he put down the needle, stood, and found the pad and the phone.

Ring Janine at home today. She says you have number. M.

'Right,' Henry said, 'I will.' And tried unsuccessfully to banish all feelings of guilt.

Janine answered on the fourth ring. After a few seconds of chat that Henry knew was just chat, she took a breath, as if she was both pausing and preparing.

'Look, Henry,' she said, 'before you say anything, I'm coming down to Melbourne tomorrow to sort some things out. So do you think we could meet and I could tell you what I've got planned about the trip? My folks are driving me, so maybe you could meet them, too? I mean, you didn't really at the funeral. Everyone was so –'

'Ah, yeah,' Henry said. 'Sure.' What else could he say?

'And Henry –' Janine paused. 'I know I've kind of forced you into a lot of things lately and I'm sorry, but well, I mean I have hassled other people as well.' She laughed. 'But I know I've singled you out because – I can't say it. Yes, I can. Because I like you. There.'

Henry frowned. Shit, things got complicated quickly around this place.

'No, you haven't forced me into anything,' he said. 'I promise. So where do you want to meet? You tell me.'

'Well, I'm not sure where you live, Henry.' Janine's relief was obvious. 'But I'll be staying with my cousin in Richmond. Is that far from you? If it is, I can meet you somewhere else, no problem. You just say.'

'No, Richmond's close.' Henry was already working out how he could get there by train if he couldn't get the car. 'I can get there easily. When and where? Just tell me.' Henry could hear people in the background. Someone laughed. A door shut, maybe a fridge door, bottles rattling.

'Hang on. I'll just ask Maureen, my cousin. She's at our place. We're all going into town tomorrow. She knows all the places.'

Henry waited, looking out into the backyard, able only to see the top of the fence and the neighbours' shrubs. Janine picked up again.

'Right, Maureen says *the* . . . High On Richmond Hill cafe is good and pretty casual.' Janine gave Henry the address and phone number. 'How about twelve-thirty? I'm looking forward to seeing you. A few things have happened. I'll fill you in tomorrow. Thanks, Henry. I'm sorry if I've caused you any trouble, I really am, but I would like to see you. I'll buy you lunch.'

'You haven't caused me any trouble.' Henry wanted her to know he meant what he said. 'I swear. I'll see you tomorrow. Bye.' He hit the button, wondering what the hell would happen next.

Henry watched Janine's mother and father leave the restaurant. They turned and waved before walking away, Janine's dad bulky in a new-looking denim shirt, her mother small and neat in a black cardigan and skirt, her dark hair coiled neatly at the back of her head. For a moment Janine was silent, fiddling with a spoon, as if it was possible her parents might still be able to hear her.

'They're all right,' she said. 'They just wanted to meet you – I mean, *again*, just in case you do decide to come with me. When and *if* I do decide to go.'

'Yeah, they're fine.' Henry felt that Janine was giving him the upper hand in the conversation. He wished she would just relax. 'You'll go,' he said. 'Because I know you want to. And so do I. But,' he hastily added, 'I haven't quite got things sussed yet.'

Janine rested her arms on the tablecloth. Henry saw she wore a bracelet of mauve stones linked with gold. He liked it.

'Look, I'll tell you exactly what I'm thinking, Henry.' She put her hand above her heart. 'I'm thinking of going a month before Christmas and staying, well, I don't know, maybe two weeks or maybe two months, it all depends. On a number of things.'

A month before Christmas; Henry calculated he'd be finished uni by then. Or close to it.

'Right,' he said, noticing she wore a number of rings on various fingers, none that he could decipher for meaning or significance. 'Be cold over there then,' he added. 'I reckon. Winter, you know. The opposite.'

'Yeah, true, Einstein.' Janine grinned. 'But hey, I've got a footy jumper. And then I might go somewhere warm, but anyway –' she took a deep breath. 'I've applied to do nursing here next year, in Melbourne, so if I get in I'll be back. And if I do I'll be living here.' She indicated the suburb outside. 'There, I mean. Richmond. With Maureen. She's got a room I can have, and she's a nurse herself, so it'd be perfect. Time has come for me to leave old Stratty and the Rosewood.' Janine lifted a finger. 'Listen. Can you hear Cecelia?'

Henry processed this new information as fast as he could.

'Wow,' he said. 'It's all happening. It sounds great. Where do you do nursing? How?'

Janine sipped water. 'Through university. I just thought I had to make a move. You know, before it's too late. Time to see the big wide world.'

Henry was aware of an underlying sadness in Janine that hardly wavered. It was there when she walked in, it was there now in her face, a faint tiredness, a slowing of how she moved and spoke. He could feel himself, unwisely perhaps, about to commit to something that he had not really thought through – but stuff it.

'I'll go with you,' he said. 'To France. As *long* –' he finished with a rush, 'as it's after exams.' He shrugged as if the decision was like a coat he was putting on. 'I will. I've always wanted to go. With you.' He couldn't help a smile. 'Let's go. Why not?' He knew why not, but he ignored whatever sensible, negative, reasons he had stacked up, Henry-style, ready to put forward. 'It'll be fantastic.'

He waited for a reaction, expecting to see Janine smile, but instead he saw tears spill through her eyelashes.

'Oh, Henry –' she wiped her eyes with the side of a finger. 'I'm sorry. I mean. I'm not even upset.' She produced a tiny smile. 'I'm actually the happiest I've been for months.' She shook her head, not as if she was confused, but as if things had become clear. 'Truly, Henry. It's just that you're doing what Trot would've done. He would've come just because I wanted to go. And you're doing the same thing. And that's – you've – made me so happy.' She laughed, her cheeks shiny. 'Oh God, I'm such a mess.'

'I've always wanted to go,' Henry said again. 'It's just that, well, I didn't think I could. You know, with Trot and those things. I didn't know whether it'd be, you know, okay with you and everyone. The timing.'

Janine dabbed at her face with a serviette, her eyes bright.

'Trot and you are separate.' She pushed back her hair, then straightened her chair to the table. 'Well, you're not separate in that you're the two best guys I've ever met, but you are separate because I loved Trot and I still love him, but you're – I don't know –' she glanced up and around as if she might find the appropriate words on the plate glass windows. 'You're a best friend, Henry. You're better than that.' She moved forward. 'Look, I'm sorry. I've been an absolute freak-show since he went.'

Henry nodded, not so much to show that he understood, but to demonstrate that it was all right for her to say whatever she wanted.

'Going to France,' he said, testing the idea. 'God, I've never really been anywhere before. Canada once. When I was thirteen.'

'Well, you're doing better than me.' Janine took a tissue from her bag. 'I haven't even been to Queensland. Will we have another coffee? Maybe a drink? I could do with one. D'you want a beer? My shout. Since I just stressed you to the max.'

A beer sounded good to Henry.

'Yeah, since I'm not driving the train. Why not?'

Janine gave up trying to attract the attention of the waiter, who was too far away to see her.

'I'll grab him in a minute.' She touched her cheeks with her fingertips. 'I bet my make-up's atrocious. I'll go and fix it in a sec. So what will your folks say? If they really don't want you to go I'd accept that. I mean, they haven't even met me.'

Henry was not prepared to concede that his folks ran his life.

'As long as I don't drop my course,' he said, 'I can't see that they can complain. I guess they'd like to meet you, though.' He laughed. 'Maybe just do that at the airport?'

'Yeah, right.' Janine signalled to the waiter, then turned back to the table. 'Think about it again, Henry, and talk to your folks. I'll be back in town, anyway, to sort my course out.' Her face had brightened, although Henry could still see where tears had run. 'It would be a buzz to go wouldn't it? I mean, to really go.'

'Yeah. Absolutely.' Henry felt something click into place, like a small block dropping into a small block-shaped slot. Decision made. Nothing could stop him now. 'It'll be big.' He looked at Janine, small-framed in her white dress, her shoulders dark-skinned and smooth, her face dominated by her blue eyes. 'And you'll go well down here. Really well. You'll be fantastic.'

Henry was not surprised by his parents' opinion of the proposed trip. He could see why they didn't think it was very sensible – so could he, in some ways – but he knew that his reasons for going were honest and reasonable.

'Yes, I can see your studies won't suffer,' Walt said. 'As long as you do come back when you say you will. But I'm also a little unsure about the basis of it, like your mum. I'd want to be quite sure you've got it pretty well planned out before I give it the green light.'

'I'm not even so worried about the planning, Henry.' Marg sat in her usual armchair, a reading lamp leaning over her like a concerned sunflower. 'But what about Marcelle? Is she – are you?' Henry's mother crossed her legs and smoothed her skirt. 'Or is she not part of the picture at the moment?'

'We've broken up,' Henry said, from where he sat in a chair identical to his mother's. 'So, well, that's all right.'

'Oh, okay.' Marg seemed a bit taken aback. 'But Janine, who we haven't even met – I mean, I know it's a few months since she lost her boyfriend, Henry, but are you sure it's going to be all right, for you to, ah, travel with her?'

Henry knew his mum did not actually mean *travel*.

'Sure. It'll be fine.' He laughed. 'She works in a motel so she'll know all about bookings and things. You know, twin beds, and all that stuff.' There, he'd bloody said it. Now he wanted to swing away from the whole subject. 'Anyway, she'll be down in Melbourne next week. She's doing nursing here next year. So you can meet her then. Next week. Not next year.'

'Sure. We'd like to do that.' Walt wore his thoughtful, reasonable, face. 'You'll plough through whatever money you've saved, Henry. It won't go far in Europe, let me tell you.'

Henry supposed his dad was right. 'I'll do some work on the weekends, if I can. Before I go.' This was better, safer, ground. 'And the next holidays. And now I'm gunna go and do some study.' Henry pushed up out of his chair. 'Look, it's only gunna be for a couple of weeks. It's no big deal. It's just a trip.' He knew this wasn't quite true. 'It'll be fine. I'll see you later.' And he left the lounge, knowing that Marg and Walt had already marked more than a few mental bullet-points for further discussion.

In his room he sat, feet up, and looked out the night-dark window. Well, he was going to France, but he was *not* taking Trot's *place*. But he knew, in a way, he was. How else could he look at it? But this was just how things had turned out; there was nothing he, or anybody else, could do about the situation. Trot was gone.

Henry thought of Andy Lansell, and although Andy's death was like a part of the collective death of all soldiers, Henry knew that wasn't the reality. He tried to imagine, through the years, across the world, Andy dying as an individual. Perhaps he died instantly, perhaps not, maybe as badly injured as Trot must've been, his eyes losing their last sight of the world like Trot's, his ears hearing their last sounds, and then his life was gone and Henry knew that Andy wasn't a mythical ANZAC, although his death had made him one – he was just a young guy who'd been brave enough to put himself in a place where there was a chance he could get killed, and he was.

Henry wondered *why* exactly he and Janine were going to France. What was it all about? What would it achieve? Did it really make any sense? All he could come up with was that it *seemed* like a good thing to do.

Maybe it was as simple as acknowledging that Andy Lansell had really lived and done what he'd done. Maybe it was enough that he, Henry, liked Janine and would go with her because the trip meant a lot to her. You tried to help your friends, didn't you? And it wasn't as if you had to be related to someone to visit their grave or respect what they had done. All you had to do was be able to think about them, and imagine their lives.

August 8 1918.
Villers-Bretonneux, France.

Darcy's birthday. Go forward in half an hour. Feel a bit jittery. Hope to do well. There's a million blokes here.

'What's the bloody date today?' Andy asked, as he and Darcy and Bob, with their battalion lay down on grass soaked by heavy mist, in full battle gear, at the white tape that marked their jumping-off point. The mist, cold and damp, soft on his face, reminded him of mornings on the farm – except in Strattford there was not the ominous roaring of manoeuvering tanks, and the low murmur of thousands of waiting men.

'The date, mate?' Darcy put his rifle aside, took out his cigarette tin, and selected a smoke. 'I'll tell ya what the date is. It's the eighth of bloody August.' Darcy lit up. 'My bloody birthday.

Thanks for rememberin', boys. Better be a cake when this little bunfight's over, or I'm takin' me bat and ball, and goin' home.'

Andy and Bob wished him happy birthday.

'I'll make a note of it for next year.' Andy touched his tunic pocket where his diary was. 'We'll probably still be here.' Fear made his words brittle.

He had, like everyone else in the battalion, taken the blessing given to them by the chaplain, but it hadn't noticeably reduced his fear or reassured him that God was truly on their side. Or if he was, Andy reckoned he was showing his support in a pretty even-handed way. Still, any help was better than no help. He was alive, wasn't he?

Darcy looked off into the mist. 'Yeah, look, boys, I don't mind goin' in against the might of the bloody German army on this, me one special day of the year, but Jesus, I do hate getting a wet arse. Now why aren't there any fuckin' foldin' chairs?'

Andy had to laugh. 'We go at eight.' He looked at his watch, the one his grandfather had given him years ago. 'Ten minutes. I saw Ripper a moment ago with the other sergeants. Jesus. Listen to the bloody tanks.'

Behind the troops, hidden in the fog, the tanks growled like caged bears and the higher droning note of aeroplanes coming and going was ceaseless. Andy could feel vibrations through the earth as if tremendous weights were being dragged over it. Something was happening to the whole world, it seemed. Or maybe just the half that was behind them.

'They run us over I won't be happy,' Darcy said, cradling his rifle. 'That'd be a good start.'

'Nine minutes.' Ripper looked along the line of pale faces. 'Good on ya, boys. You're gunna do good today like yers always do. I think we're gunna have a good shot at this. I'm hopin' things will be real good for us.'

The mist began to move, then, like curtains being drawn, it slowly lifted, the sun visible, the sky blue, miles of green and gold countryside appearing miraculously. Men began to shout.

'Look at that! Bloody look at that! Get the harvester out, boys!'

Andy, like everyone else, looked to the front, his gaze carried on and upwards by the wheat-covered spurs and fields that rose to the wrecked town of Villers-Bretonneaux.

As the mist lifted the scale of the attack became obvious. Tanks and armoured cars made their way forward, and on the slopes, thousands of infantrymen prepared to move.

'Look behind yers,' said some gruff voice. 'It must be friggin' Christmas!'

Andy looked, and saw beyond the tanks, hundreds of batteries of horse-drawn artillery and thousands more troops in formation. It was the most amazing sight he had ever seen, and when the call came to move, he went forward in a daze. Ripper rolled his arm over as if he was bowling a leg break.

'Come on, 77th! Steady as she goes, boys. And good bloody luck.'

As part of the line that looked to be miles long, Andy, Darcy and Bob set off up the slope, their task to move up to, and then on through the battalions that had attacked and consolidated earlier. Hardly a shell fell and there was not a German in sight, apart from groups of prisoners Andy could see coming back down the roads, making way as tanks, artillery, and troops flooded forward.

'This is the bloody life!' Bob munched an apple, the dew bright on his boots. 'This is what I joined the army for. Battles with no shootin'. Gees, whadda ya reckon, Darce? Happy birthday, eh?' He elbowed Andy. 'One, two, three. Ha-*peee* birthday to you, happy birthday to you, happy birthday, dear Darcy, happy birthday to you!'

As the battalions advanced, the song wove its way up and down the line as if it was being sung in rounds, every man shouting it out, the sound of it like an anthem, louder than the tanks and the guns that had opened up somewhere along the plateau. Andy hoped the Germans could hear it. Shit, they'd run a mile. Here come the lunatics.

Andy walked on up the slope, the ground unbroken, sunshine warm on his shoulders as if the attack was something ordained. He watched as aeroplanes flew in straight lines to the north, and inwardly allowed himself to consider, briefly, if this attack might just possibly be the last of the war, as Ripper had said. The Germans appeared to have been totally overrun. He could see hundreds of prisoners coming down the slope, some in greatcoats, most bareheaded, or wearing flat-topped caps, escorted by soldiers walking with the butts of their rifles on their hips.

'And there they are, boys.' Ripper came up from behind, smoking, wearing a tin hat with a bullet hole in it. 'Our enemy. Gees, they don't look much, do they? Sad and sorry lot, I'm pleased to say.'

'I like 'em like that,' Darcy said. 'With no guns.' He held his own rifle as if he had no intention of using it. 'They strike me as a lot more easy to get on with.'

After forty minutes climbing, the battalion reached the high ground, the red brick ruins of the smashed village as bright as a wound. Along an old Roman road, arrow-straight, more and more artillery came, the horses at a canter, the sound of harness slapping and ringing like birdsong in contrast to the booming of the guns. It was obvious to Andy that the advance had pushed on fast and without much opposition, although there was a scattering of a few bloodied dead, Australian and British as well as German, some roughly covered with coats or capes, others lying, arms outflung, eyes glazing in the sun. But the casualties appeared to have been slight. Compared to up north.

'You blokes won't lay a tackle!' a skinny private in his undershirt shouted as the boys came up and passed over a newly dug trench. 'You blokes won't get a bloody kick. We've already done all the hard yards.'

'They 'eard we was coming,' Ripper stopped. 'So whadda ya diggin' in 'ere for anyway? The front line'll be bloody miles on when we're finished.'

The private glanced around. 'Yeah, well, we like it 'ere, don't we? So we're stoppin'. Good luck, boys. Off yers go.' He waved. 'Bring us back some sausages. Go on. Bugger off now.'

Andy's battalion moved on, one battalion among many, the men spreading like ants across the country that was divided by roads, fields, a railway line, and flanked by woods of sullen green. The sky seemed large and providential, the day a special one; Andy figuring there was a pretty good chance that they'd all make it through to tea time.

'This'll do me.' Ripper fell in beside. 'Surely this has gotta be –'

Ripper and Andy went to ground as bullets whipped and snapped around them, Andy hearing hard smacks as men were hit, the rattle of equipment as they fell, the sudden grunting and moaning of the wounded, and the calls for stretcher bearers that went up like the sound of dogs baying.

Ripper craned his neck, trying to see what was happening.

'But it's bleedin' bloody obvious we haven't done with the bastards yet,' he said. 'I think we'd better scarper. And 'ope the boys further on up can deal with this minor inconvenience.'

Another swathe of bullets flicked close overhead.

'Fuckin' 'ell,' Ripper added, his cheek on the ground, 'this business is really gettin' on my nerves.'

thirty-two

On the last Saturday in October, Henry put his sailboard on the roof of the Volvo and drove down to the bay. The day was blustery, the wind blowing from the south-west, the sea pushing into the shore in thick choppy waves. Henry rigged up, kneeling in the coarse sand.

He thought about the trip to France and felt a current of excitement. It was happening; he had brushed aside his parents' concerns, he had been putting in hours at the factory, the flights had been booked, and his passport renewed. He was going, with Janine, and that spooked him as much as it excited him. When he had told Marcelle she had responded with silence, then she had wished him luck, and hung up. He had not heard from her since and tried to not think too deeply about how he had treated her. He expected he would feel guilty about it for a long time. And so he should, he supposed.

Henry carried his board to the water, stepped on and sailed

away, looking up to watch his sail and suddenly thoughts of all things except what he was doing disappeared – yet, he could feel his life, and for a moment he knew it to be beautiful, good, and fortunate. He nodded to himself, knowing the value that could exist in a single moment. He was lucky. There was no denying that.

After a quietly successful dinner with his parents, Henry drove Janine back to her cousin's house in Richmond. He kept thinking how good she looked.

'D'you think it'll be a bit strange living down here?' he asked, watching the tail lights of the car ahead. 'Like, it might take you a while to get used to it.'

'Well –' Janine drew the word out as if it was a sigh, 'it sure feels strange organising the next three years of your life, I know that.' She looked out at the houses and the Gothic-looking plane trees. 'And it's awful doing it without Trot. It makes me feel so guilty. Like, *he's* gone, so *now* I get my act together. But I guess I stayed in Stratty for him, anyway.'

'Yeah, I guess so.' Henry felt awkward. 'But, you know, you're just trying to sort things out. And you have to do that.'

'Yep, I guess.' Janine turned away from the passing houses and sat without saying a word until the song on the radio finished. 'Can I turn that off, Henry? The music? D'you mind?'

Henry hit the button. 'Nope. Not at all.'

'You know,' Janine said, 'I went out to where it happened a couple of times. I didn't put flowers there or anything.' She spoke without looking at him. 'I just went there and stood. It's really quite a beautiful part of the road. The grass is high and the trees are really big and old and there's a little bridge that's been there forever. It's just a bit of farmland, really. Kind of innocent and nice.'

Henry was aware of trying to drive as safely as he could.

He also felt a bit of a wuss driving along in a Volvo when he thought about Trot's car, which was definitely a hard-goer.

'And I just stood there.' Janine spoke as if she was analysing her own behaviour. 'Sometimes in the day, a couple of times at night, and all I could think was I wish Trot was *here*, like – you know, with me, so we could look at the place and he could tell me what happened, and how it was and all that, and then I could go away knowing everything, and I'm sure that would've made me feel a lot better.' Janine glanced over. 'I'm a nut-case, I know.'

Henry lifted a hand. 'No, you're fine. Most people would do that sort of thing, I think. Probably. They do. I know they do.'

Without fuss, Janine wiped her face with a tissue she had taken from her bag.

'But he didn't turn up, the old Trotter. It was just me and the cows and the trees, and the next thing I know, I'm in bloody Melbourne.' She gave Henry a mock-solemn look, then poked him with a fingertip. 'With you, Henry. And the overseas thing coming up. And the air clear with Cecelia. Shit, I'm turning over new leaves everywhere. It must be spring.'

Henry watched the road, the geography of intersecting roads complex.

'And we're goin' to France,' he said, as if it was something he'd just read on a billboard. 'In what? Two months? One? It's amazing.'

'And together,' Janine added, as if that was another line from the same poster. 'Whatever *that* means.' She laughed, looking at the city, the buildings lit up in bright towering layers. 'So what's the worst thing that could happen? Really? C'mon? So bring on December, I say.'

August 8 1918.
Villers-Bretonneux, France.

Darcy's birthday. Go forward in half an hour. Feel a bit jittery. Hope to do well. There's a million blokes here.

Resting by a hedge somewhere in a field beyond Villers-Brett. The day goes on. Bloody hungry.

All day long, at walking pace, the attack continued, the sun shining implacably as the Allied force forged ahead, fought for, claimed, then passed over square miles of territory, the roads and fields crawling with tanks, artillery, ambulances, lorries, and horse-drawn limbers – all and everything existing under the relentless thundering of the barrage, the howling shells, and drumfire on German positions close and far.

Andy's section, with Ripper, slowly worked their way up a railway line, machine gun fire coming down at them from a cutting a quarter of a mile ahead. Bullets passed in hissing hordes, stinging and zipping, whining as they ricocheted, or smacked blindly into branches, the ground, and the boys' cover. Overhead, single German shells arced to crash into the fields where Canadians advanced, the sun catching on bayonets as if the wavy green crop was a sparkling sea.

In a ditch, the boys crouched, trying to get a clear sight on the position of the machine gun. Andy's mouth was dry, gummed-up so thickly he couldn't even spit. He thought of the baby, as he often did in any relatively quiet moment anywhere, and the thought stopped him, stilled him, then wrenched at him. If only he could get home! But the possibility was so remote it wasn't even laughable.

'If I can just see where that bloody gun is,' Ripper said, tightening a puttee that was hanging over his boot, 'then we can work out a way to winkle 'em outta there. But I ain't chargin' up the track like the 11:05 to fuckin' Ferntree Gully or we'll all get knocked, and the rest of the boys comin' up behind us. We'll give it a couple of minutes and see what might happen.' Ripper took a mouthful from his drink bottle, capped it, and wiped his mouth. 'Because I can hear the little wheels of a little tanky, which might be a bloody big help in a situation like this.'

Andy rose cautiously to the edge of the ditch, and peered through the weeds to catch sight of, he reckoned, the pale spitting muzzle of the German gun. It was dug into the top of the embankment, sited to rake the line for a thousand yards, and could probably cover the fields on at least one side as well. Stealthily, he eased his rifle up, used the edge of the ditch and his upturned hand as a rest, and began to fire, ignoring the fear of getting shot in the face as he tried to steady the foresight and lock it onto the dugout that was probably sandbagged and almost bullet-proof. At the fourth shot, the machine gun stopped, then started again, a hail of bullets skipping down the line, twanging off the rails, cracking off the stone ballast, and scything through the grass. Andy dropped back down into the ditch, swallowed, and began to reload.

'Well,' said Ripper approvingly, 'at least you got his attention. Now where's that tank, I wonder? I can hear him. Come on, bubba, come to Ripper.'

By the sound of it, the tank was a Whippet, Andy thought, small and fast, coming up through the field on the other side of the tracks to where the boys had gone to ground.

'We wait till it goes past.' Ripper looked at his watch. 'And when the gun turns on it we line this bank and then we into 'em as hard as we can. Right. Get ready.'

Andy crouched, head down, and pushed home a fresh magazine, all the time listening to the hard, grinding, squeaking sound of the tank as it drew level with their position. It went on, machine gun firing, the furious ticking and spanging of bullets flying off its armour like hail.

'Into it, boys!' Ripper was up, elbows propped, firing, and in five seconds the entire rifle company lined the ditch and was shooting at the tiny, busy, candle-like flame visible against the dark bank of the cutting.

Andy fired shot after shot, sometimes having to wait as the smoke of the ten other Lee Enfields obscured his aim, and then Ripper called them not forward out of the ditch, but sideways, to scramble over a wooden fence that separated the railway line from the field where the Canadians advanced.

'Up here!' Ripper pointed along the fence line that ran parallel to the train line. 'Go low! Go a hundred yards and drop. Go!'

Andy ran, back aching, equipment bouncing, crouching, to stop where Ripper stopped, behind a copse skewered by three or four poplar trees. From where he lay, looking back to the south-east, Andy could see the Canadians clearly, like toy soldiers in the distance, in deep artillery formation, platoons deployed in diamonds, men like pieces spread evenly over a twenty-acre draughtsboard, never slowing, never hesitating, the scattered crackle of small-arms fire spreading along their front. Ripper lay down his rifle and took out his cigarette tin.

'Smoko, boys.' He smiled, his teeth as filthy as a farm animal's, his eyes steady, but red-rimmed and ruined-looking. 'We'll let that tank hop into it for a couple of rounds, then we'll go and see what else has to be done. Hopefully she'll be all clear and we can then let this big mob of Canadians go on through. Otherwise –' Ripper sucked deeply on his cigarette and blew out a thin stream of smoke, 'we'll have to try and bomb the bastards out of there. Which I do not relish. Meanwhile, boys, relax. Eat, drink, load up. Make a model boat.'

Andy had a few sips of water. At either end of the copse, Ripper had sent a man to observe, the two soldiers prone in the grass, rifles aimed along the tracks, bayonets like single silver flames. The rumble of the guns never stopped although it faded in and out of Andy's consciousness, a permanent feature of the place, like surf on a coastline but louder, wider-ranging, deeper, and infinitely more threatening. He watched the massed Canadians, the occasional man dropping to become a lump as he was sniped, left by the rest for the stretcher bearers and ambulances that would come through immediately after the division had gone on.

'All right, boys.' Ripper squatted, rasped his hand across his face, and coughed. 'I guess we better go. We'll keep on up the fence and see what we can see. The cover's not bad. Keep your bloody heads down.'

Along the fence they travelled until Ripper stopped behind a lump of earth that offered good cover. The railway line entered the cutting thirty or forty yards in front of them, disappearing between the tall earthen banks. Again they stopped. Andy could hear machine guns firing, but there was too much other noise for him to tell by the note if they were German guns or Allied.

Ripper moved to the edge of the bank, looked over for five seconds then squatted down again, pushing back his helmet as if some cool air might loosen his thoughts.

'Right.' He nodded at Andy and Darcy. 'Right, you blokes – *fuck!*'

There was a smacking sound like a fist hitting flesh and Collie Richmond, a rifleman about Andy's size and age, writhed as if he had been speared, a watery gurgle coming from his throat, his fists clenched, his eyes vibrating, the whites bulging. Andy could see the spreading blotch of darkness below Collie's armpit. The single bullet had come from up the line. Panic flared, the boys scrambled around the mound, another bullet hissing between them, then another that took the heel off someone's boot as they threw themselves down flat.

'Christ, this won't do.' Ripper peered around. 'If that machine gun gets a line on us we'll be bloody mincemeat. Right, boys – shit, I don't like this.' Ripper nodded toward the strip of shrubs, trees, and grass. 'Right. Back in amongst this stuff here –'

There was a sound like a pumpkin being whacked with a bat, Collie's head jerking.

'*You* —' Darcy coughed out, his voice choked with disbelief, 'you fuckin' *bastard*.'

Andy felt an intensity of hate that was so far beyond anger it chilled him, not displacing his fear, but combining the two feelings into something that felt like it was corroding his head from inside out. He could feel hate in his mouth, in his throat. He could smell it coming off himself. He did not even think about what he wanted to do to the German sniper.

'Rush in twos and threes up the line,' Ripper said. 'Stay in the scrubby shit then cross the line as soon as we get to the start of the cutting. If that MG's still there they won't be able to get a sight on us. Andy, Bobby-boy, with me. You right?'

Andy knelt and nodded, hardly knowing himself, seeming to exist outside his body, or to have reduced himself to a tiny inhabitant controlling his body like a puppeteer. With Ripper and Bob, he rushed around the mound and into the thin scrub, feeling his boots tearing into the soil, small branches whipping against his arms and legs, his stomach swilling like a bag of blood.

'Keep goin'!' Ripper yelled. 'I'll go back and keep the other boys movin'. See yers in a minute or so up the other end.'

Andy ran, crouching and crawling, battering his way forward through the vegetation until he had made it to the start of the cutting. With Bob, he crossed the line and lay down flat.

'Can't hear that gun.' Bob was intent on the way ahead. 'They couldn't get a line of fire on us down here any — hey, there goes the bastard!'

A hundred yards away, a German soldier ran across the line, delicately bounding over the rails, rifle in hand. Bob was up like a sprinter out of the blocks.

'Bloody after him!'

Andy ran with Bob in the shadow of the embankment, almost falling over the wreckage of the machine gun and crew that they, or the tank more likely, had blasted out of the shoulder of the cutting. Andy, with barely a flicker of thought, bayoneted two bleeding gunners who were attempting to salvage the weapon, then ran on, making it to the end of the cutting to stop and look down over fields that sloped down to a stream before rising again. The roofs of an intact village stood out like models on a ridge a mile away. Andy scanned the ground for the sniper, or signs of other Germans, but could see none.

'He's gone.' He sat, sweat soaking, lice moving in the moist heat. 'Geez, bloody thirsty.' He took out his water bottle. 'So now what?' He drank, the water warm, tinny, and exquisite. 'Where's the rest of the bloody battalion, then?'

'Spread out along the railway line, I s'pose.' Bob also drank. 'We better wait.'

Andy gave a fleeting thought to the machine gunners he'd killed, then tried to think about what he and Bob would do next.

'I guess Ripper'll have us work up off the Canadians' flank here,' he said. 'God, look at 'em. There must be a bloody million.'

The Canadians moved over the tracks in a formation that extended for miles, the occasional pop and crackle of distant rifle fire coming from their front. Andy could see tiny distant dark figures labouring up a hill. Germans, he thought. Out of range. Not even worth having a crack at. Bob lit a cigarette.

'I would've liked to get a shot at the bastard who knocked Collie,' he said reflectively. 'Maybe the Canadas'll flush him out from the creek.' He sat up, managing to rest his pack against a small stump. 'Sick of this bloody luggage, too. Look. Here comes Rip and the others. Reckon they'll believe us if we tell 'em we took that machine gun out by ourselves? Military Medal, maybe. Good for a root those things, they say.'

Andy looked at his bayonet, a thin layer of blood along its length like old paint. The sensation of killing the Germans existed in his hands and arms, of plunging the blade in, and having to drag it out. In a way, he felt strengthened by what he'd done, at the same time he knew he'd spend the rest of his life trying to forget it.

'D'you ever think we'd ever be doing this kind of thing?' he said. 'Blowed if I did. I can't believe we have.'

'No, we have.' Bob cradled his water bottle in one hand, rifle in the other. 'You done good, Andy.' He offered his water, which Andy declined. 'You're a brave bastard, mate. You'll do me. We'll get the job done, don't worry about that. And pick the pieces up later.'

thirty-three

For some reason Henry couldn't exactly nail down, he found himself working harder at his essays and assignments than he had been. He guessed it was to show his parents that even when he was going to do something that was basically against their will, i.e., go on the trip, he was still Henry Lyon, obedient, career-minded student.

He guessed he was in trouble when Walt and Marg sidled into the kitchen from the lounge room. Henry put the jaffle into the jaffle maker and shut the lid.

'Whatever it is,' he said, 'get off my case.'

'Henry, we're not on your case.' Walt stood in the door-way. 'I don't think you understand perhaps how difficult this whole thing may turn out to be. It seems pretty complex for a number of reasons. I'm sure you can see that.'

'Your dad has a point –' Marg made a flanking man-oeuvre, over to the bench. She took out a green tea bag from a tin, draped it in a cup, and stood holding a spoon. 'Especially since Janine –'

Henry abandoned his snack. God, he'd leave it rather than go through all this again.

'I'm not changing my mind.' He did not want to have this conversation. 'So forget it. I'm going. Overseas and out of here. I'll see you later.' He walked out, leaving behind silence he counted as success, and his jaffle, which he was missing already.

In his room, he leant against his bed and thought about the trip. He was going to get on a plane with Janine, they were going to land at de Gaulle airport in Paris, catch a train to the north and then – hey, he didn't know what then, but he was going and maybe he would come home before Christmas and maybe he wouldn't.

On an impulse, he rang Janine, his mood improving as soon as he heard her voice.

'I've given up trying to explain to people why I'm goin' on this trip,' he said. 'If I said I was just going to Queensland for two weeks partying, everything'd be cool, but this? Bloody hell, you'd think I was going to the moon.'

'Just tell 'em to get stuffed, Henry. And if they have a problem with that, tell 'em to go see Cecelia Hainsworth in the front bar of the Stratty Hotel, and she'll sort them out, because *we* are goin' *around* the *world*.'

Henry felt his feelings jump like a spike on a graph.

August 8 1918.
Villers-Bretonneux, France.

Darcy's birthday. Go forward in half an hour. Feel a bit jittery. Hope to do well. There's a million blokes here.

Resting by a hedge somewhere in a field beyond Villers-Brett. The day goes on. Bloody hungry.

In a different paddock. Still bloody hungry.

Andy, with the rest of his section, five or six yards between each man, moved down the sloping field toward the stream. Out to his left, on similar contours, hundreds of other infantrymen from the battalion either slowed down or sped up to straighten the line.

'Yeah, this is lookin' better.' Ripper spat with satisfaction. 'Slow down!' he shouted to his left. 'We're not a patrol, ya bloody greyhounds, we're part of an *organised* attack. Now where are me bloody tanks gone?'

'There's a couple up further,' Darcy said. 'Or least, they got our colours on 'em. And they're still goin' all right.'

Every minute German shells, singly or in strung-out groups like racing pigeons, blasted high overhead to explode far behind the body of the advance. Occasionally, one fell close — then, perhaps from a newly-sited battery, shells began to fall amongst the Canadians who marched nervelessly through the bombardment, leaving fifteen or twenty men behind, some moving, some not. Without pause, the Allied guns boomed and blasted, kicking up a vast low-hanging haze over the land ahead.

'How far on's this blue line s'posed to be, Rip?' a white-headed rifleman called Floss asked. 'We been walkin' for bloody hours.'

'Two mile.' Ripper did not take his eyes off the trees in front. 'And then we gotta go on through that to the red. We still got a big day in front of us, boys. Doncha's all just wish yer'd joined the bloody flyin' circus?'

'Not particularly.' Bob pointed upwards. 'Look at that.'

In sky the colour of blue satin, there was a smoke trail like a long black rip. Other dots circled like silvery insects playing out some dizzy autumn game.

'Yeah, well I didn't say it was *safer*.' Ripper turned his attention back to the country in front. 'I just said it was *easier*.'

Andy was too tired to laugh. He watched the trees, the stream shining between them.

'*Fritzy!*' someone yelled. 'Two o'clock, five hundred yards! Comin' outta the back of that 'ay shed and headin' for the trees!'

Andy, like eighty or ninety others in the line, knelt or lay down, and began to fire. The Germans were within range but moved quickly, Andy catching them in his sights, but finding it hard to make them out against a backdrop of trees. He fired, the noise of massed rifles seeming to roll out the blue smoke of muzzle blasts like a cloud. A few Germans, he saw, had dropped, the survivors disappearing into a wood that by now hundreds of men were pouring fire into.

Andy stopped shooting and got up, the volleys easing until it was more like a carnival shooting gallery, the odd shot popping. Floss pointed downhill, the slope slick-looking with sunshine.

'Souvenirs, boys. See 'em comin' outta the scrub by the creek? Look at 'em, hands-up doin' the Hokey-Pokey.' He gestured grandly to the Germans, rifle slung over his shoulder. 'Come on up, fellers! I'll swap ya a smoke for ya bloody gun any day.'

Andy watched the surrendering soldiers moving toward the advancing infantry until they were absorbed then passed over, a couple of riflemen dispatched to escort them to the rear. He was amazed that the prisoners were just men, harmless and soft-looking without weapons, many bareheaded, quite a few with their shirts hanging out.

'They're like bloody fish those Fritz,' Darcy said. 'Under-sized when ya get 'em on the bank. But Jesus crikey Moses, see 'em comin' at ya at night and ya think it's forty full-backs from bloody Bairnsdale.'

Andy heard bullets hiss and whisper, then the low stuttering bark of a German machine gun. The men moved quickly for the trees, soldiers stooping to hoist or drag the wounded. High on the hill Andy could see the German post, the machine gun being fired from behind what looked like a section of stonewall, but was probably a fortified pillbox.

'*My* blokes,' Ripper yelled, his face hard, 'go downstream then work up that gully. Pincer 'em in and hopefully a bloody tank can —'

A shell came screaming in over the trees at so low a trajectory that Andy was buffeted by its wind, then knocked over as it exploded forty yards up the hill. Shrapnel whizzed, smacking into trees, clipping off branches, a soldier in the line suddenly spinning three hundred and sixty degrees.

'*Fuck!*' Darcy shouted from where he lay, his head sideways. 'They're firin' that bastard from a bloody hundred yards away. Don't they read the bloody handbook? They're supposed to be two miles back behind the bloody lines. And there's cow shit here.' He looked at his hand. 'And I'm bloody covered in it.'

Shivers shook Andy. His skeleton felt like it was rattling. He tried to stand, then hearing another shell coming like a train, he threw himself face down, the explosion feeling like a split in his skull. He got up, ears ringing.

'*Outta* here for Christ's sakes.' Ripper moved amongst the men. 'Get down there.' He gestured toward the stream and trees. 'Then up that first fuckin' gully.'

Andy stumbled into the shade of the trees and set off downstream. Being in the place was like an embrace, the flowing water drawing his eyes, drawing his whole being. Sometimes he thought he could hear it, a mesmerising whisper that came to him when the barrage lulled, the light and dark of the place soothing until another shell came screaming in to blow a crater out of the hill, throwing dirt and toppling a tree. Pushed by fear, Andy jogged on with Floss.

'The second we stop,' Floss said. 'I am gunna stick my head in that water and drink a bloody gallon. I don't give a shit how many dead bastards are in it. If I don't wet me whistle soon I'll bloody die anyway.'

Andy grinned, his mouth dry and sick-tasting.

'Fuck it, let's stop now.' He stopped running. 'They can stick that field gun up their arse.'

Floss pulled up. 'Yeah. Sideways. And fire it.'

'Whadda you blokes up to?' Another infantryman, lines in his face like creases in leather, stopped. 'Jesus, I'll never start up again. I'm just about knackered.'

'We're drinkin'.' Floss headed for the stream. 'Mad if yer don't, Lylie. It's here, it's free, and it's wet.'

Andy, with Floss and Lyle, and then a fourth private, got down on all fours to slurp like cattle. To Andy it was like drinking happiness; the coolness, the tang of dirt and pasture, was so far beyond being refreshing he felt like he had been blessed, that he would never forget this water for as long as he lived. He looked down into it, able to see tiny fragments trundling along the bottom as he listened to the boys saying how good it was. Andy washed his face, wishing he could submerge himself in it for a day.

'Better get goin',' he said. 'And catch up to bloody Ripper.'

'If we have to.' Floss got up, his face shiny with water.

Behind them another explosion rocked the hill.

'I wish that bastard'd piss off.' Floss dried his face on his tunic. 'It's givin' me a bloody headache, that gun, and I am not jokin'.'

thirty-four

Henry slogged his way through exams and assignments, slogged his way in and out of the city in the heat, and at night he added things that he was going to take to France to a list. And then he was walking down Swanston Street on a Thursday afternoon with Marcus, his university year finished.

'I'm bloody exhausted,' he said, the wind blowing grit into his face. 'When do you finish? Tomorrow? Or Friday?'

Marcus pushed a hand back through his hair.

'Next Monday. So when d'you go? Away, I mean?'

'Saturday week.' Henry shook his head as if to clear his vision. 'It's amazing. I can't believe it.'

Marcus didn't argue. 'Yeah, you brought it off. You're goin'.' He gave Henry a look that slid away. 'It should be interesting.'

Henry decided to change the subject.

'We'll have a beer on Monday. I'll come in. I've gotta get

a couple of things for the trip, anyway.'

Marcus stepped around a courier's bike parked on the footpath,

'Cool. We might even have a few. So where do you first lob?'

'Paris,' Henry said, 'then up north. You know, where that Andy guy is buried. And then, who knows?' He looked around at the intersecting flat-walled canyons of the central business district. 'Depends on what Janine wants to do. I'm sure we can work something out.'

Marcus clicked his tongue. 'I'm sure you can. Anyway, mate, there's my tram. See yer.'

Henry watched Marcus head off, then crossed to the station entrance that reminded him of a steel and glass monster. In just over a week he'd be on a jumbo jet. And now, the difference was, he almost believed it.

Henry's mobile buzzed as he walked home, the sound of Marcelle's voice stopping him in his tracks.

'I just rang to say hello,' she said. 'And to wish you luck, I guess. So, well, good luck.'

'Thanks.' Henry was somewhat stunned to be having this conversation. 'Yeah, I hope it'll be good.' His mind kept flashing back to their last encounter. 'So what are you up to? How's work? You, ah, seeing anybody?' He paused. 'I mean, I know you're *seeing* people. Shit, you work in the city. There are millions of them in there everyday.'

Marcelle laughed and Henry was relieved.

'Well, hey, you know. I go out. Yeah, I am kind of seeing someone. Anyway, have a safe trip, Henry. Maybe you could ring me one day and tell me how it all went?'

'Yeah, sure, I will.' Henry guessed he'd sound like an idiot if he said he wouldn't. 'I will. See you, Marcelle. Thanks for the call. Bye.' He finished the call and walked on, looking somewhere out into mid-air as he slipped his phone back into his pocket.

She was a brilliant girl. In her own way. In lots of ways. He was glad she sounded happy. It let him off the hook. He was grateful. He guessed he didn't deserve to get off so lightly.

August 8 1918,
Villers-Bretonneux, France.

Darcy's birthday. Go forward in half an hour. Feel a bit jittery. Hope to do well. There's a million blokes here.

Resting by a hedge somewhere in a field beyond Villers-Brett. The day goes on. Bloody hungry.

In a different paddock. Still bloody hungry.

Machine guns raked the slopes, and from loopholes German riflemen sniped at the advancing troops, catching Canadians and Australians in the open. Andy climbed up the gully, his section spread out, every few seconds a pair of men dropping to provide covering fire as the others tried to close in on the fortified position. Below him, he saw a tin helmet flip and a digger slide back, dark blood trickling from sweat-flattened red hair. Andy allowed himself to acknowledge what he had seen, but had let the thought go even before Ripper had stopped swearing.

'Get up here, boys!' Ripper windmilled an arm. 'Get in where it's steep and geddown! And get that fuckin' Lewis gun! I want to *rip* those bastards *outta* there.'

A big, red-faced sergeant from another section scrambled up the gully, so furious-looking, so focussed on the German position that Andy was sure he would be sniped before he could start firing, but no bullet dropped him, although Andy heard a couple smack into the ground close by. Ten yards behind, a private came labouring up the gully with a haversack of ammunition. Andy could hear him wheezing, his helmet slipping sideways.

'Look after me, Jesus,' the infantryman was muttering. 'Look after me, Jesus.'

Andy dropped down next to Darcy and began to fire as the sergeant with the Lewis gun started up, immediately blowing chunks of concrete from the slit in the pillbox.

'That'll rattle their brains a bit,' someone said. 'Shit, now there's two goin' at it. Beautiful.'

A second automatic weapon was firing on the German machine guns, the slit obscured by dust and flying chips, Andy imagining the bullets ricocheting around inside the concrete dug-out. The machine gun stopped, but the fire from down the hill seemed to intensify and now, as if rising from the ground, German soldiers staggered into the open from the rear of the position, hands up.

'I don't like their chances.' Darcy looked up over his rifle. 'I think they may've left their run just a little bit too late. Oh, well, they gotta white flag now. That might help.'

All fire on the position stopped. For a minute nothing happened as the German garrison made their way down the slope, hands in the air, many of them wounded. Andy saw a Canadian soldier run to the pillbox, toss a grenade then squat, the explosion muffled but loud, smoke and dust wafting out to drift away on the warm afternoon air.

'And on we go.' Ripper stretched, then inserted a cigarette into his mouth. 'After I've had a bloody leak, that is. Geez and not a tree to be found.'

thirty-five

'This does *not* seem real,' Janine said, as she and Henry walked past glittering glass, metal and chrome Duty Free shops that lined the way to the various airport gate lounges. 'We're on *airport* time now.' She grabbed Henry's hand, but let it go almost immediately. 'God, it's a bit scary. And back there, with the folks and all that. That was pretty hard, wasn't it?'

Henry agreed. He also felt strange, isolated and vulnerable, and was secretly worried that perhaps they had embarked on something that they might not be able to handle. He had felt a lump rise in his throat when saying goodbye to his parents, and Marcus and Nick, but he'd managed to defeat the possibility of crying with willpower and jokes.

'It'll be fine,' he said. 'We sit in here in the lounge, we sit on the plane, we get off. Cool. We're there. There's our plane.' He checked the number on an overhead screen. The rich smell of coffee wafted from a small cafe. People wandered around or read books.

For half an hour they waited, saying little, then boarded the 747 to sit and wait again. Then, with a rocket-like rush, the plane took off and steadied, as if fixing its final course for France. Henry watched Janine as she gazed out of the window. He saw that she was crying, but he said nothing.

The aeroplane was descending – to Henry it felt like it was sinking – toward dull grey-brown ground visible through patchy cloud, the outskirts of the city visible but remote. *France.* He felt a kind of a nervous fear that he had never experienced before, a fear that managed to penetrate his tiredness, yet did not give him energy. Home – *Australia* – was twenty thousand k away, which was a concept he could not entirely come to grips with. He was in France. Or he was just about to be.

'God, well, what can you say?' He was excited, but bone-tired. 'My eyes feel like they're full of sand.' He blinked wide-ly, but it made no difference. He felt like they had been flying, apart from a three-hour stop in Singapore, for weeks.

Janine squeezed his hand. 'We made it. All this way without a shower. God, I feel like I've been dragged behind a ute through a paddock.' She looked out of the window. 'Trot would've got a kick out of this, wouldn't he? He would've thought it was the biggest joke on earth, him about to hang out in Paris for a night.' Janine slumped, put a hand to her face. 'You'll have to forgive me, Henry, if I say things –'

Henry shook his head. 'Yeah, no, it's okay. Yeah, he would've liked it. I dunno how he would've gone speaking French, though. And –' Henry slid his magazine back into the seat pocket in front, 'you don't smell, either. Although I reckon –' he sniffed, 'I do.'

Around them people prepared for landing. Henry could feel an air of expectation and excitement and he noticed, or thought that he noticed, that Australian accents and phrases seemed to have become the order of the day. He stretched, pushing his fingers toward the cabin roof, admitting to himself that if he'd been on his own he would have been absolutely terrified. He sat, buckled in, as the plane continued down through cloud.

No point panicking, he told himself. Just take things as they come. And hey, he thought, if this wasn't the biggest adventure in his life, then he didn't know what was. He had flown *around* the world. He was *not* in Australia. He was in another country. Or he was just about to be.

With a thump, the jumbo jet touched down.

August 8 1918.
Villers-Bretonneux, France.

Darcy's birthday. Go forward in half an hour. Feel a bit jittery. Hope to do well. There's a million blokes here.

Resting by a hedge somewhere in a field beyond Villers-Brett. The day goes on. Bloody hungry.

In a different paddock. Still bloody hungry.

Still hungry. Bloody thirsty now.

The battalion entered the blue line, a shallow old trench held up in places by panels of hand-woven sticks. Here they rested, soldiers taking water bottles and food from the haversacks of freshly killed soldiers.

'Ten minutes,' Ripper said, walking along the meandering ditch. 'Ten minutes, boys. Then we form up and go on.'

Andy rested, drinking from a German water bottle. He passed it on to Bob.

'To the victor the spoils.' Bob tilted the tin container. 'Cheers. And on we go, for ever and ever.'

Along the line the men rose, the smokers lighting up, the battalion proceeding forward in a zigzag pattern like the teeth of a saw. Andy and Darcy, in the middle ranks, strolled along, with nothing to shoot at but a fox as they worked through crops and over farms. Then the line wheeled to the east to lend fire on a wood where German machine gunners were raking the Canadians. Tanks waddled forward, and in a gully massed troops seemed to have skewered sunlight, carrying it forward on their bayonets as they stormed into the trees, their yells distant and child-like.

'At least – ' Darcy stopped talking, the sound of shells rendering words obsolete.

Men lay down in swathes, wrapping their arms around their heads, Andy flinching at the explosions, shockwaves rippling through him, and then there was a blast of heat and a kick to his side that seemed to smash him out of time and existence – before he found that he was flat on his back looking at the sky, his hearing muffled, the pain in his chest so massive he acknowledged it with short grunting breaths and tears.

Beneath him the ground bucked and shuddered. He looked up into the sky that was a piercing, perfect, blue, but he did not see it. In the chink left to him that pain had not taken, he tried to think of his parents and home, and for a moment he gratefully held a picture of Kooyong and his mother and father and Emily, then he saw Cecelia, and then Cecelia became Frances-Jane, before all were swept away by a gale of pain that had him gasping.

Darcy, Bob, and Ripper peered down at him, a jigsaw pattern of sky between them. He felt they might be shouting at him, but he could hear nothing but odds and ends of words and sounds. He tried to speak, but did not know if he had succeeded.

Then he was being lifted, the pain tearing screams out of him, and he knew, somewhere down very deep, that he was not going to be able to overcome whatever had happened to him. It was much too much, and in a way — he felt apologetic for this — he wished it were over already. He knew that was not what he should be thinking, but he had identified the truth: that already he had been separated from the world and was floating away, slowly, on his way to somewhere else.

Yet he was still who he was, although he didn't think he would be for very much longer. Everything was slowing, the quickness of all things mired in pain, and a kind of a choking hopelessness and helplessness that frightened him a lot. He was moving closer and closer to his very core. He could not help it. The force against him was insurmountable.

He could see Darcy halfway between himself and the sky, a scattering of Darcy's blood dripping down onto his face, and he could hear words, but the words flew away like small dark birds. Then he was being carried, Darcy walking alongside, cradling a bleeding arm, and it occurred to Andy that the war was over, that he was free of it, that it had released him. It was, despite the pain he was feeling, time to consider his life.

He didn't so much think of the people who loved him and the people he loved, he experienced it. It washed through him, the love of the boys, his parents, his sister, his grandparents, Cecelia and Frances-Jane, and there was the baby, his baby, who brought a wild, primitive, sweeping love that he could not fathom, but only experience.

He was only emotion now — in thought and memory, of the present and of the past. His life of doing was over. It would not be added to now, but he did know he had done his duty — but that was like a second of his life, and that second was gone. It was love he was remembering; he remembered his people and the land as love, his horses grazing under the gums, his mum and dad, Emily, all the girls, his mates — Andy could hear Darcy. Darcy, with one hand, was putting a greatcoat over him.

'You're gunna be *orright* Andy.' Darcy's face was dead-white under grime. 'Boys're takin' ya back to VB. Just stay with me, mate, orright?' He got hold of Andy's hand. 'Don't leave me. Just 'ang on tight and you'll be right.' He replaced Andy's hand on top of the heavy coat. 'I'm comin' back with ya, cobber. I'll be with ya every step of the way.'

Andy, with great effort, moved his hand to settle on top of his tunic pocket.

'In here, Darce. Take my stuff.'

Darcy shook his head, his face twisted, a broad smear of blood on his neck.

'No, I won't. You'll be back in the fuckin' field 'ospital in half an hour, because there's motor ambulances back here. And then the doctors'll look after ya. So don't you go givin' me no letters nor no diary. You'll need it tomorrow. Ya can fill it in yaself, mate. I don't want it and I won't take it, because I swear to yer on the bible everythin's gunna be orright.'

Andy wanted to nod. Yes, *things* would be all right – things would be – but not himself, in his particular case. Whatever had hit him had hit him too hard. He could feel what it had done to him. It had really caught him. He doubted anybody could take it. He knew he couldn't. He would try, but when he did try, like Darcy asked, he felt himself falling further back. It was better to be like this, moving away like a leaf in a current, allowing himself to be taken downstream.

thirty-six

The train moved through the countryside at a moderate speed, as if the driver had decided, for reasons of his own, that this pace was ideal.

'It doesn't look *all* that different from the land around home,' Janine observed as she watched the fields pass, most empty of crops. 'I mean, it does a bit, and it looks *colder*, but it's got the small hills and the colours are kind of the same, you know, the greens and the ground and the fences. But darker, in a way. I guess they get a lot more rain here. And less sun.'

Henry watched the landscape unfold as the train made its way along at its medium pace. It was quite hypnotic, the blending of his thoughts with the passing of farm houses, barns, roads, and trees. Yes, perhaps the place *didn't* look all that different from places he'd seen before, but he *knew* it was. It amazed him that he was on a French train going through the French countryside under a French sky.

'The trees are different though, aren't they?' He pointed to a row beside a narrow road. 'Poplars, maybe. And the hedges. It's like, more organised. And the towns, like, they're everywhere. And little.' He could see a village on a small plateau, its spire the highest point, the rest of the town seeming to entirely fit under a spreading umbrella of foliage. Beyond the village, along a road, he could see a – well, he guessed it was a wood. 'And there's a *wood*.' He grinned. 'You know, you couldn't call it the bush, could you? It's kind of darker, too. Different trees. Closer together.' Henry looked at everything, trying to absorb it all.

'Andy might've come along this way, I guess.' Janine's breath huffed faintly on the window. 'Where we're going. I mean, they fought in Villers however-you-say-it, so maybe they came down, or went up, whatever, this train line. Although they probably would've walked, I s'pose. It's amazing, isn't it? To be here. To actually be *here*.' She pushed the tips of her fingers against the glass.

Henry looked where she looked. He could feel her warmth at his shoulder.

'Yeah, it's hard to believe that this is where it all happened.' A red brick farmhouse passed, complete with a courtyard and a trailer piled with what he thought were potatoes. 'Or up further a few k, anyway. And here we are.'

Janine took hold of his hand, hers small, warm, and firm. He could feel her rings, the pressure of them cool and tight.

'Thanks for coming, Henry.' She smiled into his face, her breath minty from Tic Tacs. 'I would never have got here without you.' She lifted his hand and held it in both of hers. 'You're my mate, Henry. You really are. You've done everything you could've for me.' She squeezed his hand once, then let it go. 'You stood by me even when you hardly knew me.'

Henry cut loose with a grin. It seemed like the only thing to do. He was happy to be here. It seemed like a huge thing to have done, but they were here, in France, rocking along in a train and everything seemed to be going okay.

'I wanted to come,' he said. 'I always did.' The train, he saw, was moving through a railway cutting. 'We must be getting close. The guy at Lille said we'd be getting there at about four. At *least* I think that's what he said.' Henry had done French at school for one year, but basically had understood nothing that had been said to him since arriving at the airport, apart from, '*bonjour*'. 'Perhaps we should get our stuff ready?'

'Yeah, let's get set.' Janine let Henry get up. 'Hate to miss it.'

The train was slowing. Henry heard its whistle. Janine bent to look out of the window.

'There's a little town on this hill. So. That might be it, then.'

'Might be.' Henry picked up his bag.

The train came into a station, their carriage coming to a halt a short way beyond a dark brick station house. Henry could see a carpark beyond it, trees, and a road climbing up a small hill. The station master stood by the central gate, methodically smoking a cigarette.

'It's nice, isn't it?' Janine helped Henry out with the bags. 'And *cold*.' She laughed. 'Feel that air.' She did. 'God, I hope we've got everything.' She dragged her coat from where she had wound it through the handles of her bag and put it on. Behind them the train pulled away.

Henry put on his jacket. He saw that already the afternoon was turning into evening, a touch of mist coming down. The sound of the departing train was a distant clicking. Leaving the station, he and Janine walked past a big brick house that stood belligerently behind locked gates. Slowly they headed along a road that led toward the centre of the town.

'It's quiet.' Henry's bag bumped his knee. 'It smells good.' He sniffed. 'Grass. Cows. Tractors.'

Hardly a car passed, only a few people were on the streets, mostly carrying shopping. Henry saw a woman draw the curtains of a red-brick house. He tried to imagine the place in 1918, totally destroyed as troops fought back and forth right through it, over the very spot on which he was standing probably – but the images he came up with were not convincing. A woman nodded to them, Henry nodded back.

'We'll have to find out where Andy's cemetery is exactly,' Janine said. 'By the looks of that little map I've got it's pretty close.' Around them, roads headed off in different directions. 'I think we could walk. We'll go out there tomorrow, will we? I hope it's a nice day.'

'Sure.' Henry was looking for street signs, hoping to locate Melbourne Street, which he found surprisingly easily. A small hotel, three storeys high, stood on the corner. 'That's it. The place with the slate roof.'

'Let's go, then.' Janine gave Henry a look he couldn't work out, which she added a grin to. 'Because A, I'm hungry and B, I'm looking forward to just sitting down where it's quiet for a while.' She looked up the road, about to cross.

'Yeah, I'm bloody starving.' Henry was also tired. 'So let's go *book* in.' He blushed, but refused to recognise that he had.

Janine laughed. 'Oh, c'mon, Henry.' She dragged on his arm. 'What's your problem?'

Henry and Janine sat facing each other on their single beds, their knees not quite touching. The room was dim, the evening sky visible through the single narrow window. Janine turned on the bedside lamp. She stood to gaze down on the street and a small park. In the dusk a seat painted yellow, blue, and green stood out.

'It really is hard to imagine what happened around here, isn't it?' she said. 'All the battles and stuff. The guys getting killed. It's just so quiet.'

'Yeah, impossible really, I guess.' Henry could see out the window from where he sat. 'I s'pose you just have to know that it did, and like, well, here we are anyway.'

'On the train today –' Janine ran her hand along the window sill, her elbow moving the flimsy lace curtain, 'you know how I said you were my mate, Henry? Well, I mean, you *are* of course –' she gave him a brief smile, 'but you're more than that.' She pushed her hair back over her shoulders and took a deep breath. 'Only I don't know how to say what I really think – of you – because I don't even know what to *allow* myself to think. And I certainly don't know what I can *do* about it. If you know what I mean. At the moment.'

To Henry, the quiet of the room seemed to be an extension of the quietness of the town, and he did admit to himself – there was no point denying it – that he wished Janine would kiss him, and then they would see where things would take them, but he was not going to make the first move. He felt, in typical Henry Lyon fashion, already guilty. Still . . .

'I'm kind of the same,' he said. 'But I know, I mean, with Trot and everything, that it's complicated. And I don't want to, well, barge in. I don't want to –' he looked directly at Janine, 'wreck things. Like, even before they've –' Shut up, he told himself. You've said too much already.

Janine sat down again. Henry guessed that she would be thinking of Trot, because what else would she be thinking about?

'I just wanted you to know, Henry,' she said calmly. 'It's hard for me to even talk about this stuff. It's a situation I never thought I'd be in.' She touched his kneecap. 'And for you, I would imagine. Unless you do this kind of thing every holiday?'

'No, it's a first.' Henry could feel as much as see that night was coming down. Outside, everything looked sombre and cold. He wondered if it might snow. 'It was a big thing that happened to you,' he added. 'To Trot, I mean. But to you, as well.'

'Yes,' she said. 'It was.' She looked at her hands, then she looked at Henry. 'Nothing is ever simple.' She took off her earrings and put them down under the lamp. 'But at some point I guess you have to stop thinking and just do. But you know, Henry, this thing is not about what other people think. This thing – you and me – is not about things that happened earlier this year. It's not about Trot anymore. It's about us. So. Kiss me. If you want to.'

August 8 1918.
Villers-Bretonneux, France.

Darcy's birthday. Go forward in half an hour. Feel a bit jittery. Hope to do well. There's a million blokes here.

Resting by a hedge somewhere in a field beyond Villers-Brett. The day goes on. Bloody hungry.

In a different paddock. Still bloody hungry.

Still hungry. Bloody thirsty now.

Andy lay looking up at the sagging green roof of the field hospital. The large tent was lit with lamps that swayed as the wind pushed and pulled at the walls, the slapping of canvas a sound he found comforting and not unfamiliar. A nursing sister moved slowly between the stretchers, stopping, stooping, talking. From somewhere close someone called out, then subsided into silence. His own pain was immense and cold. It had taken him over, but it had dulled. He did not know where Darcy was, but he wished he would come back.

Andy could not order his thoughts. He found himself roaming the farm with the horses, then he was on the veranda with Cecelia, at a dance with Frances-Jane, now he was talking to his father, then he was at the railway station, and now there was the sudden flaring orange flash of guns on a dark horizon, he was drinking in the Stratty pub, he was at school bringing in the wood for the pot-belly stove, he was playing football, he was kneeling, sniping at Germans, he was drinking from that stream with Floss, he was here.

He managed to scratch his cheek, the sensation large and intense. The blankets pressed down on him heavily, but without warmth. He watched the sister move toward him, immaculate and calm, her face lined and dark, bringing kindness with her that Andy felt through his face. She held his hand, the warmth moving deep into his arm. She spoke, although he did not know what she said.

'Water,' Andy whispered, forming the word carefully.

'Water,' she replied. 'I'll get you some right now.' And she was gone from his sight, then she was back, to lift his head and tilt the glass.

She allowed him a few mouthfuls, then knelt beside him, between the stretcher beds that were set out in rows.

'You can shut your eyes, Andy,' she said. 'You're safe now. If you feel that you want to shut your eyes it will be all right. I won't leave you. I will be here. You can rest.'

'Where's Darce?' The words felt solid in his mouth. They did not seem to go away.

The sister looked to a place that Andy could not see. The ceiling of the hospital was hazy to him. He felt he might be in a cloud, green like the colour of cut grass.

'He's getting his arm dressed,' the sister said, 'He will be back as soon as the doctor has finished. I will bring him when it's done. His wound is quite serious.'

When Andy looked again, the nurse was gone, and the canvas roof of the tent had changed into the hills around Strattford, the trees mere puffs of colour, more blue than green, the sky silver, his house shining like a white beacon at the end of the track, him walking toward it, through the farm, the horses by the fence as he headed for home.

thirty-seven

Henry and Janine walked away from the village, the day grey and cold, on their way to a small war cemetery marked on their map as 'Crucifix Corner'. Neither said much, the only sound the crunch of their boots in the roadside gravel. Ahead, Henry could see the walled cemetery. It was set back from the road in a field, a stand of trees at the back like sentinels. Around it the land dipped gently and rose smoothly, a wood visible, and the road, with one tractor moving along it, continued on straight and even.

'This was all a battlefield,' Janine said, and patted her coat pocket, 'according to the book. And then out thatta-way.' She pointed to the north. 'It's kind'a confusing, though. Like, what happened when and where and who was doing it.'

On their way to the cemetery they had seen old muddy shell casings piled in the corner of a paddock, thrown there, Henry guessed, by the farmer. He and Janine had gone over to look at the pile of cylinders that were obviously no great novelty in the area – but he was unable to gauge his reaction to seeing the real thing that was obviously so easily found, and so casually discarded. He'd looked around, perhaps expecting to see something or someone official, to say, yes, these shells were fired here eighty-five years ago, a few of the many, many millions – but there was no one, just the empty shells in the corner and the farmland spreading out.

Henry had reached through the fence to touch one. All the men, he thought, who had carried, loaded, and fired these shells were dead. All gone from here. All gone from everywhere, most probably.

Janine stopped at the entrance to the cemetery. Henry could see between the stone posts that the place was beautifully kept, the graves in meticulous rows, with walkways of lawn, and roses at every headstone. The Australian gravestones were rectangular, light grey and rounded on top, identical to each other. There were about a hundred, Henry estimated.

'Well, here we are.' The wind blew through her hair. 'After all this time. So. In we go, I guess.'

Slowly they went along the rows, reading the names and inscriptions until they stopped at a headstone with A R Lansell inscribed sharply upon it. His rank, number, and his age, given as twenty, and the date of August the ninth, 1918, was also recorded. An inscription read, A SON OF AUSTRALIA – ALWAYS LOVED.

Henry stood and Janine knelt, hands on her knees, the solemnity of the place underscored by the low sighing of the wind in bare branches. Janine traced the words and dates with a fingertip. Henry saw a tear slip down her cheek.

'Well, we're here, Andy,' she said, and took Andy's diary out of her pocket. 'And we brought your diary, too. All the way from Strattford. It helped us get here. No one forgot you, either, back home. You're still talked about. Who you were and what you did. And Henry and I came all the way to, um, thank you. To know where you are and see what kind of place you're in, and it's really quite beautiful. And Cecelia helped. She made sure I got here.'

In the quietness, surrounded by the reality of what had happened, Henry could still not come to terms with the immensity of the thing or its violence. He needed to see the men come swinging down the road as they had been, young, in uniform, with rifles, with cigarettes, with muddy boots and bristling bayonets, their talk loud in the bitterly cold air. But he knew there would be no passing ghost battalion or the cracking thunder of a barrage. There was only this place, the wind stirring, and time passing on, and the silent fields.

'We're going to go now.' Janine got to her feet, the knees of her jeans damp. 'But we'll come back again tomorrow, Andy. And there's a tree for you in Strattford – I'm sorry it's not a gumtree. And a memorial. And Cecelia forgave you years and years ago. She told me that. And I can tell you that she never stopped loving you. I promise. No one did. We'll be back tomorrow, all right? To see you and the boys.' She turned to Henry. 'It's hard to take in what it all means, isn't it?'

He nodded. The door of history remained shut, although occasionally he felt it give a fraction, offering him a glimmer of understanding.

'You kind of expect it to be more ghostly or something,' he said. 'For there to be, I don't know, echoes or sounds. To be more things around. You know, ruins. But there's not.'

Janine nodded. She glanced around as she held her hair back from her face.

'I dunno. In the sound of the –' she shrugged. 'There's something here. And the cold. I can't explain it. And the dark-ness of those trees in that wood.' She pointed along the road. 'Well, there's *something* all around here, but it's nothing you can get hold of, is it? You can only know it. But its worth knowing. It was worth coming.'

The tops of the headstones formed a perfect pattern to Henry's right. He couldn't help but think of soldiers ranked in lines.

'Yeah, it's amazing,' he said. 'To be here.'

At four in the morning, as more wounded were being brought in, Andy lay his hand on his tunic pocket. This time Darcy nodded, took hold of his hand, and pressed his thumbs gently into the palm.

'No worries, mate. Old Darce'll look after everythin'.' Darcy ran his tongue over his lips and blinked a couple of times. 'You just remember all the ones that love ya, Andy. There's us here and there's everyone at home, yer mum and dad, and Cecelia and Frances-Jane and the little baby, and there'll be the boys waitin' for ya over the way, and Emily – and Andy, I wish ta Jesus Christ we never come over 'ere in the first place, but we bloody did. And I'm bloody sorry.'

Darcy sniffed harshly and looked up at the slow-moving ceiling of the tent. Beside him, another soldier coughed and further away, another vomited.

'But ya done yer best, Andy.' Darcy's voice rode the flapping of the tent like a boat in waves. 'And by Jesus I'm proud to be yer mate. And don't worry, I'll tell everyone what ya done, especially little Eliza. And Sister Marjorie here –' Darcy tilted his head, 'says that if ya want to close yer eyes now it's fine, because ya done more than your fair share, so ya can just take it easy now, mate, and I won't be going nowhere. And me and Bobby-boy'll look after yer little girl and everythin'll be sweet. So just shut yer eyes because –'

The sister put a hand on Darcy's shoulder.

'I'll leave you for a little while, Darcy, all right? You can see that Andy's died, can't you? I'm so very sorry. Would you like me to shut his eyes? I think it would be best now.'

Darcy nodded. 'Yeah, if yer wouldn't mind, Sister.' He gently pushed his thumbs up and down in Andy's cupped hand. 'I can do a lot of things, but I don't think I can do that.'

Darcy stood, reached down, and rested his fingertips on Andy's forehead.

'See ya, Lanse,' he said quietly. 'I'm gunna miss yer, mate. And don't worry, I'll take yer little book back home for ya. It won't get lost.' Darcy patted Andy's folded hands. 'Anyway, cobber, ya done yer job like ya always did, and we, ah, *everyone*, loves ya, all right? So rest easy now because ya earned it. And maybe we'll catch up again down the track.' Darcy nodded, looking at Andy's settled face. 'Down the bloody track, mate.' Then he walked away between the stretchers, retrieving his cigarettes and matches from a pocket as he went.

At the exit, Darcy held up a hand to the sister as she and two stretcher-bearers made their way between the rows of men. Then he was outside, the flash of guns temporarily lost to him as he lit up. For a few moments, he let his eyes adjust to the gloom, then holding his cigarette and Andy's diary in one hand, his injured arm hurting like hell, he angled the page into the dim light spilling from the tent, and slid the small pencil from its sleeve. Under Andy's last entry he wrote as neatly as he could,

On this day, the 9th of August, 1918, Private Andrew Richard Lansell, volunteer soldier of the AIF, died at Villers-Bretonneux Field Hospital, France, of wounds received in battle. He was one of the best. He always was, and he always will be.

epilogue

Henry looked down at the temperature gauge as he closed in on Strattford. It was holding steady as it had done all the way up from Melbourne, but he pulled over anyway, stopping between the familiar lines of the memorial trees. He got out, leant against the Volvo, and looked up the road.

There weren't too many places, he thought, where you could actually see where the past, the present, and perhaps your future met, but this was one. There was no explaining it really. There were just the things that happened and how you reacted to them. That was it. That was your life. He looked along the Avenue of Honour. And there was what you were going to do with your life from now on. Which was plenty, he hoped. Plenty.